UNCHARTED SEAS

Also by Emilie Loring, in Large Print:

As Long As I Live
Behind the Cloud
A Candle in Her Heart
Give Me One Summer
I Hear Adventure Calling
Rainbow at Dusk
Stars in Your Eyes
With Banners
Bright Skies
Key To Many Doors
Throw Wide The Door
Lighted Windows

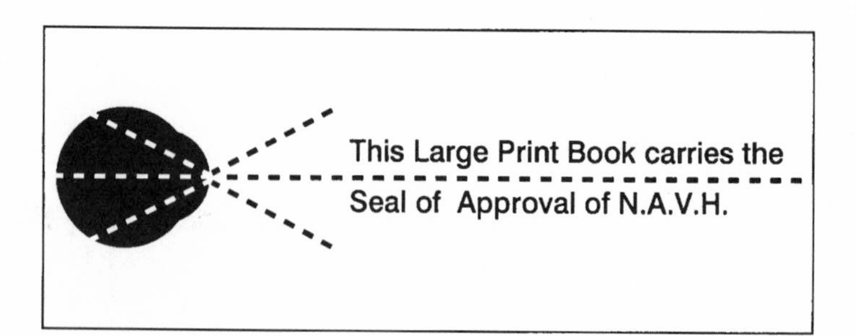

UNCHARTED SEAS

EMILIE LORING

Thorndike Press • Thorndike, Maine

Published in 2000 by arrangement with Little Brown and Company, Inc.

Thorndike Press Large Print Romance Series.

The tree indicium is a trademark of Thorndike Press.

The text of this Large Print edition is unabridged.
Other aspects of the book may vary from the original edition.

Set in 16 pt. Plantin.

Printed in the United States on permanent paper.

Library of Congress Cataloging-in-Publication Data

Loring, Emilie Baker.
Uncharted seas / Emilie Loring.
p. cm.
ISBN 0-7862-2663-3 (lg. print : hc : alk. paper)
1. Large type books. I. Title
PS3523.O645 U53 2000
813′.52—dc21 00-036459

"Dreams are the source of much of the new thinking, new convictions, new power in the world. They send the adventurous out on uncharted seas, dangerous seas, and it is danger, not security, which develops strength in mind and spirit."

Uncharted Seas

Chapter I

"Out fourteen!" announced the operator as he slid open the door of the elevator. He cocked his boyish head in its rakishly tipped, lavishly braided cap at the only other occupant of the car, a girl in a smart raincoat and a close green hat.

For the fraction of a moment Sandra Duval hesitated. Did every girl when trying for a position for the first time feel shivery, she wondered?

"Step quick, lady! Step quick!"

She barely cleared the door before it clanged. She heard the boy snicker as the cage shot up. Had she appeared dazed? Standing alone in the corridor of the huge office building she felt a small and lonely soul in a big, indifferent world.

"Step quick, lady! Step quick!" she prodded herself.

The laughter which the repetition of the

crisp command brought to her eyes lingered in their dark depths as she opened a door which proclaimed in gold letters to a more or less interested world that Damon and Hoyt were Bankers and Investors. Doors were curious things. One never knew what one might find behind them.

Directly behind this one a girl sat at a switchboard. Sandra had time only to appreciate her grooming, to rejoice that she, herself, was distinctly soigné before the operator inquired:

"Appointment? Who'd you want to see?"

"Mr. Damon. He wrote me to call this morning."

"In answer to the ad.?"

"The ad.? No."

"My mistake. I thought you'd come about an advertisement he has been running. Ten applicants already this morning and there were twenty yesterday. All the dames in the city who don't usually answer an ad. an' most of 'em who do have flocked here. Gee, must be a lot needing work." The worldly wise eyes of the operator appraised Sandra from head to foot.

"I'll ask if the boss is ready for you. Name?"

"Sandra Duval."

The girl did something to a switchboard

and spoke into the transmitter. She pulled out a plug.

"Wait until the present applicant comes out then B.D. will see you."

"B.D.?"

"B. Damon. He's the man you want, isn't he? He's the senior member of the firm. N.H., the junior partner, is away. Here she comes now. Say, I'll bet she didn't make the grade."

A young, slender woman in black, her close turban pulled down over platinum blonde hair, averted her face quickly as she passed, but not before Sandra had noted her angrily brilliant eyes set in artificial shadows. As she slammed the outer door behind her the operator sniffed.

"She doesn't care what she pays for perfume, does she? *Noel de Nuit!* She cut her own throat when she went into B.D.'s office scented like a sachet. He must have been marked before birth with a hatred of perfume. Gosh, she was mad! I felt as if corked-up TNT had given me the once-over when she looked at me. Treat that dame rough and she's all set to go off with a bang. Your turn. Second door to the right!"

What would this friend of her father's be like, Sandra had just time to wonder before she opened a door in response to a gruff, "Come in!" Through two wide open windows from which dripped a silver fringe of rain, came the drill of riveters, the hum of traffic, the whir of a propeller. On the wall which was not book-lined hung an exceptionally fine engraving of Daniel Webster. A man, tipped back in a swivel chair, was staring at it. His white hair bushed on a massive head; his coat hung loosely on his spare shoulders. He knew that she was there. How long before he would swing around and face her?

"Why didn't you turn off the water before you came in?" He waved a long, bony hand toward the downpour.

"The plumbers are on a strike. Couldn't get one on the job," Sandra countered quickly. If all business interviews opened like this, getting a position promised to be a lark.

He came about with a chuckle. His keen eyes, behind glass islands entirely surrounded by bone rims, seemed to bore into her brain; his skin was ruddy; his mustache, designed on the walrus plan, was white. A slightly older man than her father, she decided. He emitted a sound which might mean anything, and indicated the chair which faced him.

"Sit down." He touched a button. A boy whisked in.

"Close the windows."

The hum and stir of the city were shut out. What a relief! "Now I can think. My brain must be hitting on every cylinder if I am to convince this man that I am capable of filling a position," Sandra told herself.

"So you are Jim Duval's daughter! I am deeply touched that with his multitude of friends he sent you to me. His valiant spirit shines in your eyes between those long, sooty lashes so like his. I suppose he told you of the Three Musketeers of Melton?"

"Scores of times. You were Athos, weren't you? A boy named Mark Hoyt was Porthos, and . . ."

"And the youngest of the bunch, Jimmy Duval, was D'Artagnan. Those were the days! But Jim's interests took him abroad; in spite of the magic millions he had conjured from the earth, Mark Hoyt died a broken-hearted man; Aramis is a country minister; and I — well, here I am."

Sandra wondered if he cleared his voice from habit or if the memory of those youthful loyalties had caught him by the throat.

"What can I do for you, Miss Sandra?"

"As I wrote you, I need a position. First,

because I must keep so busy that I won't miss my father; second, because during the last year of his life his investments dwindled. My small income will provide bread but I would like jam with it. I had jam yesterday, I may have jam tomorrow, but I want jam today."

"Know your Alice In Wonderland, don't you? I like that." He picked up two letters from the desk, one of which she recognized as hers, the other one that her father had written to him. "You've had an interesting life traveling about the world. Jim Duval was a gay companion in the old days. He writes that your only fault is a too tender heart, that you're apt to champion the under-dog. That's a mistake, Miss Sandra, usually the under-dog is under because he won't cultivate spiritual and moral muscle."

Sandra laughed. "Behold a reformed woman! I have determined that when I take a position I shall be non-partisan, absolutely hard-boiled."

"Hmp! You look it! Now about work. There is nothing like it to ease heartache and to close the door on problems. Any previous condition of servitude?" His voice creaked, as if somewhat rusty from disuse, but his eyes twinkled. Already Sandra liked him tremendously.

"No, sir."

"What can you do? Office work?"

"I am not fitted to cope with the hectic skyscraper world yet. I had thought I might make good as a social secretary."

"I had the same thought when I wrote you to come this morning." He pushed a newspaper clipping across the desk. "Read that."

> WANTED: Social secretary. The position has unusual possibilities and is intended to interest those who usually would not answer an advertisement.

Sandra nodded approval. "It seems a perfect answer to this maiden's prayer, doesn't it?"

He regarded her from beneath shaggy brows. She was reminded of a bird-of-prey about to pounce on his kill. "You come from New England stock. Depuritanized by your life abroad?"

"Not wholly. I am still kept awake by my conscience if I indulge in coffee at night."

She liked his chuckle. It cheered her as she had not been cheered since she had been left alone.

"You'll need a conscience where you are

going — if you decide to go."

Sandra's spirit spread wings. Would the decision be left to her?

"A woman — she'll never see forty again — wants a secretary, one socially broken, who can attend to her correspondence, welcome her guests, sporting, business, professional — rarely purely social — and help her select her clothes. She goes all over the country exhibiting her horses. She has discovered that the costume of the driver adds to or detracts from the effect of the ensemble. I forgot one important qualification. Do you ride?"

"I have ridden all my life all kinds and conditions of horses. I hate to talk about myself, but I'm a demon equestrienne."

"Hmp! Have a nice sense of humor, haven't you? That was one of your father's assets. Ever been about stables? Know anything of the inner circles of turfdom?"

"Dad and I had a few friends among the racing set, but I have never seen the inside of a great stable. When I was a child he owned horses. For him there was glamour in the mere word Thoroughbred. He could have told you the height, weight, and speed of every notable horse."

"The Musketeers were all tarred with the same brush. Porthos — Mark . . ." He drummed on the desk with broad-tipped fingers, as if considering how much he would tell her. Reserve triumphed. His eyes came back to her.

"One more question. Any sentimental entanglements?"

"No, sir. I have seen so many ex-marrieds in my travels that the contemplation of the holy estate of matrimony leaves me cold."

"Those were somewhat the sentiments of the last secretary we sent to Seven Chimneys — that is the name of the place — and I haven't forgotten what happened to her. The house is in the town — a town largely given over to the Sport of Kings — in which your father and I grew up, but it was built after he left."

"Seven Chimneys. Dad never spoke of that, but wasn't there an old house somewhere which had a ghost and an underground passage?"

"There was. It belonged to the family of Mark. We boys used to haunt the place hoping to see the wraith. One night we put across a fair imitation, scared a woman almost to death, and got a licking from the caretaker."

"Dad used to tell that story with such realistic effect that I could actually feel my hair rise. It would seem a little like going h-home to go to Melton to live."

Sandra devoutedly hoped that he had not noticed the quaver in her voice. Nothing valiant about that. Damon went on as if oblivious of her emotion:

"Melton is not so New Englandish as it was in your father's time; it is so near the state line that commuting to the metropolis is easy. Mrs. Pat Newsome — ever heard of her?"

"Newsome? Newsome? The name sounds familiar. Did my father know her?"

"No. She came to the town long after he left. I am engaging a secretary for her. She hasn't always had money. She knows the horse business from A to Z, but when it comes to social amenities she falls down. She realizes it. I have told you what she wants socially. Interested to hear the rest?"

"My mind is on tiptoe with excitement."

"I like your enthusiasm. Most of the young women I know hide their feelings, they have 'em all right, I'm all for present-day youth, but they're not heartwarming. To get back to the job; the salary is two hundred a month and your living. You will be expected to dress as a daughter of the house should, and it is quite a house to dress up to, palatial describes it. As the mistress is addicted to rages — tantrums they were called in my youth, temperament is the polite word now — sometimes they walk out in a bunch, the servants, not the rages."

"The job seems to be getting bigger and busier every minute."

"It's big and busy, all right. There is no finer stable in the country. Mrs. Pat shows her own horses in both saddle and harness classes. What do you think about it? You may be sure I wouldn't let you go — that dates me, doesn't it — if I thought the environment would hurt you. Could you go today?"

No one with even a modicum of common sense would doubt the honesty and stability of Mr. Damon; besides, hadn't her father sent her to him? Sandra rose.

"Yes, sir. I could start for the Milky Way at a moment's notice. That is what traveling about the world does for one."

"Then I will phone Mrs. Pat — that is the name she is known by; she was Marte Patten before she married the first time — to meet the afternoon train. Only two a day. Your salary will be paid monthly. The cheques will come from this office." He pushed papers about his desk and cleared his throat.

"You will find complications at Seven Chimneys which will require tact. Mrs. Newsome is at present encouraging a claimant to her first husband's estate. She is doing it to spite the heir with whom she has quarreled. Women — some women — are like that. It's a mess. There's bound to be trouble. She — I won't tell you more, better that you should go unprejudiced. You may be able to help. Still want to go?"

"More than ever. Already my imagination is pulling on its seven league boots. Are you a horse man too?"

His chuckle was the nicest of the many nice things about him.

"Not a horse man, Miss Sandra, a gentleman fond of horses. I'm like that chap in the poem:

" 'He could tell you all the horses
That had run at all the courses
When they ever held a meeting
Since the racing year began.'

"Need an advance in salary?"

"No, thank you."

He pushed a typewritten slip across the desk. "There are the directions for getting to Seven Chimneys. You will like it. I'm sure you'll like it. But another fact you should know before you go: most of the people who knew your father are gone; his old home has been pulled down. You won't see much social life, not that there isn't any; there is the usual smart set, hectic young moderns with racing and hunting their paramount interest, with contract and dancing giving the horses a run for their money. The late depression has chastened them slightly but hasn't changed their interests. The chic women drive superbly, pilot planes, entertain faultlessly, have books, politics, plays at their tongues' ends, and to their everlasting credit be it said, are devoted mothers and good neighbors, except that — well, just now they are giving Mrs. Newsome the cold shoulder because of their loyalty to some one else."

"Thank you for telling me, Mr. Damon, but that makes no difference to me. I am going in a business capacity, not social, even though I am to dress as a daughter of the house should."

"Glad you take it that way. I will see you at Seven Chimneys, but come to me for help at any time as you would have gone to your father."

Sandra fought a wave of emotion. Her

heart, which had been twisted and bruised battling through months thickly fogged with anxiety, still flinched under the touch of memory. She thought her contracted throat never would release her voice, but it came.

"Thank you, Mr. Damon." She blinked back tears and smiled. "I was terribly low in my mind, now I'm tingling with the anticipation of adventure. Know the feeling?"

"Hmp! That's your father all over. You and I will be great friends. I forgot to ask, do you drive a car?"

"Yes, and I have piloted a plane."

"Great Scott, you youngsters are modern! The girl I married — and am still living with — you see, some of us stick to the vows we took 'reverently, discreetly, soberly, and in the fear of God' — can't even now get used to being on the street alone after dark. Different times, different brands of courage. Good luck to you."

"Thank you." Sandra paused at the door. "By the way, what happened to the last secretary you sent to Seven Chimneys?"

Standing, he leaned slightly forward, his palms on the desk. He reminded her of a grim war lord, dominant, ruthless.

"She fell in love with young Newsome. Watch your step."

Chapter II

Sandra stepped to the platform; the porter dropped her worn and travel-labeled bags, held out his hand for a tip, picked up his stool, and jumped back to the Pullman. The baggage man plumped a saddle beside the luggage and pulled himself up to the rear car as the train picked up speed and with an ear-splitting whistle shot straight for what looked to be an impenetrable wilderness.

She regarded the parallel lines of shining steel snaking back the way she had come and the small building huddled close to the track. Evidently this was one of the stations which a paternalistic railroad organization dropped into an apparent wilderness for the use of its rich and great patrons.

How still the world was! She listened. No sound of an approaching automobile. Mr. Damon had assured her that Mrs.

Newsome would have one waiting. She couldn't have made a mistake in the train because there were only two daily, and the conductor had made no comment when he had taken her ticket. Something must have happened to the car.

"Robinson Crusoe marooned on his desert island," she said aloud. She paced the platform, watching the smooth road which shot from the dense woods only to plunge into them again a few rods farther on. She looked up at the sky. The weather-man was attempting a welcome if her employer had slipped up. The sun was functioning on an in-and-out program. The air was glorious, washed clean by the recent rain, overstuffed with the spicy scent of pine and balsam and the refreshing smell of wet grass. Diamond drops glittered on twig and leaf. What should she do if no one came? There were no wires to indicate a telephone, no station master. Not another train today. That thought didn't help. She would walk. In which direction?

A car coming! A high powered car if the velvety hum was an indication of its class. Sandra instinctively settled her green hat, clutched her hand-bag a little tighter as a shining black roadster shot from among the dense trees.

"Enter Man Friday," she said to herself as she noted the solitary driver. A little chill of excitement prickled through her veins. She would have asked Mr. Damon more about the family to which she was going had she not been trained to respect a man's business time as if every minute were a grain of gold. Perhaps this was "young Newsome." Must she begin to watch her step at once? Taking one's first job was thrilling.

The car purred to a stop. The man pulled his soft cap a little lower over his eyes before he stepped to the platform. His short leather jacket was weather-stained; worn o.d. breeches were tucked into muddy high boots. He crossed to the saddle, settled it under his arm, and started for the car.

Sandra regarded him incredulously. Of all things! Didn't he see her or was he ignoring her? As he deposited his burden tenderly in the rumble, she reminded crisply:

"I'm here."

He turned and awkwardly touched the cap pulled so low that only a nose and an inflexible line of mouth were visible.

"So I see, Miss."

That "Miss" placed him. A groom.

"Weren't you sent to meet me? I am expected at Mrs. Newsome's."

"Are you, Miss? That's funny. Seven Chimneys is the next place to where I work. I didn't see nothing of a car as I come along. Sure you're expected?"

The hint of suspicion in the voice was maddening. "Expected. Do you think I would step off a train in this uninhabited spot if I were not? I was engaged by Mr. Damon this morning as a secretary for Mrs. Newsome. I have been waiting for hours and hours."

His lips twitched as he glanced at his wrist watch. Sandra qualified:

"It has seemed like hours anyway. What are you going to do about it?"

He looked at her bestickered bags, at the rumble of the car from which protruded the saddle. She suggested hurriedly:

"If you will take me — never mind the bags, Mrs. Newsome will send for them — you needn't even drive me to the house; leave me at the gate and I will walk the rest of the way."

Had he heard what she said? He appeared to be intently concerned as to the safety of a robin swaying on the tip of a pine. His glance came back to the luggage.

He motioned toward the car.

"Get in, Miss. I'll take you to Seven Chimneys. Guess my boss won't mind if I'm a bit late getting that saddle home."

Without waiting to know if she accepted his offer, be picked up her bags and piled them into the rumble.

"Ready, Miss."

"Your boss has a nice taste in automobiles," Sandra approved as the roadster slid forward. She had a feeling that this taciturn man would be interesting if he could be made to talk. He had a determined chin and a clean-cut nose, a nose in a thousand. His hands were gloved. Too bad — a man's hands told so much.

"It's a good car," he agreed shortly.

The road stretched ahead smooth and black through woods cleared of underbrush. In spite of the light which a sulky sun was turning on and off at its temperamental pleasure, perhaps because of it, the surroundings were gloomy, portentously gloomy. Sandra's satisfaction at her victory chilled. How long before they would be out of these woods? How like her to leap at a way out of a dilemma, without stopping to think where she might land.

She cast a furtive glance at the man behind the wheel. He had seemed afraid that she might see his eyes. Perhaps he had stolen the car!

"We'll be out of this road soon, Miss, and then you'll see some of the most handsome scenery in the world."

Handsome scenery! That was too obvious, it was out of character with his voice and face. The man wasn't a groom. He was acting a part. Why? She would play up to him. She wasn't such a bad actress herself. She agreed cordially:

"I have heard that it was beautiful. It is a great horse country, isn't it? Lots of breeding and racing and hunting?"

At last she had made him really look at her. She had but a momentary glimpse of the clearest gray eyes she had ever seen, before he was gazing straight ahead again.

"Yes, Miss. Your boss, Mrs. Newsome, has one of the finest stables in the country."

"So Mr. Damon told me. Ever since I heard her name this morning I have been tormented by a hazy memory. 'Newsome? Newsome? What have I heard about a Mrs. Newsome?' Every time I think I have the connection it dodges round the corner of a brain cell — if brain cells have corners. Oh-o-o, you didn't say enough for it! It is beautiful!"

They had shot into open country. Rolling fields, green as jade, swept off to woods which ridged darkly. Billow on billow of smoky hills shadowed with purple valleys, lightly hooded with thinning clouds, added a touch of grandeur to the horizon. In the foreground spooned a river, so glittering and still that it might have been a silver sash dropped by a giantess in flight.

"Look! A rainbow! See the reflection in the water! I never see an arc of gorgeous color like that without visualizing the finale of Das Rheingold — that's an opera by Wagner; Wagner was a great musician —" She couldn't resist the patronizing explanation, he deserved it for trying to deceive her. "A rainbow bridge spans the valley, and as the gods stride across it to Walhalla illumined by the setting sun, harps and strings unite in shimmering loveliness, and from below rises the song of the Rhine Daughters." She sang in a low, husky voice:

" 'Rheingold!
Reines Gold!
O leuchtete noch
In der Tiefe dein laut'rer Tand!' "

"That's pretty. It must be great to know

so much about the world, Miss."

Sandra disciplined a laugh. He was going strong. She confided:

"I am just foolish enough to take the rainbow as a good omen for myself. One end has disappeared into that old vine-covered stone house which looks as if it might have been picked up in Sussex and dropped here. Oh, I wonder —"

"What, Miss?" The question was curt.

"Nothing but an absurd feeling that I had seen it before. You have felt that way haven't you, about a place you know you never have seen?"

"Sure. Perhaps the rainbow's a good omen for the house too, Miss. Don't the Bible say, 'I do set my bow in the clouds, and it shall be for a token of a covenant between me and the earth?' Excuse me, Miss, it just slipped out. When I was a boy my folks made me learn a verse of the Bible a day. What's so funny about that, Miss?"

Sandra caught back a laugh. Why spoil his belief in his impersonation? She hastened to reassure:

"Nothing. Sometimes, when I'm — I'm much interested, I draw in my breath like that. Who lives in that old stone house?"

"A man named Hoyt."

Hoyt had been the name of one of her father's boy pals. Better not let this taciturn man know that she was interested. "Does he appreciate that adorable place? Is he a horse — a gentleman fond of horses?"

"He is, Miss. He keeps a few Thoroughbreds. I work for him."

The last statement was curt. Sandra regarded the man's profile. His jaw was set; his eyes looked straight ahead; he was as redly bronze as an Indian; she could see the pulse throbbing in his throat above his low collar. She would hate to clash wills with him, he would be so — so undentable. Perhaps he had owned horses himself and had lost them in the unstable world of the race track.

"Tell me about the old house. It looks as if it were drenched in history."

"It is. It has an underground passage."

It was as she had suspected, the house about which her father had told her. "Really? They have just unearthed something like that in Virginia; they think that it must have been a secret exit for the king's rulers in pre-revolutionary days."

"Is that so, Miss? This old house has a ghost too."

"Marvelous! I wonder — I wonder if

some day I may see it, the house, I'm not keen about the ghost. Perhaps Mrs. Newsome will take me there."

"Mrs. Newsome won't!"

The words flashed between them like a shining blade. Their bitterness widened Sandra's eyes.

"I'm sorry. Evidently I've made a social blunder. You see, I forget that I am merely a secretary."

"I didn't mean that. Nice job, secretary. Always thought I'd like to be one, but, of course, I ain't got the education."

He was getting better and better, fairly eating up his part.

"What did you mean? Is this place small-town enough to harbor feuds and family quarrels?"

"Oh, these rich folks don't have enough to do to keep 'em out of mischief, so they get to fighting among themselves."

"You think then that virtue walks hand in hand with flivver incomes and vice with Rolls Royce affluence — or words to that effect?"

"Poking fun at me, aren't you, Miss? I'm on. There are family quarrels here, all right. Look to the left. There is Seven Chimneys."

"How charming! Modernized colonial.

Is that old too?"

"No. One of the sons of the family that owned Stone House built that thirty odd years ago when he made a fortune. You'll get a better view after we enter the drive."

"But we won't enter the drive. Leave me at the gate with the luggage. I will walk to the house and send some one for the bags. If your boss and Mrs. Newsome are enemies, Mr. Hoyt might not like it."

"He would like letting a lady walk less than having one of his hands enter the Newsome place, Miss." He turned the car between elaborate iron grilles. "Now you can see the house."

Mr. Damon had not exaggerated. Seven Chimneys was palatial, Sandra agreed. It loomed at the end of the tree-bordered drive in which silver pools left by the late rain glinted like magic mirrors in the filtered sunshine. The top of the impressive porch had a lacy iron railing which enclosed a balcony from which opened a beautiful Palladian window. Moving clouds cast purple shadows on the roof; the house was of stone and clapboard, overgrown with vines, gay with window-boxes. She counted the chimneys. Seven.

The car drew up under the porte cochère. The driver jumped out and set her bags on the steps. Sandra opened her purse. For fear that he might see the gleam of laughter in her eyes, she kept them on the bill she offered.

"Thanks heaps. Please take this for smokes or talkies."

From under her lashes she could see his face darken with color.

"It won't bite."

"Won't it, Miss? Then I'll take it." He touched his cap. "Thank you, Miss. It will be smokes. Better not let Mrs. Newsome know that Mr. Hoyt's trainer brought you here." He touched his cap again, stepped into the roadster, and sent it humming back along the way they had come.

A trainer! That explained the unyielding line of the man's mouth, explained his attempt at deception. It was abundantly evident that he was a one-time horse owner down on his luck and super-sensitive about his change of fortune. She shouldn't have tipped him, but hadn't he deserved it for thinking her too dumb to recognize a gentleman when she met one?

She looked up at the spreading fan-light above the door with its tracery of leading, delicate as fairy lace. Curious things doors, one never knew what lay behind them, she thought, as she had thought once before that day, and pressed the bell.

Gorgeous country. She had the feeling of being on top of the world. The turquoise sky, clotted with what looked like aqueous cream whips, seemed so near that one might reach up and touch it. The sun, no longer sulking, was turning the countryside to gold — a countryside patched with lush fields, striped with miles of bridle paths. Nearby, emerald lawns, dotted with clumps of mammoth trees which suggested Sherwood Forest, Robin Hood and his Merry Men, sloped to the river which mirrored the ghostly white birches on its shore; beyond it, dusky woods splotched with whirls of pearly mist stretched to loping purple hills. Toward the east were stables, long, low, white, a tanbark fairway at their backs.

The end of the rainbow appeared still to touch the roof of the old stone house which seemed near enough to Seven Chimneys to suggest a dower-house. Against the now limpid blue heavens a golden weathercock on its barn glinted and spun indecisively as if considering whether to broadcast a cloudy or a fair tomorrow; a track circled behind the building.

Sandra's eyes followed the horizon, the arc of color. The sweep, the glory, the majesty of her surroundings swept over her spirit like mighty fingers on the strings of a harp. She felt as if she had emerged from a thunderous cloud into light and beauty. Rainbow splendor! She would accept it as an omen that the dark, tragic days of this last year never would be repeated. No matter what lay beyond, she was glad that she had come to the town which once had been her father's home, if only to feel this sense of a beckoning future.

A butler opened the door — a somewhat sloppy butler if the spots on his waistcoat were an indication; he was not in character with the perfection of the house and grounds. His skin was ruddy with especial emphasis on his nose; his deep-set eyes were black, his thinning hair iron-gray.

"The new secretary?" he inquired.

He might yesterday have left the British Isles if his pompous voice and enunciation were the criterion, but his manner was late-American.

"Yes. Please tell Mrs. Newsome that Miss Duval is here." Her memory picked up the name. Resumed its chant. "Newsome? Newsome? What have I heard about Mrs. Pat Newsome?"

The butler scowled at the bags on the steps. "Don't that chauffeur know better than to leave them in front?" He attempted a placating smile. "Sorry to keep you waiting. Madame is expecting you. This way."

Sandra followed him along a hall, rugless, tiled. He was noiseless; the click of her heels resounded through the stillness. Some one was dreaming on a violin. Cascades of scales, minor chords like the croon of a lonely spirit set her heart throbbing like a muted drum, brought back the bewildering sense of the uncertainty of what lay ahead, she thought she had broken free from forever.

Reflected in a priceless Chippendale mirror above a console in the hall was the fair head of the musician bent over a deep reddish-brown violin against the background of a mimosa tree. Beyond a beautifully wrought iron door she could see a terrace, gay with white bamboo and scarlet, a loggia at one side with what seemed to be a lodge at the end. They bordered a hedged garden alight with gold-shot haze that, in turn, surrounded a pool the parapet of which was patched with cushions.

On the threshold of a library the butler paused as if expecting to find some one within. The music, nearer now, made a soft accompaniment to Sandra's impressions. It was a room of magnificent distances — for a room. Light through tall, beautifully designed windows cast arabesques of color on the velvet rug. Two walls, book-lined to the beamed ceiling, were provided with sliding steps. Against another was a built-in desk, intricately carved, with a profusion of doors and drawers. A beautiful cabinet of red Chinese lacquer made a spot of brilliant color. On a table near a window was a half completed picture puzzle with a mass of unconnected pieces. Against the dark panels above the mantel hung a painting of a woman in a gauzy ballet costume. The flesh tones were crude and violent.

The picture was a false note in the room, besides being too small for the space where it hung. Was the mistress of the house responsible for placing it there? The flicker of flames in the fireplace cast fantastic shadows on the long ottoman in front of it, transforming the figure of the dancer from a thing of paint and canvas to a living, breathing personality.

Sandra's heart quickened its beat. Something about the room was depressing. The vines brushing against the windows became an eerie tapping. One felt that there might be eyes peering from the doors which opened on the richly hung musicians gallery, muffled footsteps on the stairs which wound up to it.

The violin soared into a passionate finale. A woman's voice, its stridency and impatience intensified by contrast to the music, complained:

"Why do you play like that, as if you were frightfully unhappy? Have I given you the best violin teachers to be had, or haven't I? Did I send you to Berlin for six months, or didn't I? Haven't I given you a generous allowance? Yes or no? And do you care what I feel or think or do?"

Sandra resisted a childish impulse to clap her hands over her ears. Was Mrs. Newsome talking? There was the sound of wood flung on wood, a low furious exclamation, and a man came through the doorway connecting the two rooms — a short, slim young man in riding clothes. The musician whom she had seen in the mirror!

He stopped as he saw her; the two police dogs with him stood motionless except for the slight bristling of hair along their backs, the cocking of their ears. His face, which had been livid, went brick-red. His hair was so fair as to seem white; his mouth under a golden wisp of mustache was crimson as if rouged; his intensely blue eyes, above which his brows met in a straight line, were set in little sunbursts of wrinkles at the corners.

Possibly he was in the late twenties, but he seemed too boyish for that age, Sandra decided. Evidently he was a gentleman of uncertain temper. One would do well to cross to the other side of the street when one suspected he was irritated, as unquestionably he was now. Who wouldn't be after being the object of the tirade she had just overheard? She wasn't mistaken this time; this must be "young Newsome," heir to his mother's rages as well as to her fortune — but a musician to his sensitive finger-tips.

The butler reminded: "This way, Miss." His tone was slightly peremptory. Small wonder. How long had she and the man been staring at each other? He must have had the same thought for like sudden sunshine a smile crinkled his eyes, revealed his perfect teeth. He touched his hair in a salute, said with a hint of swaggering gaiety:

"Welcome to our city, lady."

His engaging grin was contagious; Sandra smiled an impulsive response. Before she could answer he whistled to the dogs.

"Come on, fellas, we're blocking traffic."

She heard his footsteps on the tiled floor of the hall, the pad-pad of his four-footed companions, the clang of an iron door. The sound echoed through the still room. It added a macabre touch to her impressions of the house in which she was to earn her living.

Until the slump in her father's investments, her life had been as neatly arranged as the itinerary of a personally conducted tour; she had a curious presentiment that after today she never would be quite the same person again, that the old pattern would be torn to shreds and a new pattern substituted. It was a curious sensation. Perhaps she was making too much of it, perhaps every girl upon taking a position for the first time felt as if she were setting sail on uncharted seas.

"Nice job, secretary."

The trainer's voice echoed through her mind. Had he meant to discourage or warn her when he had said:

"There are family quarrels here, all right."

Chapter III

A woman was seated on a divan in the room Sandra entered — a room with a large studio window flanked by gold mimosa trees which made a charming frame for the gay garden beyond. In one corner was a concert grand piano upon which lay a violin. There were flowers, odd pieces of furniture, ceramics from all over the world. Little recesses in the walls were painted a luscious orange pink which appeared again in the rug and between the ceiling beams and in the glass curtains. The licking tongues of flame in the fireplace were reflected in the tea-service of ebony and silver on a small table.

The woman set down her cup. Behind her, rosy light glowed softly through the window. Mr. Damon had been right. Mrs. Pat Newsome — if this were she — never would see forty again, Sandra decided. A dynamic personality; even seated, she seemed to radiate energy. The Roman type. Hair, yellow and brittle, showed beneath the brim of a brown felt hat which matched in color her tweed coat and skirt; heavy, muddy brogues accentuated the size of her feet. No makeup. No lipstick. Her face was flabby; even in the rose light from the curtains the skin looked pasty; her greenish brown eyes gave the impression of tears just below the surface; her mouth had a bitter curl at the corners. It was evident that she was horribly unhappy. Was her son worrying her?

"Miss Duval? I am Mrs. Pat Newsome. Huckins, pull forward that chair."

"Yes, Madame, unless possibly the young lady would like to freshen up in her room first."

His tone was patronizing. Angry color surged in his employer's face, making it almost pretty. Sandra flung herself into the breach.

"I am quite ready for tea. The air since I left the stuffy train has been like champagne, all bubbles and sparkles. I got ravenously hungry while I waited for the car —"

"Wasn't the limousine waiting for you?" Mrs. Newsome's eyes flashed lightning signals of approaching storm.

Sandra groaned in spirit. Now she had done it, she had conjured a hurricane out of nowhere.

"There was nothing on wheels or on legs visible except a fat robin when I stepped from the train. While I was wondering in which direction to walk, a man in a roadster drove up. 'He looks hard as a rock but any port in a storm,' I said to myself, and proceeded to inveigle him into bringing me here. He took a lot of persuading, but here I am."

She felt as if she had been talking through ages of time as she drew off her gloves. Suppose she were asked the name of the good Samaritan?

"I'll know why Daniel, the chauffeur, didn't meet the train before he and I are an hour older. I run a boarding house for servants. Can I get anything done the way I want it? Not a chance!"

Had Mrs. Newsome started on one of her rages? Sandra allowed a faint trace of weariness to creep into her voice.

"Might I have tea? I was too busy packing to stop for luncheon. I would be consumed with mortification to faint from hunger on your threshold."

Her plea switched the woman's mood.

She smiled. She might be crude but she had sense enough to recognize the light touch when she heard it.

"Poor child, no one ever accused Pat Newsome of turning away from the starving. Get out, Huckins. We will serve ourselves."

The butler fussed at a table before he departed with a last backward glance.

"He's gone, thank heaven! He has been here two months and I still want to hit him every time he comes into the room. Can't make out why a man with his rummy nose stays in a house in which liquor isn't served — if I served it, how could I justly fire a trainer, or a swipe, or an exercise boy, when I smelled it on his breath? A man who's been tippling has no place in stables like mine, he might ruin a Thoroughbred — they've had the sense to rule it out in the hard riding set here; no drinking now before a hunt. Huckins is not too good at his job but he stays — I've never kept a butler so long before. Because he once worked for an earl and for a countess he's snooty. If he were in the stables I'd soon put him in his place."

Her tone, which had been surly to the servant, was crisp, curt, businesslike. The personnel magician had waved his adjustment wand and she was back in her element. She poured tea, inquired Sandra's preferences as to trimmings, loaded her plate with sandwiches and cakes. The requirements of hospitality fulfilled, she crossed her knees, extracted a long, thin cigar from a box of Chinese lacquer and lighted it. She pushed a silver container toward the girl.

"Cigarette? You smoke of course?"

"I can, but as I don't really care for it, it seems senseless to acquire the habit." Sandra regarded her employer with steadily mounting interest. She had seen many women in Spain and England smoke cigars — that meant nothing; it was the woman's change of personality which was astounding.

"Like horses?" Mrs. Newsome inquired.

"Immensely. I never feel so fratty with them as I do with dogs, perhaps because I do not understand them so well, but I love them. I have ridden all my life."

"B. Damon, when he phoned, told me that you could pilot a plane."

Was that all he had told her? Evidently Mrs. Newsome did not know that he had been a friend of her father. "I have done more or less of it."

"You won't have a chance for that here.

Were you told before you came what you had to do?"

"Sketchily. I would like to know from you."

The stimulation of the hot, aromatic tea, the delicious sandwiches had changed the feeling of dread, which had hung over Sandra's spirit like a fog since she had entered the house, into the larky anticipation of adventure she had felt in Damon and Hoyt's office. Life here offered interesting possibilities, unless she were mistaken.

Mrs. Newsome watched a ring of smoke thin to a pale violet haze. "You are to take care of my correspondence, greet and entertain guests — the housekeeper attends to the assignment of rooms, the hiring and firing of the servants — advise me as to the clothes I need for every occasion — I don't trust my maid, good as she is — and — and make this great ark of a place into a home, the sort of home which will keep a young man off the street."

Her tone was bitter, her eyes haggard. Young Newsome evidently had his mother worried. Sandra encouraged:

"I should think that any one would be glad to stay here. The grounds are perfection."

The woman kicked over a foot-rest as

she rose. Feet slightly apart, hands deep in the pockets of her tweed coat, she backed against the mantel. Her greenish brown eyes were specked with fire.

"Perfection! Outside! Why? Because everything on this place except this house and the stables is managed by Nicholas Hoyt. Of course you know that his uncle married me because I could look after his horses?"

The widow of Mark Hoyt! Why hadn't Mr. Damon told her, Sandra wondered, before she answered:

"I don't know anything about you. I came because the position sounded interesting."

"Well, he did. I looked after him too until he died. He left me the income from a trust fund, this place for my life or as long as I wanted it, and the stables, except for the racing stock and the cups and trophies which went to Nicholas with everything else. That was all right; the breeding of Thoroughbreds is quite a different proposition from breeding saddle and show horses which is my job. He left Stone House to Nick with instructions that he was to take all care of keeping this place up. I tried to be nice to my nephew-in-law, but would he have it? Not he. He hasn't been inside this house since — I ask you, isn't even an endowed widow entitled to some degree of personal liberty? To marry again if she wants to?"

"Why not, in this go-getter age when the meek no longer inherit the earth?"

"Say, I'm going to like you, you're a bright child. I'm telling you all this about Nicholas before some one else gets a chance to prejudice you against me. The smart set here has gone solid for him and is cutting me. He's polite enough, I could wring his neck, but — well, something has turned up which may bring him down in a crash of the blood and sand variety. There may not even be pieces to pick up. It will be all right with me."

Sandra was hotly uncomfortable. She felt as if she had opened a door marked Private. Was it Mrs. Newsome's custom to strip her heart bare on such short acquaintance? What would she say if she knew that an employee of the hated nephew had brought her secretary from the station? What a disagreeable person the Hoyt heir must be. She disliked him already. And she had suggested to the trainer that some time Mrs. Newsome might take her to see Stone House. Knowing of the feud between the two branches of the Hoyt family, no wonder he had growled:

"Mrs. Newsome won't!"

She had been here less than half an hour, but already she divined that her principal task would be to act as a shock absorber between her employer and the objects of her rages. She had better begin at once.

"I want to help in every way possible, Mrs. Newsome. If you will tell me what my duties are, I will soon get into the swing of them."

"Call me Mrs. Pat. Ever worked before?"

"No."

"What have you been doing?"

"Traveling with my father since my mother's death. He died two months ago."

"Any relatives?"

"Distant ones only."

"Glad of that. They won't try to get you away by telling you that you are burying yourself here; that's what happened to the last secretary."

That was not what Mr. Damon had told her, but why not accept her employer's version, Sandra asked herself.

"Ben Damon phoned that he had fallen for you at once, said that your gay spirit affected him like champagne. Now that I've seen you I understand what he meant. I like you. Don't get peeved and walk out on me if I'm rough. I have to be rough or I wouldn't get anything done. Some of the servants were here when Mr. Hoyt was alive and they resent me. Dan, the chauffeur, is one of them. But I'll show 'em!"

Her voice rose. Sandra hurriedly set a little backfire.

"It must be difficult to find just the right men to care for your marvelous horses."

"Difficult! You don't know the half. If it weren't for my head man Mac Donovan, I would have to spend the night in the stable when a mare is about to foal. I wouldn't dare trust her to any one else. If Nick were friendly, we could do so much together."

For a moment she had forgotten her anger. Sandra ventured:

"Couldn't you make friends with him?"

Mrs. Pat sniffed. "Too late now. I suppose Ben Damon put you wise to complications here?"

"He merely touched on them. He was more interested in engaging a secretary for you."

"I'm surprised that he bothered to find me one as his sympathies are all with Nicholas. They are business partners and co-trustees of the estate of my first husband, Mark Hoyt. He was a widower when I married him. In his youth he made piles of money in mines, after which he married. There was one son — Philip. When he was three, father, mother, and child went abroad. They took with them a nurse, Anne Pardoe, a French woman who had taken care of the boy since he was born. Mark and his wife went to Egypt, leaving Philip in a small town in southern France with the woman. She had relatives there. After they left, the child was horribly burned while playing round a bonfire. He died —"

"What a tragedy for the mother and father!"

"I'll say it was! I suppose you think I'm crazy to run on like this, but I've got to talk. I can't talk to Curtis; he drives me mad — you heard me lashing at him, I knew you had by your face. Estelle Carter, who is staying in the house, would be as responsive as a hit-and-you-have-her-doll at a county fair; she has no interest in women, only in men. We met her abroad, and when she said she had once lived in this town, like a fool I asked her to visit us. I guess old man Trouble nudged my elbow. I have no real friends. No one but jocks and trainers and swipes to yell at. I shall go goofy if I don't let loose to some one." She dropped her head on her arms crossed on the mantel.

Sandra swallowed hard and blinked back tears. The outburst was a recurrence of the storm she had interrupted by her arrival. She had thought that during the months since her father's death she had plumbed the depths of loneliness, but never had she known loneliness of the spirit like this. There was desolation in it and heartache unbelievable. Could she help? If in no other way, she could by encouraging the woman to unburden her mind. She asked gently:

"Did the parents get back in time to see their child alive?"

Mrs. Newsome squared around. Tears had left shadowy furrows on her cheeks. She brushed at them.

"No. Anne Pardoe claimed that she tried to reach them but they were in the desert. She lost her nerve; terrified at the thought of what Mark Hoyt might do when he saw that mound in the church yard, she ran away with a lover."

"How idiotic! Straight out of the age of innocence. No modern woman would elude consequences in that fashion. She would face the music, knowing that even if fright suggested a get-away the radio would catch her somewhere."

"Sure she would, but this happened thirty years ago. When the Hoyts returned, they were frantic — Mark told me this before I married him. The doctor who attended the child, the minister who had officiated at the burial had been crushed under falling walls. The relatives of the Pardoe woman knew nothing more than what the nurse had written."

"How could the Hoyts bear it?"

"Had to, didn't they? It's surprising what a lot of lickings humans can stand. Now, along comes a Kentuckian with old, faint scars of burns on his shoulders, claiming that he is the son of Mark Hoyt, that the child did not die in France but was so seriously injured that Anne Pardoe, intimidated by her lover who had reason to leave the country in a hurry, fled with him and the boy to Buenos Aires, leaving a mound in the church yard and a letter behind her. It was a small village and she could get away with it. Later the three came to the United States." A telephone buzzed. "Now what do they want?" She crossed the room, manipulated buttons in a niche and talked.

Sandra tingled with impatience. She had heard from her father that Mark Hoyt had lost his son, but of course he had not known of this claimant. Was this the complication to which Mr. Damon had referred? He had said: "There's bound to be trouble." Would she meet the long-lost heir? What a curious person her employer was. Mr. Damon had been right when he had warned the new secretary to watch her step.

With a muttered imprecation Mrs. Newsome left the telephone. "I'm going to the stables. A filly has the colic and they want me to give the little thing its medicine. There's always something taking the joy out of life in this business. I've phoned the housekeeper to show you your rooms. We dine at seven-thirty. Come to the library when you are ready, it is more homelike than the drawing room. Dress for dinner. Mr. Newsome — did you meet him in the library as you came through?"

Sparks in her eyes. Was she suspicious of every one? Poor unhappy woman.

"It couldn't be called meeting. Your son was —"

"My son! Where do you get that 'son' stuff? Curtis Newsome is my husband!"

Chapter IV

At a window of the room into which the creaking taffeta-skirted housekeeper had shown her, Sandra looked toward the west. It crimsoned suddenly in streaks as if the sun, exasperated by the slowness of the process of tinting, had flung his color-brush straight at the heavens. Dusk was stealing forward trailing an amethyst veil, delicate as malines, across a faintly primrose sky. Pinnacles of cloud, roseate now, were stabbing at the darkening dome; the once silver river rippled like molten ebony, setting a-quiver the birch leaves reflected on its surface. The windows of Stone House were faintly luminous from the afterglow. They seemed like lidless old eyes watching for home-comers.

The girl's mind still twinged from her unfortunate mistake in regard to the relation of her employer to the man who had spoken to her in the library. She had some excuse — he must be at least fifteen years younger than his wife. If she hadn't had the impression so firmly in her mind, she would have realized as she listened to Mrs. Newsome's story of her marriage to Mark Hoyt that she couldn't have had a son his age. She smiled as she remembered his engaging grin. He was likable.

'Why had she said anything? Comment had been unnecessary. It would have been much more to the point had nice Mr. Damon warned, "Watch your tongue!" instead of "Watch your step!"

She turned impatiently from the window. It would get her nowhere to stand here regretting. She had much better busy herself unpacking. She glanced at her luggage. Should she wait until morning? She might find a note of dismissal with possibly a return fare on her breakfast tray. Lucky she had not accepted the salary advance offered. Perhaps the rainbow had not been an omen of brightening skies for her after all. Perhaps the future had not beckoned but had held up a warning hand.

Not entirely because it imperiled her tenure of the position she so much needed and desired was she sorry that she had assumed that the youthful man was her employer's son; she was sorry to have hurt the woman, and her voice had shown that she was hurt. She hated to hurt any one. Life took care of that. It kept such a lot of heartaches up its sleeve which it dealt out impartially like cards from a pack, making sure each human got a few in his hand to make of them what he could.

The fact that Nicholas Hoyt's roadster had brought the new secretary from the station would not help the situation if Mrs. Newsome heard of it. Was it her custom to shoot her first husband's nephew full of poisoned arrows as she had this afternoon? With a family feud and a long-lost son hovering in the offing the atmosphere creaked with drama.

Even the gentleman trainer from the Hoyt stables had hinted at it. Of course he would take the side of his "boss." His face had been in the background of her mind ever since she had stepped from the roadster; all following events had been superimposed on it. The line of his mouth had done the trick. He looked like a man secure in his own strength, one who would rather enjoy plunging headlong into trouble to champion a cause.

She glanced about the rooms. She had been so perturbed when she entered that she had not noticed them. How lovely!

The decorator had seen to it that they were gay and foolish in spots, dignified in others, but charming always. Perhaps it was because she was home-hungry that she loved them already, loved the little balconies outside the French windows, the cool green walls touched with silver, the turquoise hangings, the turquoise draping of the crystal and silver laden *poudreuse* of the boudoir. There was delicate apricot on a chair or two, apricot cushions on the chaise longue and softly shaded lamps on small tables. The dressing room was wardrobe-walled; the bath was the color of amber-green waves with a shower curtain of shimmering silver fabric; beyond was a room ivory and apricot with a moleskin cover on the bed.

Comfort in the lap of luxury. It would be wonderful to settle down for a while here and feel the warm arms of a home close about her. If ever again she had money ahead she would have a *pied-a-terre* somewhere. No more traveling from place to place for her.

Settle down! Here? She wouldn't be allowed to after her blunder. Only another woman could understand how her mistake had cut Mrs. Newsome's pride. Suppose she had to start all over again looking for a position? What of it? Her father had said the last day they had been together:

"Remember, Sandy, that the future holds nothing that your unconquerable soul, your faith, your trust cannot meet."

Had she an unconquerable soul? Time alone would tell.

" 'The King of France and forty
thousand men
Marched up the hill and then marched
down again,' "

she hummed defiantly.

Some one knocking. Perhaps Mrs. Newsome would not wait until morning; hadn't Mr. Damon warned of her rages? Perhaps this was a personally conducted return ticket. Maddening to have fallen down the first hour on her first job. Sandra bit her lips to steady them before she called:

"Come in!"

A maid entered, an elderly maid in black silk gown and an incredibly fine muslin apron. Her crinkly hair, which once must have been red, was streaked with gray; her eyes were a twinkling brown; her lips parted on blatantly false teeth.

"I'm Bridie, the head chambermaid,

Miss. I came to see if I might'n help ye unpack. The housekeeper thought ye looked kinder white."

Sandra felt as a condemned hero of fiction is supposed to feel when a reprieve is waved in his face. Why not unpack? It wouldn't take her long to put her things back into her bags if she had to leave in the morning. She controlled an impulse to hug the friendly woman.

"Thank you, Bridie, I would like your help if you have time to spare. Here are the keys." Tears rushed to her eyes. She blinked furiously. "What is the matter?" she indignantly demanded of herself. "Second childhood?" Apparently she had a talent for registering emotion, she should have tried Hollywood, she would not have been obliged to resort to glycerine tears with her present supply of real ones. She met the maid's keen glance and smiled.

"Don't mind me, Bridie. I'm always a little upset in a strange place."

How that silly excuse would have amused her father. She upset! She, who had revelled in strange places, who never had been happier than when unpacking and arranging their few household gods in a strange city.

The woman wagged her head in comprehension. “An’ why wouldn’t ye feel strange? Lately lost yer Pa, the housekeeper tells me.” She unlocked a mammoth bag. “Sure an’ ye’ll like it here, fine. I come to this house as a gur-rl more’n twenty-five years ago, an’ I ain’t never felt no desire to leave it except to go see my folks in Ireland.”

Perched on the bench before the turquoise-draped *poudreuse,* hands clasped about one knee, Sandra smiled at the woman lifting the gowns from their tissue wrappings.

“Ireland is beautiful, Bridie. I spent months there not so long ago. Talk about horse-racing. They do it well in Dublin.”

The conversation went smoothly after that, slurring its Irish way over dropped d’s and throaty ye’s, getting more brogueish with every reminiscence, cementing friendship by love and admiration of the same places in the same country. The maid’s eyes were soft with memory as she hung the last frock in the wardrobe, placed the last pair of gold sandals on the shelf.

“Anything more I can do for ye, Miss?”

“Nothing, thank you. You have done more than unpack for me. You have cheered me unbelievably. I’m on the crest of the wave now.”

"Sure an' you look it. Your eyes are as sparklin' as a still Irish lake reflectin' stars in an Irish night sky. Don't ye get lonesome, now. Do ye like dogs, Miss?"

"Adore them."

"Then you don't never need be lonesome here. Tomorrow I'll bring Bud an' Buddy up to see you. They're big but they're like me: they're friendly with them they like, an' sure they're missing Mister Nicholas something terrible. Good-night, Miss."

Sandra looked at the door Bridie closed behind her. Tomorrow! Would she be here tomorrow? Suppose she lost this position — there were others. The woman's friendliness had left her heart in a glow, her courage gay.

Later, as she fastened a jeweled clip to the shoulder of her white dinner frock, she nodded to the velvety eyes of her mirrored reflection, eyes which still showed the strain of the last tragic year. The realization that the sheen of satin artistically accentuated the contrast between her dark hair and the magnolia tint of her skin, curled her vivid lips up at the corners.

"Beginning to feel young and flippant and gay again, aren't you?" she asked her reflection.

The shock of surprise had accomplished one thing: it had crystallized the hazy memory which had tormented her since she had heard her employer's name. With newsreel clarity had appeared the picture of herself in a London hospital, waiting to see her father, reading an account of the doping of a race horse and the fate of the trainer responsible for the ugly trick. At the end of the column had appeared a brief but spicy account of the marriage of an American widow, internationally known as a breeder and exhibitor of horses, to one of her late husband's jockeys, Curtis Newsome.

And a few hours ago she had stupidly referred to the husband as the woman's son. Had she made an unforgivable break?

The eyes she met in the mirror flashed. A deep dimple dented one corner of her mouth. She nodded approval.

"That's right — laugh. You haven't received your congè yet, and you have one friend at court — Bridie, perhaps two more — Bud and Buddy. The three B's."

She picked up the photograph of her father in its tooled leather frame which she had placed on the mantel.

"I'll keep your philosophy in mind, Jimmy Duval. 'Today is the tomorrow you were worrying about yesterday.' I'll dig in my fingers and toes and hang on. After all, the mistake was not entirely my fault. Why the dickens didn't Mr. Damon say that 'young Newsome' was the woman's husband?"

The remembrance of her *bétise* accompanied Sandra down the curved stairway, through the hall to the threshold of the library. Even with many softly shaded lights which glowed like cloudy jewels, the great room seemed sombre. Mrs. Newsome, in a black frock spattered with discs as gold as her modishly dressed hair, smiled a welcome to the girl hesitating in the doorway. Sandra sighed relief. She was forgiven.

The metamorphosis in her employer was startling. Had her maid discovered the fabled Fountain of Youth? Her skin looked firm and fresh and delicately tinted. Brilliant court earrings cascaded to her beautiful shoulders; one bare arm glistened with sumptuous bracelets. She seemed years younger than she had in the afternoon. Perhaps Curtis Newsome had seen her only in the evening before he asked her to marry him. Sandra glanced at him curiously as, attired in impeccable dinner clothes, he leaned over the puzzle table oblivious of what was going on in the room. A tall, brown-haired man was working with him.

Her eyes went back to Mrs. Newsome who was talking with a man whose back was toward the door.

"Come in, Miss Duval, and meet . . ."

The man turned.

"Philippe!" Sandra exclaimed incredulously. Was she dreaming, or was this really Philippe Rousseau whom she and her father had seen often in London?

Evidently he was as surprised as she. The whiteness of his face startled her. His usually wistful dark eyes sharpened to steel points. Once he had protested that he loved her, but, even so, seeing her wouldn't make him look as if he had seen a ghost. He had been a little shabby when she had known him; his clothes were smart in cut and material now. So quickly that she wondered if she had imagined his pallor, his color swept back.

"Sandra Duval! Of all people!" He caught her hands in his.

"I'm positively dizzy with surprise, Philippe." She returned the pressure of his hands even as she thought, "Funny that I should feel so thrilled at seeing a man who only tepidly interested me before. Is it because I'm in a strange country?"

"Why should you be surprised? Didn't I tell you last winter that my — my people had come from this town?"

Sandra's brows contracted. Had he told her that? He had appeared avidly interested in her father's stories of his boyhood days in Melton, days upon which the older man had dwelt more and more as his strength failed. His amazement at seeing her accentuated the tinge of foreign accent which gave a fascinating individuality to his voice and diction. She freed her hands, suddenly conscious that she and Philippe were being curiously regarded by Mrs. Newsome and the two men at the table. She crossed the room.

"Excuse my excitement, Mrs. Pat. Mr. Rousseau was in London with his horses last winter when I was there. And —"

"Oh, that's all right. Glad for you to meet a boy friend here. Curt, where's Estelle?"

Curtis Newsome joined his wife in front of the fireplace. "Search me. She's always late, isn't she? Greetings again, Miss Duval."

"Oh, you two met in the library, didn't you? Seems as if Estelle might be on time when she is staying in the house. She makes me mad. She's so cocksure of herself. Here she is. At last!"

Mrs. Newsome frowned at the small, exquisite girl on the threshold whose hair was the latest word in tint, Venetian gold; her skin was colorless; her lips, her glittering fingernails, her long, jeweled cigarette holder matched her coral satin shoes. Between shadowed lids her eyes glinted green. Her black frock was diaphanous. Sparkling bracelets weighted her left arm. As she smiled beguilingly at her hostess and began a pouting explanation, Sandra said in a low voice to the man who stood close beside her:

"Glamour, the lady has glamour, Philippe. Hasn't that word pushed 'IT' out of the cinema vocabulary? I have seen her type in beach frocks at St. Jean de Luz; in backless swim suits at Cap d'Antibes and the pool at Biarritz; in tweeds on the golf links at Le Torquet; in leather jackets, ski-trousers and boots in Saint Moritz; trailing gorgeous gowns, and glittering with jewels in the most up-to-date resorts of the chic internationals, but I never expected . . ."

An uncanny awareness that she was being observed checked the amused observations with which Sandra was bridging Philippe Rousseau's disturbing silence. Her eyes were drawn as to a magnet to the narrowed, speculative eyes of the tall, brown-haired man who had been at the puzzle table. Something in his expression accelerated the beat of her heart. He was suspicious of her. Why? Was he the claimant to the magic millions who was being encouraged by Mrs. Newsome? Was he really the son of Mark Hoyt, or was he an adventurer taking a long chance at winning a name and fortune? Life certainly promised to be thrilling here.

The golden girl nodded to him. "How's the fight going, Jed?" She came close to Rousseau and pretended to adjust his black tie.

"You are to take me out to dinner, Philippe."

He frowned. "Have you met Miss Duval, Estelle?"

"What a man! Trying to teach me manners, are you?"

Sandra felt her color mount as the ice-green eyes appraised her. "The new secretary? She has the cosmopolitan touch. Why will old Ben Damon insist upon strewing the pathway of youth with temptation?"

Her mocking glance at Curtis Newsome pointed the remark cruelly. He colored to his fair hair. His wife gasped. Sandra looked her contempt as the girl walked away clinging to Philippe Rousseau's arm.

"No one minds Mrs. Carter, Miss Duval." The man whose suspicious eyes had challenged her was speaking. "She prides herself on being a spade's-a-spade person, though why it is necessary always to call a thing by its right name I have yet to find out. The regal Huckins has announced dinner. Shall we follow the others?"

"After all, these spade's-a-spade persons have their uses," Sandra answered lightly. "Not until she asked you how the fight was going did I realize that possibly you were the long-lost son I have heard so much about."

He frowned down at her. "You have a curious sense of humor, Miss Duval. What's the big idea pretending that you don't know who the claimant is?"

Something in his voice had the effect of ice-cubes coasting down Sandra's spine. In an attempt to control an involuntary shiver she protested gaily:

"Looks as if we'd embarked on a twenty-questions party. I'll start it. Who is the claimant?"

"Still bluffing? Lovely ladies must be humored. The claimant is your — apparently — old friend, Philippe Rousseau."

Chapter V

"Philippe! Philippe, Mark Hoyt's son!"

The words whirled round and round in Sandra's mind. The dining room seemed to rock to their rhythm as she looked across the refectory table at Rousseau. Curious the effect he had on her. Just as the appearance of a character in grand opera is accompanied by his own special motif, so Philippe's appearance seemed always companioned by a double, a chevalier, in festive array; not excepting the dashing hat with its sweeping feather and cloak and sword.

He the long-lost son! Incredible. Why had he not mentioned the fact in the weeks he had come so often to their rooms in London? Of course his thoughts had been occupied with the horses he had brought to race, but he had listened with absorbed interest to her father's reminiscences of his youth and the exploits of the "Three Musketeers of Melton." She had thought then that he was merely showing the courtesy of a younger man to the oft-repeated tales of an invalid; now she knew that all the time he had had the knowledge of his inheritance up his sleeve.

This was the second shock since she had entered Seven Chimneys a few hours ago. She must drag her mind from this one or Mrs. Newsome would think she had engaged a dumb secretary. She forced her attention to her surroundings. The room was walled with a colorful pictorial paper. The heavily carved furniture was black with age. The decorator had gone horsey when planning the room. There were fox heads on the consoles; horse heads embellished the andirons; two prancing silver horses formed the centrepiece which held fragrant Templar roses; lights from tapers as crimson as the flowers were reflected in a thousand tiny facets on crystal. Hunting scenes were etched on the goblets; the place plates had hunting scenes in black and gold and red on their borders.

The man named "Jed" was on her left; she was at the left of Curtis Newsome who faced his wife at the other end of the table. Just opposite, Estelle Carter smoked incessantly. As her appraising green eyes alight with mockery challenged hers, Sandra hoped that she would remain a perfect lady and not give way to a primitive urge to throw something at her. Philippe Rousseau sat between the Venetian blonde and his hostess.

It was with difficulty that Sandra kept her eyes from his handsome, rather melancholy face, from the long, feminine fingers with which he smoothed his clipped mustache. Philippe heir to all this gorgeousness! It was unbelievable. The man named Jed had accused her of bluffing. Did he think her an accomplice or whatever the person is who backs up the claimant for an estate? That would be funny if — if it weren't rather terrifying.

"Miss Duval," the voice at her left sent the ice-cubes coasting again. Was this "Jed" one of those man-eating cross-examiners one read about? "Know enough of periodism to describe this room for a house beautiful magazine?"

Sandra relaxed. "Not much, at best my knowledge is spotty. I recognize the paper either as an original Zuber made in Alsace Lorraine in 1793, or a marvelous imitation. The horses in the centrepiece are 18th Century Renaissance, and the candlesticks are straight Georgian. The hunt picture set in over the mantel looks like a genuine Henry Alken. After that I'm a lost soul straying in the wilderness."

"Loud cheers. You have discovered all the points that count, the rest is Mrs. Pat's hand in the décor, like that terrible daub above the fireplace in the library."

"Then the coryphée wasn't painted for that otherwise perfect room?"

"I'll say she wasn't. Nicholas Hoyt's portrait hung there, Nick in the colors of his hunt club when he was Master of Fox Hounds. Doubtless you have heard of him?"

Was he testing her knowledge of conditions here? "One thing I haven't heard, — your name. Do you realize how frightfully handicapped I am when I want to speak to you? Of course I could say, 'Hi, Jed!' but it is rather too soon in our acquaintance, even for these informal times, isn't it?"

"Sheering away from the family complications, aren't you? Either you are a superb actress, or you really didn't know that Rousseau is claiming the Hoyt estate."

Sandra looked across the table at Philippe engrossed in conversation with his hostess. "Believe it or not, I really didn't know," she responded curtly.

"I'm on my knees in apology. I believe you. I'll bet Mrs. Pat has tried to justify herself with you already. She knows she's wrong so she is clutching her mistake tighter; that's human nature." He twisted the stem of a crystal goblet. "My name is Langdon. Jed, to you — I hope."

His laugh was delightful. If he had not commenced their acquaintance with suspicion of her, she could have liked him immensely, Sandra told herself.

"Are you here for the races?"

"Partly for the races. Of course you know that Mrs. Pat went the limit when she championed Rousseau's cause. She not only took him in here but took his stallion, Iron Man, with his jockey and trainer into her stables."

"Really! Did Philippe bring Iron Man? That gray will lead the field."

"Rousseau has another champion in you, all right, Miss Duval."

"He has. He is my friend. He was wonderful to my father and me last winter. Some one was forging Dad's name to cheques, and when . . . what is it, Mr. Langdon? Are you faint?"

Even Jed Langdon's lips were white. His laugh was shaky.

"Don't notice me, please, Miss Duval.

I'm quite all right now. I have a turn like that occasionally. Heart. Forged cheques! So it's being done in London too! Hope you didn't lose much money?"

"The bank made good — but I pity the forger if ever he is caught."

"How did Rousseau help?"

"He went with me to our consul; Dad was not able to go. He was most kind to take the trouble when he was terribly worried about his own affairs. Not one of his horses made good. The English tracks are so different from the American that it was not to be wondered at."

"He was in luck to be able to help. Aiding beauty in distress didn't go out when the new woman came in. Will you excuse me for a few moments, Mrs. Pat? Got to get a man on long distance at this hour or not at all."

"Sure, Jed, but don't make any heavy date for this evening. I'm counting on you for contract after dinner," his hostess reminded.

Sandra's eyes followed Langdon as he left the room. Some of his color had returned but he was still too white. Tragic that a man so fit as he seemed should have a tricky heart. His was not the only tragedy which was being dragged into the spotlight tonight. One felt Mrs. Newsome's unhappiness as her wistful eyes sought those of the young man slouched at the head of the table, as she listened eagerly for his voice. From her tirade earlier in the afternoon, it was easy to deduce that Nicholas Hoyt was giving his uncle's widow the cold shoulder because she had married a jockey. What business was it of his? He must be detestable. Serve him right if he lost the estate. If only Philippe could prove his claim! Could she help?

Jed Langdon returned as the last delectable course was being served.

"Better?" Sandra asked.

"Okay. Curious the way those darned attacks come and go. Sometimes I wonder if I am having proper advice. There's a man in France . . . sure, I'll play with you, Mrs. Pat. Luck at cards, like industrial activity, swings through a cycle; it is time you and I were on the up-and-up."

In the living room after dinner Estelle Carter and Curtis Newsome drifted to the piano. Philippe Rousseau was authoritatively discussing horse-breeding with his hostess; Jed Langdon was busy at the cigarette table.

Sandra opened the French window and slipped out to the terrace grotesquely patterned with the shadows of prim box-trees. The last glow of sunset color tinted the horizon; faint sounds rustled in shrubs and hedges. A perfect night. Her mind was a jumble of impressions; it was time she straightened them out. Was it only this morning that she had hesitantly entered the office of Damon and Hoyt? That episode seemed years behind her.

Voices drifted through the open windows, overtones to the sensuous rhythm of the Barcarolle from the Tales of Hoffman, played softly with exquisite feeling. Was Estelle Carter at the piano, or Curtis Newsome? Whoever it was had the touch of an artist.

She leaned against a pillar and drew a long breath of the heavenly, scented air. Flowers were pale blurs in the garden. The spray of a distant fountain glittered in the moonlight like an eruption of blue diamonds before it showered down to tinkle on the gleaming surface of a basin. From the stables drifted a faint whinny, followed a soft reply. The sky hung low like a gold-spangled canopy.

On a night like this under the stars her father seemed very near. Sandra's throat tightened. Where was he? They had been gay and understanding comrades for years.

If he had shaken his head at her stormy outbursts, he had been tenderly sympathetic with her quick, passionate repentances. Now he was gone and she was like thousands of others in these United States, a girl on her own.

"Coffee?"

"Philippe! How you startled me! No coffee, thank you. I ought to go in. Mrs. Newsome may want me. I am here to help her, you know."

Rousseau caught up a dark velvet cape lying across a chair. "I told her that I wanted to talk with you, that I had not seen you since your father — went. So that's all right. Huckins is setting out the card table. Mrs. Pat is a contract addict. Let's go down to the pool. We can talk there without being overheard. Sometimes I suspect that the very walls of this house have ears."

"The pool looks like a mammoth black mirror flecked with gold stars. I'd love to get nearer."

Side by side they crossed the terrace, descended the broad steps, followed the garden path. Once Sandra stopped to press her cheek against the golden, fragrant heart of a mammoth pink rose. Rousseau piled a scarlet cushion upon a white one on the parapet and threw the wrap over her shoulders.

"Better keep this on. It is apt to be chilly here; sometimes little mists float up from the river."

He seated himself beside her. The flame of his cigarette-lighter illuminated his face for an instant, long enough for Sandra to note his contracted brow, the deep lines etched between his nose and mouth. Did being a long lost son make him look like that?

"What was Langdon saying to you in the library before dinner?"

Suspicion stuck out of his soft voice like a jagged rock in a smooth stream. The question brought her thoughts, which had been lazily luxuriating in the scent and hushed beauty of the night, right-about-face.

"What was Mr. Langdon saying? My mind is still rocking from the shock. He said that you claim to be the son of Mark Hoyt, to be the child who, it was supposed, died in France years ago."

"Claim! I am the son of Mark Hoyt."

"How do you know? What proof have you? Mrs. Newsome told me —"

"What?"

"Of Mark Hoyt's first marriage; the

death of the child; the flight of the nurse with her lover; that a man had appeared who claimed to be Philip Hoyt. I almost had the jitters when Mr. Langdon told me that you were the claimant. When Dad used to tell you of the exploits of the Three Musketeers of Melton, talk of Mark Hoyt, why didn't you tell us that you were his son? At least you might have hinted that you had heard of him."

"I wasn't talking then, I was investigating. My mother — the woman who through the years I had thought my mother — Anne Pardoe, told me as she was dying that I was Mark Hoyt's son, that at the time of his accident she was so terrified at thought of the consequences to her when the boy's parents should see him so cruelly scarred, that, intimidated by her lover, Raoul Rousseau, who had to leave the country furtively, she had fled with him and the child to South America, leaving a mound and a letter behind her."

"What a hideous, brutal thing to do!"

"A few years later the Rousseaus moved north to Kentucky, bought an old plantation, boarded and bred horses. They brought me up as their son. In spite of the fact that they spoke French to each other, they insisted that I learn to speak, read, and write English. Now I understand why. They meant sometime to tell me the truth about my parents."

"I can't believe it's real. It sounds too old-fashioned, too like nineteenth century melodrama."

"Old-fashioned! Don't you read the papers? Don't you know that a case was recently tried in New York courts with thirteen 'rightful heirs' fighting for a fortune? Each one claimed that he was the long-lost son."

"Do you resemble either Mark Hoyt or his wife?"

"I have her dark eyes — the Hoyt eyes are gray — and hair like his. Anne Pardoe told me that I looked as he did when he was young. Even if I didn't, lack of resemblance to parents counts for nothing, often a child is a throw-back to a great-great-grandfather or a collateral."

"What does the present heir, Nicholas Hoyt, think of your story?"

"He is fighting it, of course. Who wouldn't try to hang on to a fortune? Two months before I came here, I wrote to him telling him what had been told me. Later I came in good faith with my mother's — Anne Pardoe's — diary in which day by day she had recorded her emotions of guilt and terror. I supposed that would be enough to establish my claim but Hoyt's lawyers refused to accept it as the sole evidence. Not until then did I engage counsel and bring suit to recover my inheritance."

"Of course you will come into your own, Philippe, but I can't quite understand why Mrs. Newsome invited you to stay at Seven Chimneys until your claim had been proved. It seems so disloyal to her first husband's nephew."

There was assurance and self-satisfaction in the way Rousseau stroked his clipped dark mustache.

"That was easy. I discovered that she was furious with Nicholas Hoyt because he had objected to her marrying one of his uncle's young jockeys. I didn't jump into this fight without having my campaign planned to the minutest detail. When I wrote Mrs. Newsome asking if I might come, I asked also if I might bring Iron Man to enter him against Nicholas Hoyt's Fortune in the Charity Races; then I had her cold."

"The contest may help with her, but won't it make Nicholas Hoyt more determined than ever to discredit you?"

"What can he do against that diary?"

"Has the Court passed on it?"

He smothered an imprecation. "No.

They call this a hustling country! Try to push a law case along and see how fast it is. We come to trial the day after the big races. Hoyt's counsel asked for more time. Time! Time! As if time would help them. Langdon is one of the lawyers."

"He is! That accounts for his third-degree manner. He suspects that I have come to Seven Chimneys to help you, Philippe."

"Didn't you come here for that purpose?"

It was more an assertion than a question. Something in his voice brought Sandra to her feet.

"No! No! How could I know anything about your claim? Dad gave me a letter to his old friend, Ben Damon. Mr. Damon offered me this position. It sounded interesting and I took it. I hadn't a suspicion that you were within a thousand miles of this town."

"You'll have a hard time making Hoyt and his lawyers believe that."

"They can't be so —"

"Mrs. Newsome would like you to take a hand at cards, sir. Mr. Langdon has been called to the phone for long distance."

Sandra's breath caught as she looked at the butler. His lips were set in a thin, pinched smile. A hateful smile. Had he heard Philippe's intimation that she had come to help him? She felt as if a net were closing about her.

"All right, Huckins! I'll come."

Rousseau waited until the servant had disappeared as silently as he had materialized from the shadows, before he complained irritably:

"I don't trust that butler. He's too smug. Let's forget him. Now that you are here, you will help me, won't you?"

"If I can without being disloyal to my employer."

"You can't hurt her. Whether I am judged the heir or whether Nicholas Hoyt is, will make no difference to her materially. The law would uphold the widow's rights even if I wanted to push her out, which I don't. The old Stone House will suit me till she gets through here. Coming in?"

"Not yet. I'll stay our under the stars for a while. Things have happened so fast today that like the old woman in Mother Goose I am wondering if I be really I."

"Don't stay too long, and think of me, Sandra. I'm poor, I've always been poor; don't let rich Nick Hoyt push me out of your heart. When I get this fortune . . ." He left the sentence unfinished and pressed his lips to her hand.

Sandra watched him thoughtfully as he hurried along the path. That reference to his poverty was characteristic. In London he had complained of his luck. "Luck always had been against him." She had been sorry for him. Could she help him now? He might be the son — undoubtedly he was — of the New England Hoyts, but he was incurably French in his manner. She couldn't imagine Jed Langdon or — or the gentleman trainer kissing a girl's hand like that. Why shouldn't Philippe have French manners? Hadn't he grown up as the son of the Rousseaus?

Seated on the parapet, she drew the velvet cape closer about her bare shoulders. It was chilly by the pool but incomparably lovely. The lighted windows of the house seemed like bright, kindly eyes looking down upon her; there was hardly a sound in the dusky, scented garden which was walled in by high hedges clipped to the smoothness of a velvet arras. It must have taken years and years for that hedge to grow. She had seen . . . What was that? That . . . that mist . . . floating. . . .

On her feet she clutched the cape tight about her throat. Her heart jangled to a stop. Galloped furiously on. She brushed her hand over her eyes. She was awake. Was that a shrouded white figure against the hedge? She fought creeping horror. The thing was waving a skeleton hand! It floated!

"The old house has a ghost too," the trainer had said.

Couldn't she move? The night was uncannily still. As if waiting — waiting! She must make a sound.

With a stifled shriek she fled. A voice behind her? A muffled voice? Was the thing following? She charged up the terrace steps. Pulled open the French window.

Mrs. Newsome looked up from her cards. There were four flesh and blood persons about that table. Nothing spectral about them. Sandra's world steadied.

"Been exploring, Miss Duval?" Mrs. Newsome's voice was real too.

"Yes. If you don't need me, I — I will say goodnight."

She left the room without waiting for a response. She met Jed Langdon coming down the curved stairway. He stopped.

"Calling this a day, Miss Duval? What's the matter? You're ghastly."

She met his eyes and tried to laugh. "Am I? Perhaps I have heart attacks too. Perhaps there is something about Seven Chimneys which brings them on."

She looked back as she reached her door. He was standing where she had left him, watching her with startled eyes.

Chapter VI

One week had rained itself away in a torrential downpour. Another had changed the colors in the rock garden. In the perennial borders it had brought out boltonia, fluffy clouds of it; monkshood, pale as aquamarine, purple as Persian amethysts; marigolds, running the scale of topaz tints; giant zinnias in melting aquarelles; helenium, rusty as the red of carnelian; cosmos, all mother-of-pearl or tourmaline pink; spikes of aster tataricus, looming like glorious violet mists; also it had lighted an occasional scarlet flame among the maples. August had checked out.

She had learned much in the two weeks since her arrival at Seven Chimneys, Sandra reflected, as, hands in the pockets of her honey-colored cardigan, she swung along a woodsy road into which she had turned from the highway to avoid the automobiles whoozing endlessly along the shining black macadam. It was evidently a by-path; she didn't know where it led. What difference did that make? She couldn't lose her way. The woods were fragant and still; the noise of traffic was reduced to a purr.

Lovely country. She filled her lungs with the sparkling air scented with balsam and pine, crisped with a hint of September chill. Rather nice to be on her own, not to care where the road went. Usually at this hour she was pouring tea for the cronies of the lady of the manor — she had them by the sporty score — but Mrs. Newsome, when departing early in the morning to attend a sale of horses, had told her to take the day off. Apparently she had gained the affection of her employer. Mrs. Pat consulted her, confided her deepest thoughts, thoughts so deep and intimate that sometimes her confidante scorched with embarrassment.

Mr. Damon had cautioned her to watch her step in regard to Curtis Newsome. He need not have worried; except for a nod of greeting, his wife's secretary apparently did not intrude into the world in which the youthful husband was dwelling, a world of perplexity and disappointment and high spots of gaiety which swept the other members of the household into their contagious hilarity. She had not laughed so much in months as she had since she came to Seven Chimneys. Estelle Carter was keyed to a pitch of incessant activity; when she was in the mood — and men were present — she could be fascinating. Curtis and she rode, golfed, and played tennis together. Was the girl — girl, she was a divorcee — really attracted to him, or was it the thrill of a new chase? Some of his moods were as stormy as the music of his violin. He was brutally discourteous to his wife, then remorsefully, caressingly tender.

Lately he had been consistently rude to Philippe Rousseau who was making himself quite at home on the estate he was claiming. Mrs. Pat must be aware of her husband's attitude. There had been a triumphant gleam in her eyes when Curtis had been particularly raw. Did she think that by sponsoring the "Peerless Pretender," as Estelle Carter called him, she was arousing the jealousy of the man she had married? Poor, tortured woman grasping at a straw of hope.

Life at Seven Chimneys went at a cinematic pace; it was a stirring show, a colorful pageant. Pulsing with the best sporting blood of the country, it featured the coming and going of noted and notorious stable owners; talk of the chances of green horses, show horses, harness and saddle classes; the merits of jockeys; victorious silks; past races and victors, and races and victors to come. She could sit through a discussion of equine eugenics now without changing color — at first it had seemed that embarrassment would burn her face to a crisp.

It was all so different from the conversation in the world in which she had been living, where her father's friends would fling themselves into passionate arguments on international policies, the latest scientific discovery, the science of being — that subject had been inexhaustible — they even had started an association to promote experiments in interplanetary communication. She was living in an entirely different world, a world which swept on at a breath-snatching tempo, but a world which was thrillingly interesting.

She had begun to appreciate what Mr. Damon had meant when he had spoken of the inner circles of turfdom; also she had become increasingly aware of silent animosities, underground intimacies between members of the household. So far they remained vague impressions, inaudible voices battering against some padded cell of her mind in an effort to make themselves heard. Nothing real, nothing tangible. . . .

Tangible! The word brought with it the creepy chill which shook her whenever she thought of that phantom at the pool. Sometimes when the shrouded figure hurtled through the fearful silence of her dream, she would wake out of a sound sleep, tense with horror.

She tried to reason away the memory. Of course it hadn't been a phantom; it had been a curious figment of mist from the river. Her imagination had been keyed to its highest pitch by the events of the day, and when the white thing had seemed to take shape, what more natural than that inflamed memory should fling the words of the trainer to the screen of her mind.

"The old house has a ghost too."

If any one had told her that she, Sandra Duval, could be so weak-minded as to be frightened by a bit of mist — she shut her teeth hard in an effort to hold back the creepy chill. Mist or not, it had been hideously real. Her face had startled Jed Langdon when they had met on the stairs. Had Philippe stayed with her at the pool, would he have seen it? He was a superstitious person, she had discovered during their acquaintance in London. He clutched a talisman in his left hand before a race, he had confided to her. If his horse lost, it was not the fault of the charm but the way he had held it. She had thought at first that he was joking; later she had discovered that he meant it.

Philippe's friendship was proving somewhat embarrassing. He took it for granted that she would ride with him, motor with him. She had been conscious of Jed Langdon's speculative eyes on them more than once, but now, praise be to Allah, he had gone abroad, doubtless to consult the French specialist, and she could enjoy Philippe's companionship when she had time. He was a companionable person, if a trifle moody and melancholy. He had an amusing manner with women, the Sultan manner, lordly, yet subtly protecting. He would be quite in character as master of a great fortune.

She had not met Nicholas Hoyt, but she had heard of him until she was tired of his name. She disliked him unseen for having treated his uncle's widow so shabbily; he could have stopped the social ostracism. Did he think that he could order Mrs. Pat's life? Evidently he was of the maddening dictator type.

The fight for the estate was the talk of the county. The chances that Philippe's claim would be flung out of court, what "Nick" would do if the claimant were adjudged the son were favorite topics of conversation when Mrs. Pat's friends dropped in for tea. Mostly they championed Nicholas Hoyt; they were unanimously of the opinion that his knowledge of horseflesh was uncanny. They were non-partisan when it came to Thoroughbreds — which they didn't own — and were loud in their praises of Rousseau's gray challenger, Iron Man. They treated Curtis Newsome, the one-time jockey, with the tenderness and consideration they would have bestowed on a sick colt.

A scream! The savage ferocity of the sound stopped Sandra's heart and feet at the same instant. She held her breath and listened. Where was she? She had been so absorbed in thought that she had followed the road unheedingly. There it was again! It made her think of a furious animal charging into battle. A stallion? Of course — this was a horse country. Now he was roaring — that sound was more terrible than the scream — he was thrashing wildly.

Was he being abused? She dashed forward.

The narrow road ended suddenly. Her onward rush was blocked by a heavy rail fence. She stopped, her eyes wide with amazement. In the very middle of a paddock quivered a superb black horse. He was young. He was beautifully sleek, his head was high, his powerful neck arched. His eyes rolled viciously.

Fascinated, breathless, she watched a small man climb to the top rail of the fence as another man swung to the back of the colt, who, except for quivering flanks, stood as motionless as a cast-iron statue.

Sandra's brows puckered in unbelief. Was she trespassing on Nicholas Hoyt's property? The daring rider was the trainer who had brought her from the station; she would know that unflinching mouth anywhere. His hair was rough; there was a bloody streak down one cheek.

The horse bellowed, screamed a battle challenge, reared. Her heart tore up to her throat. Would he flop over backward and crush the man in the saddle? As if in answer to her gasp of terror, the trainer brought him down with a twist of his head and his own legs.

The sleek savage roared and stood still. The silence boded tragedy. Was he thinking how he could most quickly get the man on his back under his plunging hoofs, at the mercy of his mighty teeth? Up he went, came down with a suddenness which shot the rider forward onto his glistening neck; for an instant the trainer remained draped over the ears, but his hand was wound in the flowing mane, and when the horse came up again and bellowed, he slid back into the saddle and slipped his feet into the stirrups.

In her absorption in the superb horsemanship, Sandra leaned her arms on the top rail.

"Go back! Go back!" the small man shouted hoarsely. His eyes bulged, for all the world like the round eyes of a bloodthirsty spider; his face was gray as he dropped to the outside of the railing and ran in her direction. She hastily retreated to the shade of a nearby tree, furiously embarrassed by her thoughtlessness.

The colt, apparently indifferent to the side-lines, looked around at the man on his back as if asking:

"Ready?"

There was an instant of tense stillness, broken only by the creak of leather, the strident chirp of a bird, before the horse shook his head and began to fight. An ironshod hoof struck the rails where Sandra had been leaning; he plunged, pawed, reared; he bared savage teeth; in between the beastly noises sounded the thump of the man's body going back and forth in the saddle.

So suddenly as almost to unseat his rider, he stopped, quivered. The trainer gently stroked the sweating neck; then turned him, made him canter, stop, go, walk, stop again.

"Licked, and taking it like a good sport," exulted an excited voice beside Sandra. It was the spider-eyed man. His young, hard-bitten face was transformed by a fatuous smile. With him came the effluvium of mingled leather, sawdust, sweat, and the stable. "You shouldn't have come so near this yard, Miss. I almost had heart-failure when I saw you. You might have been killed."

"I'm sorry. It was stupid of me. What a wonderful horse!"

"I'll say Curtain Call is wonderful. I've been a jock for years and I've never seen a fairer fighter. Not a dirty trick, though he wanted to throw what was on his back something terrible."

"Hi, Sharp!" the trainer shouted. He had dismounted and was holding the pawing colt by the bridle.

"Coming!" The thin legs slid over the rails in answer to the authoritative shout. A man with pompadoured white hair hovered nervously at a discreet distance; two freckled-faced, pop-eyed exercise boys peered from the door to the paddock. The jockey dropped into the yard. Curtain Call laid back his ears and watched his crablike approach with burning eyes.

"Try him," the victor commanded.

The little man leaped to the saddle. Instantly he was shot into space with the speed and accuracy of a shell from a great gun. The trainer's frown squelched the boys' laughter, and they vanished. He waited only for the jockey to pick himself up before he sprang to the colt's back. Curtain Call bellowed, looked around, rolled his eyes. With a snort which might have meant either contempt or resignation, he obeyed the touch on the rein and cantered toward the stable.

Sandra's breath came with a rush. She had not realized until that moment that she had been holding it.

"And that seems to be that!"

Startled by a voice dropping from the sky, she looked up. Curtis Newsome was peering through the leaves of a tree.

"Have you been here all the time?"

"Yeah, in a grandstand seat." He dropped to the ground. His face was alight with interest; his blue eyes sparkled; his voice was warm with enthusiasm.

"Ever see a prettier show? You've been looking on at the making of a great race horse. Another man might have busted that proud spirit."

"I'm limp as a rag-doll. Each time the colt reared, my heart shot to my throat; each time his four feet struck earth, it dropped like a lead sinker. Do you suppose it is the first time he had been ridden?"

"Suppose! Where do you get that suppose? I know. That was Curtain Call, one of the Thoroughbreds Nicholas Hoyt inherited. He's half brother to Fortune who cleaned up the field last year when running with crack two-year-olds. Fortune will be entered in the big race which is to be staged for charity at the Hunt Club track about five miles from here three weeks from now — purse of $25,000 and cups for the winning jockey and owner — if he makes good he'll be entered in the Kentucky Derby in the spring. There'll be a classy field, some of the big horses in the country, with Rousseau's Iron Man as one of the favorites. That little jock, Eddie

Sharp, who was squatting on the rail, will be up. He's good. He and Fortune are like brothers — but gosh, I wish I could ride that hoss!"

His wistful voice reminded Sandra of her first impression of his boyishness.

"Why can't you?"

"I'm not riding!" he answered curtly. "Besides, I wouldn't get the chance. You've been at Seven Chimneys two weeks; don't you know yet that any one from there would be shot at sunrise if found in the Stone House camp?"

"Is Mr. Hoyt so bitter because he may lose the fortune he expected?"

"Where did you get that dope? He's a grand guy! He was nice enough to Pat until she married me. Gosh, now we're in for it! Why didn't we beat it?"

Sandra wheeled. The trainer was vaulting the rail fence. His sweat-soaked shirt clung to his lean body; one torn sleeve flapped as he walked; locks of wet hair framed his white face. His eyes burned as he approached, but his voice pelted like icy hail.

"What are you doing here, Newsome?"

"Sorry — didn't mean to butt in — honest! Heard you were going to break the colt this afternoon. Couldn't keep away.

Gosh, you were great!"

His fervent admiration made no impression on its object.

"Who told you I was going to break Curtain Call? Who's the informer?"

For the first time he looked at Sandra. Did he think her the guilty party? She resented the bite in the question.

"Don't glare at me as if I were the little bird who chirped the news. I didn't even know that I was on sacred ground. I just stumbled on the show you staged." Admiration submerged anger. "It was wonderful!"

His eyes softened, then hardened. "Keep out, Newsome; don't let curiosity bring you — or any member of the Seven Chimneys' outfit — here again. You're all backing Rousseau and his Iron Man, aren't you? Keep away from these stables. Get that straight. I mean it."

"Oh, King, permit thy servants to depart with their heads?"

Sandra laughed up at him as she droned her mocking plea. Something swift and strong flashed from his eyes to hers. A thrill, made up of indignation, shame at her own flippancy, reluctant admiration of the man's unyielding personality, tingled through her veins.

"Go on, please, Miss. I want to speak to Mr. Newsome."

Sandra's pride smarted as she turned away. It had not been his anger which had hurt most; it had been his maddening indifference to the girl he had brought from the station, and now he practically ordered her off the place. Even a gentleman horse trainer might show a little interest.

It seemed but a moment before Curtis Newsome joined her. His cheeks were red, his eyes bright. Sandra felt his repressed excitement.

"Good gosh, I got mine! You were let off easy, being a girl."

"Mussolini, Napoleon, and the late Julius Caesar rolled into one! For a mere trainer, I'll say that the person who snubbed us with such a grand air is going some."

"Trainer! That guy's more than a trainer. You can't blame him for ordering us off. He thinks we're all tied up with Rousseau, and — and if that Kentuckian is your old friend, I wouldn't trust him around the corner when it comes to horseflesh or — anything else — that's how I feel about him, but that — the trainer doesn't know it of course."

"The day he brought me from the station he talked like a stable-boy with years of schooling yet to go. Perhaps you can explain that?"

Newsome chuckled. "You wouldn't have thought when he was laying us out cold that he likes his little joke. Search me why he was acting up to you. Didn't know, did he, that Rousseau was your friend?"

"How could he? I hadn't the faintest idea that Philippe was here."

"Is that straight?"

Sandra resented his quick gravity. "Of course it's straight. Ask Mr. Damon."

"I believe you. You can't blame Hoyt and his lawyers if they are suspicious of any one who knew Rousseau before he blew in with his race horse to claim the estate, can you? Hoyt is manager of this big property. That fella back there is his right-hand man. I'll bet he knows more about Stone House stables than the owner himself." He grinned. "If you were in Hollywood, you'd say he doubles for his boss."

"Socially?"

That was a catty question, Sandra flayed herself. Curtis Newsome apparently took it as a joke.

"I wouldn't say that. He couldn't crash

one of Pat's dinners." The laughter vanished from his eyes and voice. "Not that he would want to," he admitted morosely.

"I can't believe that he is so important — why he took . . ." Sandra derailed the remainder of the sentence. Why let Curtis Newsome know — even if she had done it as revenge — that she had tipped the understudy to the present Hoyt heir?

Would Nicholas Hoyt remain legally in possession of the estate? Speculation as to the justice of Philippe Rousseau's claim engrossed her as she walked home. Of course she believed in him, but she was getting a little tired of his constant reminders that all the world loved a rich man, that the scales of justice would tip for Nicholas Hoyt because of his background. Her thoughts whirled on and on like a merry-go-round; no sooner would she reach a conclusion than her mind went into reverse at breakneck speed only to demolish the argument she had so logically built up. The memory of the many times Philippe had encouraged her father to talk of his youthful days in Melton edged into her reflections. Curious that not once had he mentioned his interest in the town. She fed a question to Curtis Newsome now and then to keep him talking. Even in her self-absorption she gathered that he passionately admired Nicholas Hoyt, that he as fervently detested Philippe Rousseau.

When they reached Seven Chimneys, Newsome left her and swung off to the stables. She went on to the house. She lingered on the terrace for a moment to revel in the air freighted with the fragrance of many flowers, in the beauty of the river touched with the rosy reflection of a crimsoning west. Great scarlet medicine balls floated on the still water of the azure-lined pool, which mirrored each convolution of the iron rails of the balconies above. On the tanbark fairway back of the stables, trotters were being sent around for a late afternoon brisk, the drivers hunched over their withers.

Who would think, looking at this charming home, that it was rent beneath its surface by conflicting passions? Sandra stepped into the hall softly as if a footfall might disturb the present calm.

She stopped and stood motionless. Gazing into the mirror was a maid in uniform. Tragically brilliant eyes stared appraisingly back at their reflection; hair of a rusty red-brown was adorned by a strip of lace and ribbon.

Sandra blinked and looked again. She

wasn't mistaken. In spite of dyed hair, the woman was the applicant for the advertised position whom she had seen coming from Mr. Damon's office. Close beside her, as if he were whispering, stood Huckins, the butler.

Chapter VII

Bud and Buddy, the two police dogs, dashed into the roadside shrubs on predatory business bent. Sandra stopped at the iron gate in the box hedge to look at Stone House whose upper windows with their twenty-four panes seemed like kindly, unblinking eyes staring incuriously back at her. It was the first time she had seen the place at close range, it looked just as her father had described it. Giants must have hoisted the huge granite blocks into place. A batten door! Never before had she seen one out of captivity. Large-headed nails formed a diamond pattern on the weathered slabs of oak to correspond with the design of the panes of the casement windows of the lower story. A great iron ring served as a knocker. She was glad that she had dared Nicholas Hoyt's wrath as personified by his trainer; the sight of that marvelous old door was worth a risk.

From the direction of the stable drifted a man's voice singing.

She rested her arms in their pale yellow sleeves on the top of the iron gate, and listened. What a boon to the lonely or the downhearted the radio was, she thought, as the refrain cruised the air with a gusto which set her foot to beating time to the rhythm.

" 'The farmer's in the dell,
The farmer's in the dell,
Heigh o the derry oh,
The farmer's in the dell.
"The . . .' "

The song stopped abruptly. Evidently the listener thought it time for the farmer to be snapped out of the dell. Had the trainer been the listener? It was a week since he had warned Curtis Newsome and "any member of the Seven Chimneys' outfit" to keep off. It was just a week since she had seen the new maid gazing at herself in the mirror, she remembered irrelevantly. Emma, she called herself, was efficient; she rarely spoke — when she did, it was with an English accent — but whenever she was in the room, Sandra was reminded of the telephone girl's comparison of her to corked up TNT, and her slangy conclusion:

"Treat that dame rough and she's all set to go off with a bang."

The contact would not be lacking at Seven Chimneys, Sandra concluded, with a thrilled, if shivery, premonition of excitement to come. Was Huckins, the butler, especially interested in her, or had he been giving the new servant instructions merely, that first day she had seen them together? The maid might have been an automaton for all the notice Philippe Rousseau took of her. It was doubtful if the other members of the household were aware of the change in waitresses; when Mrs. Newsome was in one of her servant-eating moods — as she had been for the last week — they came and went with bewildering rapidity. It was a wonder that the butler stayed on; she was particularly raw to him. Doubtless he was picking up a small fortune in commissions.

Of course, the woman who had applied first for the position of social secretary might be in such dire stress that she would accept housework, but in that case, why dye her hair? Pride? Ought she to tell Mrs. Pat of her discovery? No. Why be little Miss Fix-it? If she told any one it should be Mr. Damon, but why tell him yet? The woman might lose the job of which probably she was in tragic need.

Sandra switched her thoughts from the waitress. She had much better consider what would happen to her if she were discovered on Stone House property. The trainer's warning to keep away had prodded her like a challenge, and here she was stepping on proscribed ground. The foray into enemy country had been her first thought when Mrs. Pat had announced her departure for a day or two. She had been summoned to Mr. Damon's office for a conference, she had explained, had added bitterly to her husband:

"Better not come with me, Curtis. Probably Nick will be there, and you hate the sight of him."

Sandra had pondered that last remark. Curtis Newsome's voice had held no hint of dislike when he had exclaimed, "He's a grand guy!" Was his wife trying to strike a spark of enmity between the two men?

With the owner in the city, and the trainer, she hoped, where he belonged, on the track or in the stables, the opportunity to approach Stone House appeared heaven-sent. It was more than a house; it was a personality. Snuggled into a perennial border lovely with pinks and blues, soft yellows, violets, the green of emeralds and tourmalines, it suggested births and toddling childhood, daring youth, home-comings, weddings, achievement, delightful old age, and lives well lived passing on to Paradise.

The dogs abandoned the squirrel they had been hunting, flung their lithe bodies against the wrought-iron gate and drew themselves up to look over. They whined and snuffled, wagged their tails riotously as a chunky woman, whose figure billowed under its dove-gray taffeta, appeared on the flagged path at the side of the house. Her arms were full of long-stemmed dahlias in varying shades of red. Her laugh was a plump chuckle as she looked at the two heads with their open mouths, dripping tongues, and snapping eyes.

"So-o there you are, Bud an' Buddy. Come down from the big house to see old Nanny O'Day, have you?" A slight touch of brogue richened, deepened her kindly voice. Her small merry eyes appraised the girl. "You're the new secretary at Seven Chimneys, aren't you, my dear? Bridie's told me about you. Come in. Come in."

She lifted the latch. Sandra drew back. She caught the dogs — who showed symptoms of being about to crash the gate — by their collars.

"Oh no, thank you. I am sure Mr. Hoyt wouldn't like it. I didn't mean to intrude. I only stopped for a moment to look at the old house. It did something to my heart, and I lingered. I had heard so much about it."

"Of course you've heard about it; who hasn't in this part of the world?" The roll of the r was a joy. "You needn't be asking pardon because you stopped; hundreds do. As for Mr. Nick's not liking it, it's a show place, he knows that. Wouldn't you like to see inside?"

Sandra's scruples as to intrusion thinned like mist under the woman's sunny personality.

"I would love to see the inside, Nanny O'Day." The dogs attempted to squeeze by her as she opened the gate. "No, boys, no! Stay outside and wait for me, and don't go teary-eyed as if I were a hard-hearted wretch, either."

"Let them come in. Well they know the place and me."

"Is Mr. Hoyt at home?"

"Even if he was, it wouldn't matter. He doesn't mind visitors so long as they don't cut pieces out of the paneling as one crazy man did the other day. Come in. Come in, an' we'll have a cup of tea."

Sandra followed the waddling figure into a hall — coolly dim after the sunny outside world — sheathed in pine boards mellowed to a dusky brown. Nanny O'Day stopped and pressed a panel under the stairway. It rolled back and revealed a dusky interior with dark blotches which were steps.

"See the stairs? They go up and then down. Indians used to be as thick as huckleberries round this country and folks took to hiding sometimes." Her voice had dropped to a dramatic whisper.

"May I go in and look? My father used to live in the village and he has told me many times about the underground passage."

"Certain, certain, my dear. Go in. Take this flashlight so you can see."

Sandra went slowly up the age-blackened stairs which creaked uncannily under her feet. The air was clear and sweet. She peeked into a sort of cubicle on the landing. She could see a bar of light. Had the opening once been a window?

Other steps descended to a bolted wooden door. Eerie shadows. Queer groaning noises in the walls. She hastily rejoined Nanny O'Day.

"Didn't take you long, my dear. There isn't much to see but every one wants to see it," the woman observed indulgently. "Come to the living room; the woodwork in that never has been changed."

Sandra controlled an absurd urge to look furtively over her shoulder at the secret panel as she followed into a room scented with tobacco. Set in the middle of one wall of bookshelves was the painting of a tight-lipped, white-collared Puritan; his eyes were as stone-gray as his clipped mustache and small goatee. A table-desk looked businesslike; a small piano was in one corner; there were lattice windows; a noisy little fire crackled and flamed on the hearth.

With profound sighs, the dogs thumped to the rug in front of the blaze, dropped their heads on their outstretched paws, and looked up at Nanny O'Day with expectant eyes. Back to them, she arranged the tall dahlias in a bronze vase, crooning over the flowers as if they were children whom she delighted to touch. The blossoms harmonized with the red leather of the old-time chairs as the firelight brightened it to scarlet, dimmed it to dark crimson. Her labor of love completed, she drew forward a small table.

"Sit down, my dear, and we'll have tea — unless you are afraid of our ghost." Her chuckle was as round and soft as her ruddy cheeks.

"A ghost!" Sandra's knees gave way. She sat down suddenly.

"Certain, certain, my dear. Doesn't every self-respecting property as old as this have a ghost? See that portrait between the books? See the mark on the man's coat just below the heart? A sword made that. Notice the eyes?"

Sandra wondered if the creepy chills which slithered along her veins were becoming chronic. She nodded and put her hand to her constricted throat even as she mentally flayed herself for being such a poor sport.

"Those eyes were peep-holes in Revolutionary days."

Sandra paid tribute to Nanny O'Day's dramatic power. She had missed her vocation; she should have gone on the stage. As if encouraged by the girl's silence, the woman elaborated:

"The portrait is hung over what was a window before the little room back of it was built on. The secret stairway I showed you runs up to that. One day Major Hoyt of the Continental Army, home for a day to hold a secret conference with superior officers — some say 'twas General Washington himself — was standing on the very spot you're on now. He looked up. The eyes of the portrait flickered!"

Sandra impulsively linked her arm in Nanny O'Day's. The woman patted her hand.

"Quick as a flash the Major plunged his sword through the picture. He heard a groan, then a thud. He rushed for the secret panel. The spring wouldn't work — it sticks even now. He shouted for the servants. It was ten minutes before they forced the door."

"Whom did they find?"

"What beautiful eyes you have, my dear; they're as velvety as black pansies. Who did the Major find? Nobody, just a pool of blood and a red trail along the underground passage and trampled mud where it comes out at the river bank."

"Did they find out who had been spying?"

"No. They suspected a member of the family who had turned king's man. No one else knew of the passage. He disappeared only to return to float about the estate, it's said, when there's treachery afoot. Then he walks as a warning to the traitor. You look white. I've talked too much. It's nothing but a story, child, nothing but a story. We'll have tea right off. I don't know what Mr. Nicholas would do to me if he knew I'd frightened you. Make yourself at home, my dear, while I put the kettle on and make some toast; our little maid is out. Like it with cinnamon?"

"Adore it. I'm not fr-frightened, really I'm not. Let me help? I haven't seen the inside of a kitchen — an honest-to-goodness kitchen — for five years. I used to love to cook."

"Certain, certain, come right along. Ours is a nice kitchen."

Sandra slipped out of her knit jacket and laid it over a chair, before she followed Nanny O'Day into the hall. She was glad to get away from the portrait. Could that thing she had seen by the pool have been real?

"Don't be silly, don't be *silly! It* only appeared when there was treachery afoot, Nanny O'Day had said. Could it be that Philippe — forget it, forget it," she told herself and dashed into the kitchen.

"Nice" was hardly the word to describe the long, deliciously cool room with its solid oak beams; it was adorable. Red geraniums in pots sunned themselves on the deep sills of the windows — windows draped in ruffled white muslin, set into the massive granite walls. A rocking chair, cushioned in red and white gingham, stood near the end of a table, which was covered with an old-fashioned red and white and blue plaided cloth on which rested a brimming work-basket and a yellow bowl heaped with eggs. One end of the room was all fire-place, with great ovens at the sides and seats at the outer edge of the nine-foot opening. A dresser, its shelves displaying pewter platters, bowls, pint-pots, porringers, and plates which shone like silver, stood against the wall opposite the windows.

A canary in a gilded cage poured out his heart in song. A fluffy white angora cat with an orange tail, on the threshold of the open door, sprang to her feet, bared her teeth, and hunched her back into an interrogation point. The dogs who had followed Sandra looked casually at each other; then as casually turned and walked softly back into the hall. Nanny O'Day chuckled.

"Bud and Buddy have had their lesson." She chirped to the bird before she explained: "That pewter was used by the Hoyts up to the Revolution; then porcelain came in. Now look at our modern kitchen!"

With faintly repressed pride she moved a three-fold screen and disclosed an electric range, refrigerator, and all the equipment an up-to-the-minute kitchen should possess.

Sandra nodded reluctant approval. "I suppose that is necessary now, but the old part is infinitely more picturesque, isn't it?"

"Certain, certain, my dear," Nanny O'Day was enveloping herself in a capacious white apron, "but the new way saves time and energy. Take this; you might spot that nice knitted dress."

Sandra doubled the sleeveless apron around her and tied the strings in a belt. She bobbed a little curtsey.

"All ready for work, ma'am."

"Sure an' it's a pity Mr. Nick isn't here to see the new cook with her pretty bare arms. Here's the bread. Cut it as you like it. I'll put on the kettle." She brought eggshell cups and saucers and set them on a tray.

"We'll take this to the living room —"

"Please let's have tea here. I'd love it."

"Just as you say, my dear. Mr. Nicholas often has his breakfast in the kitchen, and sometimes the head trainer, Mr. Parsons, and Eddie Sharp, the jockey, come for tea.

There's the phone! Some woman or girl calling Mr. Nick, of course. They don't give him a minute's peace or me either. It's:

" 'Is Mr. Hoyt there?' or 'When do you expect Mr. Hoyt?' 'The minute he comes in tell Mr. Hoyt to ring —' from morning till night.

"All I can think of is the fox with the hounds after him. I suppose it's to be expected when a bachelor is rich and young and handsome as a picture. You'll find everything you need. Go right ahead and make your tea and anything else you want; no knowin' when I'll be back; whoever it is will be wanting me to write down a message."

Sandra's eyes thoughtfully followed the plump woman as she got under way like a fussy little tug-boat. Fox and hounds! Had Nanny O'Day picked up that comparison from the pursued Nicholas Hoyt himself? What detestable conceit! Thank heaven, he was in town today. Had she run into him here, he might have thought her another hound on his trail. He and his trainer! Like master like man. So — the trainer's name was Parsons. Catch her coming to Stone House again! But now that she was here and the poor badgered fox was in his city lair, why not make the most of this adventure?

She filled the kettle, sliced bread. The bowl of eggs drew her eyes like a magnet. She was ravenously hungry. Had she forgotten how to scramble them? Nanny O'Day had handed her the freedom of the kitchen. Why not try?

Could that story of the ghostly traitor be true? Of course not. She must keep the thing out of her mind. As an aid to normal thinking she hummed under her breath as she moved back and forth across the sun-patched floor.

" 'The farmer's in the dell,' " the last word rippled as she remembered Nanny O'Day's comparison. She paraphrased:

> "The hounds are on the trail,
> The hounds are on the trail,
> Heigh o the derry oh,
> The hounds are on the trail."

The canary began to sing. The kettle began to purr. The toast began to brown. Appetizing smell! She was reaching into the pantry when she heard some one enter the kitchen. Without looking over her shoulder, she called:

"We'll have eggs with our tea, Nanny

O'Day. You never tasted anything like my scrambled —"

She turned. The trainer was at the door, his figure dark against the sunshine. She dropped a saucepan and held her hands high in pretended terror.

"D-don't s-shoot, Mr. Parsons!"

Chapter VIII

"Hands down! This ain't my day for putting folks on the spot, Miss." The man leaned against the door, twisting a cap in his hands. "Say, how did you know my name was Parsons?"

He was quite a different person from the disheveled rider she had seen breaking the colt. His hair was smoothly brushed, his riding clothes were well cut, but he was still keeping up the impersonation. She would appear as dumb as he thought her.

"Mrs. O'Day told me that Mr. Parsons, the trainer, often came in for tea. I didn't tell her that you and I were ancient enemies."

"Enemies! So that accounts for the dramatics when I appeared."

There was an ironic twist to his mouth which Sandra remembered, a warning glint in the clear gray eyes. "Dramatics" had been a slip. It was quite out of character.

"Certain, certain." She didn't realize that she was mimicking dear old Nanny O'Day until the words were spoken. This man certainly had the trick of making her flippant. "Having dared to come to Stone House in spite of your warning, Mr. Horse-breaker, I was prepared to take my punishment."

"Why did you come?"

Sandra expertly broke eggs into a bowl, measured milk, thoughtfully added salt and pepper to the mixture.

"To see this wonderful house. I had heard —" Perhaps it would be better not to tell him that she had heard of the place for years and years from her father. "Having heard that your boss was in the city, I seized the opportunity. I had forgotten that he had a savage understudy. What will you do about it — beat me?" Now why had she defied him instead of being sweetly apologetic? She turned on the heat and set the saucepan on the electric range.

"I didn't beat Curtain Call. What are you doing?"

He was rather heart-warming when he smiled — pity he didn't indulge oftener. Why not be friendly? He was not to blame for his employer's shortcomings.

"Scrambling eggs. Nanny O'Day turned me loose in this adorable kitchen, and I couldn't resist cooking. I haven't been in a real home for years, and I'm incurably domestic."

He came over to the range. "They look grand. Can you spare some?" As Sandra hesitated, he added: "I have many of my meals here; Nanny O'Day won't object."

Why not? He was the deputy manager of this huge estate. Hadn't Nanny O'Day said that he often came in for tea? He was interesting, and she liked and had spent her life among interesting men. Each time she had talked with him she had had the sensation of being gloriously alive; he had the same effect that flags flying, the approach of martial music had on her spirit.

"Get a plate. Something tells me that you won't be popular if you use that pewter," she protested as he took two pieces from the dresser.

"The best is none too good for this party. What shall I do next?"

"Put them on the table. Lay a slice of toast on each one. Now spread it lightly with the anchovy paste from the tube — not too much! That's right. Get the forks."

She heaped fluffy yellow mixture on the

toast, shook paprika over it till it blushed rosily.

"There! Isn't that fit for the gods?" She poured boiling water into the teapot, peeled off the voluminous apron, seated herself in the chair he held for her. He smiled as he sat opposite.

"You are domestic, are — ain't you? Your cheeks are pink; your eyes are — kinder sparklin'; you look's though you were havin' the time of your life." He tasted the egg. "Say, you're a swell cook!"

Sandra laughed as she filled a cup. His English had threatened to slip back to normalcy. She felt absurdly light-hearted. "I'm good — I hate to talk about myself, but I'm good," she boasted theatrically. "If I fade-out as a social secretary, I can cook."

"I'll — I'll bet Mr. Hoyt would take you on here."

Sandra stiffened. "Thank you, but I wouldn't care to work for your Mr. Hoyt."

Nanny O'Day appeared at the hall door with a dog on each side of her. They defied the spitting cat and charged at the man who had risen from his chair, thumped forepaws on his shoulders, and tried to reach his face with their rough red tongues.

"Well, Mr. Nick. Why didn't you let me

know you were back? I've been taking messages for you on the phone till I'm beat out," the woman explained reproachfully.

"Mr. *Nick!*" Sandra repeated in an incredulous whisper.

Nanny O'Day babbled on like a brook. "Certain, certain. Sure an' it's nice you two young people eatin' eggs together sociable like. I told you Mr. Nicholas liked to take a bite here in my kitchen, my dear."

"Yes, I remember." Fury crisped Sandra's voice. Nicholas Hoyt must be vastly amused at her gullibility, or did he think that she had known who he was and was just one more hound on the trail? She would show him!

"I didn't realize that it was so late, Nanny O'Day; I must be going. I left my jacket in the living room."

"Down, boys!" Hoyt pushed the dogs away, and with an authoritative "Stay here!" to the chunky little woman, followed Sandra into the living room with Bud and Buddy at his heels.

"I can't let you go like this, Miss Duval. Let me explain."

"I won't listen to explanations."

"Oh yes, you will. Having walked of your own accord into the lion's den, you'll hear what the lion has to say in explanation."

He held her knit jacket. She thrust her arms into the sleeves. She responded to his darkly intent eyes with defiant amusement.

"Did you think that you had fooled me with your English? A hint of servility in the 'Miss,' a double negative here and there, an occasional crude phrasing to add verity to the whole; that I was so stupid that I would not realize that 'I do set my bow in the clouds' was out of character, that I didn't know when I gave you that money that you were bluffing? I wasn't quite bright enough, however, I never suspected who you were. I thought you a gentleman turf man out of luck. Why waste such God-given talent on me?"

He backed against the mantel with its tall carved pilasters. He had not the air of a man whose home and fortune were threatened; he had the manner of a conquering hero. His silence infuriated Sandra.

"You have mistaken your vocation. To think that such a star actor should be lost in a mere banker! Why did you keep up the deception? Why did you forbid Curtis Newsome to tell me who you were that day at the paddock?"

"Did he tell you that?"

"He did not, but being ordinarily intelligent, I can put two and two together."

"Can you? Then you ought to be able to figure out why I didn't want you to know who I was — for a while. Mrs. Pat hasn't given me too good a reputation, has she? You needn't answer. I know."

He was maddeningly cool and authoritative. She might have known from what she had heard of him that Nicholas Hoyt would be like that. There was something in his eyes when they met hers which made her curiously shivery. Anger, of course, but anger never had affected her so before. Would she ever forget that behind his respectful gravity he must have been convulsed with mirth when he had accepted that money? Hadn't she been laughing too? He had been laughing at her this very afternoon. She hated being made ridiculous.

"How did you happen to come to Seven Chimneys? Who sent you?" Hoyt demanded.

"Who sent me? What do you mean? Don't you know that —"

"Just a minute!"

He picked up the phone in answer to a ring.

"Nicholas Hoyt speaking."

Was this another lady-hound on his trail? Sandra coughed back a nervous giggle. She watched him in fascinated interest, saw two sharp lines cut between his brows, before she realized that this was her chance to slip away.

"Hulloa, Blanche! *Wait!*"

He caught her hand and held her. She had wondered what his hands would be like; now she knew. Well-shaped, beautifully cared for, strong. Though his hold was light, it was uncompromising. Of course she could break away, but why gratify him by making a scene? She waited, apparently passive, as he talked.

"No, I didn't mean you, Blanche. . . . Dinner tomorrow? Can't. . . . You have? . . . Sure, I like 'em blonde. . . . Does it? I've turned over a new leaf; perhaps my voice shows it. I've been taking the thing too seriously. . . . Well, if you do, others don't like me that way. . . . Make it the day after and I'll come. . . . Okay! Good-bye!"

He released Sandra's hand as he laid the phone on its stand.

"You weren't playing fair to make a break for freedom when I was busy."

"Don't flatter yourself that you kept me. I remembered your suspicion. Don't you know that your own partner, Mr. Damon, sent me here?"

"Yes, but did he know that you and

Philippe Rousseau were old friends?"

Sandra never had met eyes so cold, so intent. She felt the color rush to her hair. Apparently Mr. Damon had not told Nicholas Hoyt of his friendship with her father. Neither had he told Mrs. Pat. What had been back of his reticence? She resented:

"Why should he tell you? He didn't know. Believe it or not, I never was so surprised in my life as when Philippe turned and faced me in the library at Seven Chimneys."

He sat on the corner of the flat desk and folded his arms. Sandra felt like a criminal before a judge.

"And yet Rousseau told Langdon that he had talked the matter of the inheritance over with your father before he came."

"Philippe told him that! Well, if he did, I suppose it's true — but it would be wasting breath to tell you again that I never heard of it. You wouldn't believe me."

"I'm not so sure about that. It's more important to know whether you believe Rousseau's story."

Sandra did not answer. He paced the floor as if inaction were impossible.

"You can't! Look here, do you think I'm such a poor stick that I wouldn't have been glad to have Uncle Mark's son come into his own? He would have been my cousin, almost like a brother; I've never had any one young — belong to me. I can't tell you why, but the moment I saw Rousseau I knew that he was a fake. Oh, I grant that he has plastered his claim with all the trappings appropriate to such a situation — old, old scars of burns on his shoulders; 'The strange and haunting barrier which always stood between him and the woman he had thought his mother'; 'Veiled suggestions from her as to the marvelous fortune which should be his'; 'Hints of what might happen if parents were to emerge from the mists of a far country and claim him as their son.' — All that bologna, thank God, isn't evidence; it is merely one of those difficulties in litigation which the ingenuity of the bar is supposed to overcome. He is no more Mark Hoyt's son than — than Jed Langdon is. It's a racket!"

Sandra felt as if she had been snatched up in a cloudburst of concentrated fury, and as suddenly dropped. Was Philippe a fraud? How could she be so disloyal? She said hurriedly:

"Speaking of impersonations, why the pretense that day at the station?"

"Damon had phoned that he was

sending a secretary, that I'd better look her over. We had made sure that Rousseau had heard of the advertisement; it would give him a chance to get in an ally."

"Why are you so determined to believe Phillippe dishonest?"

He ignored her indignation.

"With a claimant to the property and a strange horse here to compete in the Charity Races, we are not taking chances. I had to know what sort of secretary was coming to Seven Chimneys. After I got started, you were so patronizing — I expected at any moment you would call me 'My good man' — that it began to be corking fun, and I tried to see how good I could be."

"You were good, but not too good. And all the time you were laughing at me. Was the chauffeur's failure to meet me prearranged?"

"Just a minute! I wasn't laughing at you; I was having fun with myself. As to Dan, he is a friend of mine. He still believes me the rightful heir."

"I suppose taking that money was the peak of the — to you — humorous situation."

Not the peak, rather the foundation of a situation which something tells me may not be humorous. I carry that bill here." He put his hand over his breast pocket. "I may need it — if I lose my inheritance."

Did the gravity of his voice mean that he feared that Philippe Rousseau might win? "I must go. I hadn't forgotten that you had forbidden any one of the Seven Chimneys' outfit to step foot on your place, but Mrs. Pat is away for a day, and I had to see this adorable house."

"You're not alone at Seven Chimneys with Rousseau?"

"It could hardly be called 'alone' with sixteen servants and Mrs. Carter, could it?"

"I forgot them. You — you don't like me, do you?"

"Mad about you. What an ornament to your times!"

Her tone darkened his face with color. "You were friendly enough before you knew who I was. We'll let that ride — for the present. Glad to know that you exercise Bud and Buddy. I used to take them out — they were my uncle's pets — but when Mrs. Pat married Newsome, they remained at Seven Chimneys and I — came here."

Was the emotion in his voice real or a theatric touch to gain her sympathy?

Whichever it was, she didn't like him, she told herself; they had been antagonistic the first time they met — the kitchen episode had been but a truce. To bridge the disturbing pause, she explained lightly:

"The dogs have taken me to their hearts. Usually when I go up in the evening I find them waiting at my door. Bridie, the chambermaid, knows that I love them, so she sneaks them up to keep me company. They sleep on the two balconies. Something tells me that Huckins the butler, who is my idea of what the devil might be in his lighter moments, would spray forked blue fire from his long, sinister fingers if he caught the three B's on their way up. I asked Mrs. Pat if she objected, and she said that if any one could make up to them for missing —"

"Go on, you needn't spare my feelings; I realize that she had already slammed Nick Hoyt to you. I am not a jealous person — at least in regard to dogs. I am glad they are crazy about you; they are — they are a protection."

"Alas, it isn't all devotion; I keep a box of candy for them."

"There's that infernal phone. Be a sport; don't go until I answer.

"Nicholas Hoyt speaking. . . . When did you get back, Gladys? . . . Nope. No! . . .

Haven't a free evening this week. . . . Another visiting girl! The woods are full of them. . . . Sure, I like 'em dark. . . . Can't make it. Good-bye!"

He was frowning as he laid down the phone. His expression roused a little demon in Sandra. She hummed:

"The hounds are on the trail,
The hounds are on the trail —"

"What are you singing?"

"Was I singing? You really should have a secretary."

"Will you take the job?"

"Sorry, but 'I ain't got the education.' "

He reddened. "You haven't forgiven me for that fool trick, have you?"

"I hate being laughed at."

She was uncomfortably aware of him as he followed her through the hall with the dogs at his heels. At the door he demanded abruptly:

"So you believe that Rousseau is really Philip Hoyt?"

She deliberated — she hoped maddeningly, he was so dictatorial.

"Isn't it possible? He has charm, he has the *grand seigneur* manner. *Il y a toujours la maniére*. He has everything to make him an ideal master of this great estate."

She was a little frightened after she had said it. The eyes looking down at her blazed in a white face.

"Which is a lot of hooey any way you look at it. You're not thinking of marrying him, are you?"

"Marry him!" Sandra changed the pitch of her voice from angry scorn to amused tolerance. "Who can tell? The day has gone by when one plots the curve of one's matrimonial future."

"I suppose you are all for the modern jumping-off-in-the-dark method, now that divorce has dropped to the nickle-in-a-slot class. As you are such a partisan of Rousseau, I'll give you something to think of. You believe in him, don't you? Well, you're going to believe in Nicholas Hoyt and — like it."

Chapter IX

"Miss Duval assured you that there were no sentimental entanglements? That's your phrase, not mine," Nicholas Hoyt reminded.

Back to the mantel in the firelighted living room at Stone House, he frowned thoughtfully at Ben Damon in the big red chair. The elder man fitted the square-tipped fingers of both hands carefully together as he regarded his questioner from under shaggy brows.

"She did. So emphatically that I believed her."

"Then what do you make of her friendship with Rousseau? It couldn't be coincidence that she came to the very house that cagey Kentuckian is claiming. He must have put her on to that advertisement for a social secretary."

"Don't growl, Nick. It wasn't coincidence. I haven't told you, for reasons that do not concern you, that her father was a boyhood friend of mine and your uncle's — you've heard of Jimmy Duval, one of the Three Musketeers of Melton, haven't you?"

Laughter banished gravity from Nicholas Hoyt's eyes. "And then some. He was the leader of the gang, wasn't he? I was brought up on their escapades. Next to the ghost episode my favorite is the time they filled the gardener's hip boots with water."

Damon chuckled. "I've been round the world some since, but I never have heard a more colorful peroration than that man's when he put his foot into the boot. It was Jimmy's idea. He certainly had an imagination. Those were the days — but to get back to his daughter. I had seen Jim from time to time abroad and when he came over here, but never had met the girl. When I saw her, I thought her an ideal person for Mrs. Pat and engaged her."

The white angora cat stalked into the room. She sprang into Damon's lap, settled into the curve of her orange tail, folded her forepaws under her snowy breast, and regarded Nicholas with inscrutable topaz eyes. Damon stroked her fluffy back.

"Of course I hadn't a suspicion that Sandra Duval ever had seen or heard of Rousseau. I had a talk with her the other day and got the whole story — much — much more than she realized she was telling."

Nicholas rapped the tobacco from his pipe and refilled it. "Go on. What did she say? Don't you realize that any information about this Peerless Pretender — Estelle struck it when she dubbed Rousseau that — is of vital importance to me?"

"Take it easy, Nick! Take it easy! It seems that last year while the Duvals were in London, Rousseau presented a letter of introduction. As he had brought over a couple of racers, Jim was interested at once. The crafty Philippe — crafty is my word, not hers — encouraged the invalid to talk of his boyhood days here, of Mark Hoyt and the tragedy of the burned child, but never mentioned the reason of his interest."

"Sounds probable, doesn't it?"

"You've seen Sandra Duval. Do you think she'd lie to me?"

Nicholas crossed to the lattice window and looked out upon the garden border. The slanting sun was tinting leaves and blossoms with red gold. "No, I don't, but we can't get away from the fact that they are both at Seven Chimneys, that she believes in his claim, she admitted as much to me. I'd like to punch his head! When this case is settled, I will, no matter which way it goes."

"So that's it, is it?" In his excitement Damon pulled the cat's ear. She promptly scratched him and he as promptly dumped her on the floor.

"What's 'it'?"

"Nothing, nothing, just mumbling to myself. I don't wonder you're on edge, boy, with this fight coming on."

"You are still convinced that the diary is forged, aren't you, B.D.?"

"I'm convinced that Anne Pardoe Rousseau left enough of a diary so that, as he read, a great idea was born in the tricky mind of her son. He would be the dead Philip, if there were property enough to make it pay. He wouldn't have tried it had your Uncle Mark been living. I'll bet that Jim Duval was not the only Melton old-timer with whom Rousseau got in touch. He was bright enough to steer clear of me."

"How can we prove the diary a fake without a word in Anne Pardoe's writing with which to compare it? Didn't the expert say that the genuine and disputed writing should be put close together for comparison, to interpret the similar or different characteristics? Uncle Mark must have had slews of letters while she was taking care of the boy. Where are they? We've held off court proceedings while we searched. Experts are to examine Rousseau's evidence three weeks from now and we haven't a scrap of paper with which to prove him a liar. Where are those letters?"

"Stop walking the floor, Nick! You get on my nerves. The night your uncle collapsed, with his head on a book on the desk in the library, there were charred embers of letters on the hearth. Mrs. Pat told the doctor that Mark had seemed troubled all day; that he had said that he had received a letter which Nick must have at once, he would tell her about it later. There wasn't any 'later' for him. No trace of the trouble-letter either. Had he burned it by mistake with the others?"

"I can't believe it. There were several books on horses and racing on his desk — evidently he had been looking them over. It doesn't seem probable that he would leave them to burn a lot of old letters. But apparently he did. We've been through everything in this house and at Seven

Chimneys. When I found the concealed drawer in the library desk, I went blind with excitement for a minute — it was empty. Looks as if I would step out and the Kentuckian would step in."

He thrust his hands hard into the pockets of his coat.

"I can't believe it, B.D. It isn't so much the money I mind losing — do you suppose the Court will make me refund what I've spent — it is turning this place on which I've grown up over to that — that —"

"Take it easy, Nick. We're not washed up yet, though the fact that there is no record of Rousseau's birth in the South American village, where he says he thought he was born, helps his story. You know and I know that Jed Langdon hasn't gone abroad for his health, he's on the trail of something. Talked with Mrs. Pat since the long-lost son came?"

Nicholas Hoyt kept his eyes on the pipe he was carefully filling. Only over the phone. I don't want to see her. She might at least have waited until Rousseau had proved his claim before she fell on his neck and championed him and his racer."

"You're not quite fair to Mrs. Pat, Nick."

"Not fair! Well, I'll be darned, B.D.

You're not falling for the Pretender, are you?"

"No, but Jed and I told Mrs. Pat to take him in."

"What!"

"Don't shout. Angry as she was because of your objection to her marriage with Curt Newsome, Mrs. Pat came to me with Rousseau's letter in which he asked if he might come to Seven Chimneys and bring Iron Man to enter in the Charity Races. The letter was a masterpiece. He knew of the breach between you and your step-aunt, that your black Fortune was the favorite in the coming races."

"Was all that in the letter?"

"Not a word. I read between the lines. Mrs. Pat was so furious with you that she was all for inviting him, and Langdon and I were jubilant. To have the long-lost son where we could watch him was our meat. Of course we didn't let Mrs. Pat know that. We encouraged her to think that she had overruled our objections. Poor soul!"

Nicholas wheeled from his contemplation of the fire. "What's the matter with her? Why the sob stuff?"

"Because, fool that she's been, I'm sorry for her. She's coming out fast from the make-believe world she created for herself.

The Lord and she only know — and neither of them is telling — why she invited the Carter woman to Seven Chimneys; perhaps because she had once lived here she thought she would boost her socially."

"Estelle and Curt Newsome are playing round together, I hear. Even if you did encourage her, Mrs. Pat handed me a rotten deal when she took Rousseau in; in spite of that, I hate to see her hurt. She was on the level every minute with Uncle Mark."

"What can she expect? She tempted a young jockey, who was music-mad, with promises of leisure to study, the best violin masters, just as his winning streak broke — he'd been hanging up victories — and she had him."

"But what can Curt see in Estelle? She was an affected little thing when, as a girl, she lived here; she had a way though, one after another we boys rushed her and dropped her."

"Curt is flattered by the attention — and apparent admiration — of the type of woman he never before has seen except in expensive cars or on top of a swanky four in hand at the races, miles removed from him socially. Besides, don't forget that he is married to a woman years his senior and that Estelle is young and seductive."

"Perhaps you're right, but why is she, who has been everywhere, seen everything, encouraging Curt Newsome, who has nothing behind him?"

"She is bored. She is adrift spiritually; she grabs any new experience. Compare her cold, skeptical, worldly-wise eyes with the deep, responsive eyes of Sandra Duval. The first girl cares for nothing, believes nothing; the second has been brought up with spiritual standards which keep her steadily, confidently moving forward in our torn, shaken, slowly rebuilding world. Can't understand why, in this cosmetic age, some beautician doesn't begin to preach the cultivation of the soul as an aid to beauty. Here I am philosophizing again, when we were talking about Curtis Newsome."

"Always liked him, but when Mrs. Mark Hoyt married her late husband's jock, I went berserk. I've been a crab, I know."

"You would have cooled off long before this, Nick, if the arrival of Rousseau hadn't been fresh brush on the fire. Great Scott, how Mrs. Pat raged at you when she came with his letter! Why your uncle married Marte Patten — than whom there are worse but also more attractive women — I never could understand."

"I can. He was lonely and she talked his language, had driven his horses in shows, had grown up on a breeding farm. After his first wife died, he cared for nothing but his stables, his books, and me, and after college I was sent to New York to you to learn the ropes of high finance that I might know how to take care of the millions I was to inherit. Millions! Magic millions! Now you see them and now you don't. The last few years have shrunk them to half. If Rousseau wins, they will do the vanishing act for me."

He answered the ring of the telephone. "Nicholas Hoyt speaking . . . Hulloa, Peg! . . . Can't tomorrow. . . . Of course I want to be a good egg, but just remember that I'm a son of toil. . . . No, it's not a joke. . . . Can't. Can't dance all night, sleep in the office, and impress my clients with the fact that I'm a wizard of finance, can I? . . . After the races, gal. After the races. I'll be seeing you."

He laid the instrument on its stand. "You've heard that one about an ill wind, haven't you, B.D.? If Rousseau wins, I won't have quite so many phone calls to answer. Nick Hoyt setting out to conquer the world, with his knapsack on his shoulder, will not be in demand."

Damon rose, ran his hands through his white hair till it resembled nothing so much as an electrified brush.

"But you'll still have your share of our business. Rousseau won't win. He can't. He's a fraud. I know he's a fraud. Something will trip him. For heaven's sake, don't lose your sense of humor. Don't lose your courage, Nick."

Nicholas Hoyt disciplined an infectious laugh. "My sense of humor is functioning all right. Where'd you get the idea that I was losing courage, B.D.? I've got to win for the honor of the family, can't have a man like Rousseau representing the Hoyts. I'll win on three counts."

Damon forcibly and not too tenderly removed the white cat who was scaling his leg with indigging claws.

"Three counts! 'Where do you get three? The estate, and the Charity Race —"

"And Sandra Duval. Philippe Rousseau is quite mad about her, isn't he?"

There was a smile in Nicholas Hoyt's eyes but a sudden tightening of his jaw.

"So am I."

Chapter X

In the stillness of the old living room the red sparks singing up the chimney sounded like nothing so much as a swarm of bees. Damon stood as if taking root. His eyes under shaggy brows bored into the eyes of the younger man. Nicholas could feel the hard beating of the pulse in his own throat, the twitch of a nerve in his cheek.

"Mean that, Nick?"

"Yes. The day I met her at the station I thought her the gayest, most gallant girl I ever had met, and yet her eyes showed that her heart recently had been torn up by the roots. Having been unable to get that way about a girl or woman since my in-again-out-again college days, it's a queer break that I should fall for one who turns frosty whenever I speak to her, whose hostility can't be mistaken."

"It's one of those things that's just too

good to be true, Nick. That you should want to marry Jim Duval's daughter — it's serious, you do want to marry her, don't you?"

Nicholas' face went a dark red even as he laughed. "Now I'll say, 'Take it easy,' B.D. I do want to marry her, but isn't it the limit that I should meet the one girl I want just as I stand a chance of losing almost everything I have in the world?"

"And such a girl! Sandra Duval has an old-fashioned tenderness which is as unexpected in youth these days as an extra dividend from one's investments. You haven't lost your fortune yet, remember. Wait till the Court decides that. Think I'll invite myself to dinner at Seven Chimneys tonight. Want to see who is there, what's going on. I miss Jed's reports. Rousseau may have one or two allies on the job, I wouldn't put it past him. If ever there was an establishment infernally designed for conspirators it is the one presided over by Mrs. Pat Newsome. The servants hop in and out like fleas."

"We made sure that Rousseau heard of the ad for a social secretary we inserted in the papers. If he sent a woman after the position, she didn't get it. Why should he plant any one in the house if he is so confident that that diary is sure-fire evidence?"

"Perhaps it isn't because of the estate only. Rousseau has two irons in the fire, hasn't he? Your Fortune has ninety-nine in a hundred chances of winning those twenty-five grand stakes, hasn't he? Well, twenty-five grand would come in handy for the claimant to the Hoyt estate just now. You know as well as I that he turned everything he owned but Iron Man into cash to finance this fight, and then you ask why there should be a spy in camp. Heaven is your home, Nick, better go back, you're too unsuspicious for this mundane world."

Nicholas laughed and linked his arm in Damon's.

"Don't waste breath calling me names. Come on to the stables. Let's do a little sleuthing."

Under a brilliant blue sky, cloudless, but already flushing slightly from the ardent rays of the slanting sun, they followed the perennial-bordered stepping stones. Against an opal-tinted horizon, purple hills were as sharply defined as paper cut-outs. Pastures were beginning to turn rusty; the air was full of scent baked from the box hedge by sunshine.

Two men, smoking on a bench outside the stables, jumped to their feet and touched their caps; two freckle-faced exercise boys, shooting crap, scuttled out of sight as Damon and Hoyt entered the building. They passed the tack room, hung with saddles and harnesses. Nicholas' brows met as he noted through the glass doors of a cabinet an array of gold-lettered rosettes, blue, red, yellow, and gleaming silver cups. Would the green and white, his colors, bring in another trophy, or would Rousseau's orange and black be victorious?

Five horses left their hay and walked to their gates. Nicholas patted the nose of sleek black Curtain Call. After he had given each an apple from the barrel which stood near, four of them turned away, but a black stallion remained at the gate. Fortune.

Nicholas looked up into the great fiery eyes. How could he doubt the outcome of the race with this horse in the field? His proud neck shone like satin; his nostrils were distended, his ears thrust forward; muscles stood out like intricate cording along his slender legs. He stamped his fore foot in the straw and whinnied softly as his owner rubbed his soft nozzle. Nicholas turned quickly to the man who had come up behind him.

"Who was that, Parsons?"

The hawk-faced man with pompadoured white hair looked nervously over his shoulder; the slim jockey with him touched his cap.

"Who was what, Mr. Hoyt?"

"The man who just slipped out."

Damon laid his square-tipped fingers on his partner's shoulder. "You are having an attack of curvature of the brain, boy. There was no one here when we came in."

"Oh yes, there was. Come clean, Parsons."

The trainer grinned. "It was this way, that Kentuckian from Seven Chimneys dropped in. Slick, I calls that guy, with a line what wouldn't deceive nobody. He asks, wouldn't I show him Fortune who, he'd heard, was the favorite for the coming big race. He said, 'Of course you know I own Iron Man who's second in the betting. Thought I'd like to size up the two. No harm in that is there?'

"Sure, there's no harm, says I, and —"

"Great Scott, is Rousseau hanging round this place?"

"Hold on, B.D. Let Parsons finish. Did you show our champion?"

The trainer's head seemed in imminent danger of being split from the wideness of his grin; the jockey chuckled.

"Not the one he was expectin' to see. I put Curtain Call through his paces; he's black too. That man Rousseau thinks he's seen the champeen."

"Good boy! But don't let that man, any man, come into the place again when I am not here; get that straight, Parsons. Understand me?"

"Sure, I get you, sir."

Damon was hanging over the door of Fortune's stall. "Look at the bloom on his coat! He has filled out in the right places, Nick. Have his gate manners improved, Sharp?"

"Not too much, sir. He needs more schooling. He gets unstrung by the track band and he's choosey."

"He'll get over it. Don't let any one from Seven Chimneys sniff around here again. I'm afraid of some of them. 'When a thing has happened, even a fool can see it.' That isn't original, so you needn't make a note of it for my biography, Nick."

Nicholas Hoyt repeated to the grooms the instructions as to visitors as they left the stable. He went on a few paces and stopped.

"Go on, B.D. Just remembered something I want to tell Eddie Sharp. I'll be with you in a minute."

He turned back. He had made light of it, but the fact that Rousseau was hanging round Stone House stables had startled him. If only Jed were here. Had he gone abroad in pursuit of a clue? There were clues enough here to keep him busy if B.D.'s suggestion that the Kentuckian had allies under the roof of Seven Chimneys was true.

Sharp, in a chair precariously tipped against the wall, looked up from a newspaper as Nicholas entered the tack room. The chair came down on all fours and catapulted him to his feet.

"Cricky, Mr. Nicholas, what's up? You look like you'd got your mind set to shoot Niagara Falls in a barrel. Caught some one red-handed meddling with the colts?"

"Nothing wrong with the horses, Eddie. I — I've got a lot on my mind."

"It's that Rousseau guy who's bothering you. Think I don't know? Next time he comes sidling round these stables, we'll give him the works."

"Has he been here before today? Why haven't you told me?"

Sharp scratched a thatch of black hair; his round eyes protruded. "I've spilled the beans now. Before he went away, Mr. Langdon told Parsons if any one from.

Seven Chimneys came here, to tell nobody, 'specially not you, and that we were to treat him same's we would any other visitor, but some one was to keep an eye on him every minute. Mr. Langdon said he was working for you, sir."

"He is. Take orders from him. Has Rousseau been here many times?"

"Twice. I've never seen him. Parsons told me that he was asking a lot of questions about me, said how he'd like to talk with me. I'm not even passing the time with any one like him, if he does think he'll be boss here some day, so I've kept out of his way. He's never asked before today to see Fortune. Mr. Langdon may be right in letting him come, but I don't think so. He doesn't do anything, Parsons tells me, but come in and walk around and be terrible smiling to everybody, but he makes the grooms and swipes nervous. They know he's the owner of Iron Man and they whisper about dopes and bombs and kidnapping; they're so kinder worked up, the horses feel it."

"Come out, let's look them over again."

Five sleek, shining heads appeared simultaneously over five gates, five pairs of great liquid eyes rolled in his direction as Nicholas approached the stalls. Big black

Fortune poked his nose into his master's outstretched hand. Ping-Pong, an old hunter in the next stall, whinnied a greeting.

Sharp grinned. "Those two are stable mates, all right. We'll have to take Ping-Pong along when we go to the races to keep the champion from getting lonesome."

"We'll take him. All right, boys, get back to your eats."

One of the colts whinnied and the others answered. In the tack room Nicholas stopped.

"If Rousseau comes here again, keep out of his way, Eddie."

"Sure, I'll keep out of his way, though I don't see what he'd find out talking to me."

"Iron Man's his horse, isn't be? With a strange jockey up on Fortune, our black stallion's chance of winning wouldn't be so good. So watch out that he doesn't tempt you before race-day."

"You mean to drink, Mr. Nicholas? I wouldn't have to wait for him. Mr. Huckins asked me once, but I told him that I wasn't drinking before the races."

"Huckins! Well, I'll be —" Nicholas broke off to remind crisply: "You know what winning this race means to me, Sharp? It isn't the money only; it means a reputation for Stone House stables. I am depending upon you."

"You're depending on the right fella. I'd — I'd die for you."

"I'd much rather you would live and ride for me, Eddie Sharp. I'm trusting you to the limit. Goodnight!"

When he entered the library, Damon was standing with hands clasped behind him looking up at the Puritan who stared back at him with painted, lack-lustre eyes.

Nicholas filled and lighted his pipe. His eyes followed his partner's.

"Old chap looks as if he could bite nails, doesn't he?"

"He does. Great Scott, I wish the Stone House phantom would get on the job and give Rousseau the fright of his life. If he's the light-weight I believe him to be, he might be scared into coming across with the truth."

Nicholas' answer was drowned in the clatter of the tongs as he poked the fire.

"What are you mumbling about, Nick? I believe you're laughing at me. How can you laugh when the trial of that case is getting nearer and nearer and we haven't a scrap of paper with which to fight that diary?"

"You got me wrong, B.D. I wasn't laughing at you."

"I admit I'm contentious when it comes to anything which touches you, boy. I love you as if you were my own. It isn't losing the money I care about only; it's the idea of our being licked by Rousseau, the maddening sense of frustration. When I think of it, I feel as if I could pull Mark Hoyt from his grave, shake him till his bleached bones rattled back to life, and make him tell what he did with those letters of Anne Pardoe's."

The dark redness of Ben Damon's face startled Nicholas. He put an arm across his shoulder.

"Don't worry, B.D. I can't, I won't believe that we will lose. If we do, I'll make myself believe that Rousseau is Uncle Mark's son."

"If he is — I'm afraid he'll win Sandra —"

"Oh no, he won't! That will be another fight. I . . ." The telephone rang. Nicholas picked up the instrument.

"Stone House. . . . Hulloa yourself, Linda. . . . Still here to watch Fortune's workouts. . . . Sorry, every night filled for the next two weeks. . . . Sure, I'll be at the Hunt Club Ball. . . . Linda, do something for me . . . ? That's a rash promise. . . . Make your committee invite Mrs. Newsome to receive at the ball, will you . . . ? Don't argue. I know what I'm asking. Do it or not. Good-bye!"

He replaced the instrument and answered the question in Damon's eyes.

"Linda's reaction to my request was shrill, but she's a good sort. Mrs. Pat is known all over the world for the high standard of her horses. The owner of the Seven Chimneys stables ought to be in the receiving line at the ball. Out of partisanship for me, my friends have ostracized her. That's got to stop."

Damon regarded him from above the cigarette he was lighting. "Your viewpoint has changed in the last few weeks, Nick."

The sarcastic comment deepened Nicholas' color, but there was a smiling challenge in his eyes as they met the older man's.

"It will change more. You'll be surprised. I didn't realize until you spoke of it that Mrs. Pat's heart was being tortured. Can't stand that. You and Jed are right. I have made a big mistake staying away from Seven Chimneys. I'll eat a huge hunk of humble pie and ask Mrs. Pat if I may come to dinner."

"And then?" Damon asked eagerly.

Nicholas looked up from the pipe he was lighting. Little flames were reflected in his eyes.

"And then? I'll win out on one count at least. Guess which?"

Chapter XI

"Glory be, Miss! How you frightened me!"

Sandra, perched on the top of the high steps in front of the shelves in the library, glanced from the maid's white face to the book sprawled on the floor. She had been absorbed in a colorful account of a horse-race, when a squeak had drawn her eyes to the desk with its countless drawers and pigeonholes. Emma was running her hand over the front of it!

Maddening that she had dropped the book. Had she kept quiet, she might have discovered the reason of the woman's presence at Seven Chimneys. She had not as yet confided her suspicion to any one that Emma might be here for another purpose than that of earning her living. Time enough for that when suspicion had crystalized to conviction. Was she a tool? Whose? Huckins'? He had been standing suspiciously close the day she had seen the two together in the hall. If that were so, why was he here?

Sandra glanced at the table with its heap of jig-sawed scraps. That sort of puzzle was not needed in this house; one was assembling with humans for the pieces, unless she had missed her guess, and she was quite sure she hadn't.

"Please excuse me for disturbing you at your reading, Miss. I forgot to dust the desk this morning — I'm helping till the new parlor maid comes — and hurried in to do it. You know how the madame is if we skip anything, Miss."

The maid had come to the foot of the steps. Her manner was perfect for her position, yet she had answered an advertisement for a social secretary first. That fact needed explanation. Light from the jeweled window rested in triangular red patches on her cheek bones. The color intensified the brilliance of her eyes. There was a glint in them which twanged along the sensitive fibre of Sandra's imagination. Did she resent the fact that the girl looking down at her had secured the position she herself had wanted?

"That's all right, Emma, I was through reading. Hand me the book, will you? I'll put it back on the shelf. Thanks."

Sandra watched her as she left the room. Dusting! Afraid that "the madame" would rage at her carelessness. Evidently she had forgotten that Mrs. Pat had gone away for a few days.

" 'Curioser and curioser,' " she reflected as she carefully examined the book in her hand. Quite a drop for a volume so old and rare. She breathed a little sigh of relief. Unharmed. She replaced it on the shelf. This was the fourth on the subject of the horse she had read. Fascinating, but out of date. The next she selected would be the latest publication the shelf offered. Some day she would startle nice Mr. Damon by the amount of knowledge she had acquired from the books which his old friend had collected. How Mark Hoyt must have loved them! In each one was noted the date and place of its purchase.

She was still pondering over the maid's interest in the library desk when an half hour later, mounted on Happy Landing, the roan Mrs. Pat had set aside for her use, she drew rein on top of the hill to look down upon the colorful pattern riders were spreading over the lovely country which offered all that a hunting-mad community needed: grass meadows, open fields, a long, trying half-mile rise crowned by an in-an-out, post and rail fences, clay roads, patches of woodland. Spectators were scattering, some on foot, some on horseback — though not part of the field — and more were in automobiles.

Men in pink coats and white breeches, yellow waistcoats, women in smart brown felt hats, Scotch plaid coats, tan breeches, jack boots, were setting their horses' heads homeward. The carefully groomed mounts glistened in the sunlight. The low-headed, diversely colored hounds followed a pair of bob-tailed cobs, whose riders apparently were in animated discussion. She watched them take a stone-wall as easily as feathers lifted by a breeze. It was a beautiful wall, all gun-metal and slate color and light granite glistening with silver, one of the few hand-made things left in this mechanistic age.

What a day! Its clouds were almost silver, its blue infinite, its green had a bronze-gold tinge. A flotilla of gay autumn leaves came sailing and bobbing down the shining river. Fluffs from a milkweed pod winged away in front of her like little white fairies in a hurry as she guided Happy Landing into a wooded road, checkered with quaking shadows, where the late sunlight shone through trees whose brilliant leaves were a-flutter in the soft breeze.

Rather a pity that she couldn't have joined the hunt, she was not too bad to look at in her canary color breeches, dark blue coat, matching soft felt hat, snowy stock and black top boots. Lucky that every girl wasn't as mad about clothes as she. But she couldn't have gone had she been invited; Mrs. Newsome's social secretary had no right to accept what would not be extended to her employer. Besides, Nicholas Hoyt would be one of the riders, and since their skirmish at Stone House she had not cared to meet him. It had been more than a skirmish; it had been a declaration of war. She had tried to put him out of her mind. If he retained his inheritance, she would find another position; if he lost it, he would doubtless fade from the picture, which eventuality would be all right with her.

Apparently life went on as usual at Seven Chimneys. Horse buyers and gentlemen fond of horses came and went; enthusiasm over the approaching races was at fever-heat. Mrs. Pat was backing Iron Man enthusiastically. She had ordered neckties in orange and black for her men who would accompany the gray to the track, and all buckets and bottles which would be used were having a coat of Rousseau's colors. She was getting increasingly difficult. Curtis Newsome was gay and sombre by turns and went about with tormented eyes. Estelle Carter was bearing down hard on the glamorous note. Only Philippe Rousseau appeared untouched by the ominous forces which seemed to be gathering just beneath the surface. Sandra had a strange feeling that storms were drawing in from all points of the horizon, that the atmosphere was saturated with electricity.

Philippe was still superbly confident in his role of rightful heir restrained for a short time from slipping on the rich cloak of his inheritance. A week had passed since Nicholas Hoyt had told her that she would believe in him — and like it. The mere thought of his challenging voice and eyes sent that curious feeling of aliveness quick-stepping along her veins. One would never have known by his manner that day that just as Fortune stood to win or lose a race, his owner stood to win or lose a fortune.

Was Philippe making progress in establishing his claim? She had noticed yesterday at tea that Mrs. Pat's cronies were beginning to count him as one of themselves. They had been excited over Iron

Man's victory in a tryout. Piggy Pike, his jockey, had held the gray just off the pace and had pegged back a roan named Five Up as they turned into the straight. Then Iron Man had bounded forward as if touched by a spring, had stretched out and won.

Sandra preened with self-satisfaction. That summing up had not been so bad. It showed the effects of browsing among the books on horses and racing in the library. She had been at Seven Chimneys but twenty-four hours when she had determined that she would know something of horseflesh that she might look intelligent at least when champions of the turf were mentioned. That brought her back to Emma again. Why had she been in the library?

Happy Landing nibbled at late pink-topped clover as Sandra pulled up outside a rail fence to watch the brood mares and baby Thoroughbreds grazing in a green pasture. A few colts were running round nose to tail. Astonishing how they had grown since she first had seen them a few weeks ago. Beside a water hole a small stallion nipped not too playfully at a peaceably grazing colt, whereupon a young filly let her heels fly to land squarely on the midsection of the offender who galloped away squealing.

Again the eternal triangle. Interesting and fascinating business, this raising of Thoroughbreds. That aggressive young stallion might be a potential Gallant Fox, a Twenty Grand, or, wonder of wonders, a Man O' War.

She touched the roan lightly with the crop; he bounded forward in response. Was that the gilt weathercock of Stone House stables glinting above the trees? She had not realized that she was so near. She would love to stop for a chat with adorable Nanny O'Day — better not, she might meet Nicholas Hoyt.

Who would ride Fortune for him? The jockey who had spoken to her that day at the paddock? She was beginning to understand some of the subtleties of the turf, but she still felt like a rank outsider looking through a window. As the days passed, her sense of aloneness grew rather than diminished. Sometimes when she woke in the night and couldn't sleep, she would get panicky, thinking distorted thoughts of what illness would mean; it seemed as if she could hear the hours hurrying along. It made one curiously shivery to realize that one was the last of one's family. The dogs and Irish Bridie were her only confidantes, but she could not say to them:

"Do you remember when . . . ?"

There was no one with whom she could talk over subjective things, presentiments, impulses. Her godmother was a fashionable, vague sort of person who would not have recognized an ideal had it tapped her on the shoulder. Of course a normal girl shouldn't spend a moment fearing the future, but perhaps she had not yet returned to normalcy after the heart-twisting experiences of the last year; perhaps she should have married — foolish thought; who? Why worry when her horse was sprinting — her eyelashes felt as if they were being uprooted — when the air was glorious?

A whirling spiral of dry leaves skittered across the road. With a sharp whir of wings a partridge followed. The combination was too much for Happy Landing. He recoiled with a suddenness which sent his rider over his head. Before she realized what had happened, she was sitting on the ground gripping her left shoulder.

A man with a gun burst through the underbrush. "I heard a thud . . ." Philippe Rousseau recognized her, dropped to one knee beside her. "Sandra! What happened?"

"A happy landing. See it? Speed but no control." She giggled foolishly. The laughter faded from her eyes. She bit her lips. The pain in her shoulder was gruelling if she moved her left arm, but he must not know. The roan stood with low-hung head as if overcome with shame.

"We were going like the wind. A partridge startled the poor dear, and my mind was hundreds — of miles from here. From — the — the way I feel . . . it has stepped out . . . altogether now. My brain — is a nice — great . . . empty room. It was not his fault . . . he is beautifully mannered. Doesn't he . . . look contrite?"

"Don't try to talk! Stop laughing! Are you hurt?" Rousseau laid his hand on hers. She shook it off. Something within her suddenly rebelled against his touch. His eyes narrowed, his voice grated along her nerves.

"What's the matter? You haven't gone back on your old friend, have you? Has the big shot set you against me?"

"The big — s-shot?" Sandra shut her eyes. She must have hit her head when she fell. If only she could dig her toes and fingers in and hang on to her whirling senses.

"I mean Nicholas Hoyt, of course. What has he been saying about me?"

His voice sawed into her mind; then his head described a parabola and righted. The wave of unconsciousness frightened her. "You are not faint. You . . . never fainted in your life . . . remember," she told herself over and over.

"If you would get me some water . . . instead of growling and imagining all sorts of . . . absurd things, it would be more to the . . . the point, Philippe."

"You said something then." He stood up and looked down at her. "You are hurt. You're white as a sheet."

"Don't stand there telling me how I look! I shall begin to think . . . I am faint. Ever heard of mental . . . control? Get me some water. I can . . . hear the tinkle of a brook."

"I'm sorry. I'll get it." He broke through the brush and disappeared.

What made the trees so unsteady? Was that a horseman approaching, or was she seeing things? No. He was real. He was coming on at a gallop. If only those tricky trees would keep quiet.

"Drink this!" Something burned down her throat. She looked up into gray eyes. The proximity of Nicholas Hoyt, the man she so cordially disliked, cleared her mind as nothing else could have done. She struggled to her feet. He regarded her with a frown. He was terrifyingly tall and impressive in his pink coat and white breeches. His polished boots were slightly spattered; a tiny dab of mud, like the patch of an old-time belle, under one of his eyes, increased its clear brilliance. He looked from her to Happy Landing nibbling by the side of the road.

"Did he throw you?"

"It wasn't Happy Landing's fault . . . I was dreaming. A partridge flew across the road. Haven't I . . . said that before? He stopped. . . ." Something seemed to whirl inside her brain. — "I shot over his head. I often . . . get off that way. Simplest stunt . . . in the world." — How hazy things seemed. — "Want me . . . to show you?" She caught at his sleeve to steady herself.

"Not now. Where did you hit?"

"My shoulder . . . perhaps . . . my head." She bit her lips and closed her eyes. She seemed to be floating in a thick fog.

"Don't talk. Here, Board Boy!"

The hunter came close. Nicholas Hoyt caught Sandra gently round the waist and lifted her to the horse's back. He kept one arm about her as he mounted.

"Which shoulder?" he asked gruffly.

Her lips barely formed the word "Left."

He shifted her position gently. As he picked up the reins, Philippe Rousseau emerged from the bushes. Water trickled from his cap as the two men stared at each other.

"Put my girl down!" The belligerence of the Kentuckian's voice brought Sandra out of the haze in which she was aimlessly drifting. The blaze in his eyes frightened her.

"You . . . better put me . . . down, really you'd . . . better," she warned in a shaken whisper which trailed off into a hard drawn breath. In answer, the arm about her tightened.

"Ride Miss Duval's horse back to the stable — Rousseau. I'll take her to Stone House; it's nearer."

"Rousseau! It won't be Rousseau long — now." The hatred and defiance in the repetition pierced Sandra's consciousness. She must separate them; Philippe had a gun. She clutched at the pink sleeve about her. She rallied her strength; not as a heroine of romance did she plead, instead she demanded impatiently:

"Are you two . . . going to — glare at each other, while I — I . . ."

In her excitement she twitched her injured shoulder. Her head dropped back against something heavenly warm and alive, something which pressed close against her cheek, something behind which she could hear the hard, throb, throb as of a distant drum. Through a haze, stabbed with fiery spurts of pain, cut a voice.

"Get out of the way, Rousseau, or I'll run you down. Can't you see that Miss Duval is unconscious?"

"I'll have her out of your house before night. . . ."

Sandra struggled to clear her senses. Who had said that? How easily the horse stepped. There was no pain in her shoulder. She looked up into eyes dark with concern.

"Is it hurting horribly?"

Her lips twisted in what she hoped was a sporting smile. "Wouldn't know — I had a shoulder . . ." She clinched her teeth on a moan.

How long had she been in the dark? She struggled to clear her senses. Of course that was not chunky Nanny O'Day crooning over her, tenderly loosening her blouse. Her shoulder . . . did the hatchet-faced Puritan realize how it hurt? He was looking down upon her . . . dead eyes . . . had Nanny said that they once had been live eyes? Live eyes — eyes of the thing she had seen at the pool! She tried to cover her face. Some one caught her hand, some one said huskily:

"Don't move it, darling."

It seemed a year or two before the doctor arrived. His hands were gentle, but — she sniffed greedily at the sickish stuff he held to her nose. That eased the pain — eased. . . .

Was she a bubble coming up for air? Curious. Were those men's voices? What were they saying?

"Nothing serious, evidently been through a tremendous nervous strain, kept up like a Thoroughbred in a race. Now that it's over she's gone to pieces, emotionally exhausted, that's all. Happens that way sometimes. Nothing in that dislocated shoulder to make you look so white, Nick. It snapped into place all right. No. No concussion. Dazed by pain and shock. What's that phoney claimant coming here for?"

Down, down again into smothering space. When next the bubble rose, Sandra forced her eyes open. How dim the room was! Was that Philippe Rousseau? Was the little fat man with a hand on his arm the doctor? Where was Nicholas Hoyt? How far away their voices seemed!

"I tell you, she can't be moved."

"Mrs. Newsome would want her taken to Seven Chimneys." Philippe's voice; the bubble recognized it.

"It makes no difference what any one but the doctor wants. He says that Miss Duval is not to be moved tonight. She stays here."

She was glad she wasn't combating the ultimatum which came from behind her head. Nicholas Hoyt, of course. Curious that she didn't care where she stayed. Some one was lifting her. She was close in tender arms, close in a refuge from all terrifying things — loneliness, fear, pain. Distant music . . . flags flying . . . Ooch! The bang of a door made her jump. How it hurt!

Now she was floating through space. Heavenly to have her head down again. Her right hand was gripped tight. The touch held her mind steady. It must be Philippe. He had said that he loved her. But — she had hated his touch when — she — had fallen. — Things were jumbled. Hadn't she been thinking of marriage just before . . . She must hold tight . . . to something or she would float away again.

She drew closer the hand holding hers, cuddled her cheek against it. Said drowsily in a voice which came from a great distance:

"I think perhaps . . . I'd better marry you . . ."

Curious how the fingers under her cheek twitched; curious how deep, how fathoms deep a husky voice seemed:

"I think perhaps you'd better, darling."

Darling! Some one had called her that before . . . Some one bent and kissed her gently on her lips. In a blind, unreasoning effort to evade the passion of response which shook her, she jerked away. What had she said? She didn't really love Philippe. Pain tore through the haze. She sank back into smothering space.

Chapter XII

Sandra, her left arm in a sling, leaned her head, which still had its merry-go-round seconds, against the red leather back of a chair in the library at Stone House. She watched the reflection of licking tongues of flame in the melon-pattern silver tea-service on a table near the window. Late sunlight sifted through the diamond panes to checker the lace cloth with gold. One vagrant ray warmed the slaty eyes of the portrait of the Puritan between the bookshelves.

They caught and held the girl's for a moment. She turned her head away with a little shiver. Through the feverish hours since the accident, the phantom figure she had seen at the pool had flitted and quaked and waved. Should she tell Mr. Damon of the experience? This was her chance. Back to the fire, he was frowning thoughtfully at space.

She couldn't do it. He had called her valiant the first day they had met. There had been no valor in the way she had scuttled from that pool. Were she to tell him, doubtless he would scoff to himself:

"Hmp! Neurotic! Never would have thought it of Jim Duval's daughter."

No, she would not confide in him yet — if ever.

He looked at her sharply — had her mind touched his — and straightened as if shrugging a load from his shoulders. His eyes behind the strong lenses shone with friendly light.

"How are you feeling, Sandra?"

"Wonderful, thank you. My shoulder is stiff but not painful; my mind is quite clear again, praise be to Allah! I feel as if my thinking machine had been smothered in cotton wool for an aeon or two, but you assure me that Happy Landing playfully tossed me over his head only two days ago. Nanny O'Day says that you arrived soon after I was carried upstairs. It was sweet of you to come."

"I had to know how you were. Aren't you my protegee? Wasn't I responsible for your going to Seven Chimneys? Nick phoned me immediately after he brought you here and suggested that I come and stay until you went back to the other house. Guess he feared you might be kidnaped."

"Kidnaped! Who would want me?"

"Is that merely a rhetorical question, or are you asking for information? I will leave it for you to answer. You are a lovely sight in that pale blue costume. I like to see women in velvet."

"I'm thrilled that I please you. Bridie brought these pyjamas from Seven Chimneys. She's a dear. She wept salty tears over me till I feared I would do the Lot's-wife act."

"She is a privileged character. She came here when Nick was a boy. She worships him. Has Mrs. Newsome phoned?"

"Yes, from town. She returns to Seven Chimneys at noon tomorrow, but the car is to come for me in the morning. She wanted to send it today, but evidently she had talked with the doctor and he had vetoed that."

"She was swearing mad, I suspect, when she heard that you were in the camp of the enemy?"

"Had she been broadcasting over the radio, she would have been cut off at the second word for using language unfit for the air."

"It is a treat to hear you laugh. I suppose you've been told hundreds of times that you have a lovely laugh. You will be glad to return to Seven Chimneys?"

"Yes. I like my work there; besides, I want to help on that eight hundred piece jig-saw puzzle Mrs. Pat brought back from town the last time she came. She thinks that puzzles keep her husband interested. They do. At any time when he isn't practicing, you may find Curtis Newsome bending over that table. We've all picked up the germ. Philippe, Mrs. Carter, and I stop when we go through the library to fit in a piece or two."

"A picture puzzle! Going back to second childhood?"

"Jeer if you like, but wait till you have tried it. One can't read or be in the open all one's spare time, and I'm never conscious of an inferiority complex until I start to play cards at Seven Chimneys, Mrs. Pat and her pals are such demons at the game. I have sent to New York for a puzzle for Nanny O'Day. She will love it. She will need diversion after my departure. She must be worn to shreds. I'll wager she has been up and down stairs a thousand times since my spectacular arrival. She has taken care of me as if I were a baby."

"Or a young filly. She is as horse-mad as the rest of us. Doubtless she has had the time of her life. It must have been a let-up for Nick. Usually she spends her time fussing over him. He is the very light of her eyes."

"Too bad that he wasn't here to enjoy the respite. As you know, he fled from the invalid."

"Hmp! You an invalid! Put you in a race today and I'll bet you'd pound past the judges with a good head to spare. You don't hit it off with Nick, do you?"

Sandra resented the touch of acid humor in the question. She rose, went to the piano, and to emphasize her indifference, ran her fingers lightly over the keys. "It is mutual. The first time we met he pretended he was a trainer —"

"And a crack-a-jack trainer he is, my dear."

"I mean a professional trainer. He disliked me at once. I felt it, and all he saw was my outer self on parade. I was flippant and indignant at being obliged to accept his ungracious help. After a few moments I realized that for some reason he was playing a part, though I couldn't understand why a mere secretary was worth the trouble. I resented it. It may have been my fault but I was in the mood to see small things large."

"And you are letting resentment befog your common sense now. The man who claims he is Philip Hoyt made a grand row because you were brought here when you were hurt. He insisted that his friendship with your father gave him a prior right to look after you. The fact that Nick showed him the door when he burst into this room to renew his protest didn't serve as oil on the troubled waters. Great Scott, he acted as if he thought bandits had snitched you! Can't you imagine what he would have said had Nicholas stayed on here? As for Nick's pretending he was a trainer the day you two met, don't blame him. Lay the whip on me. I phoned him to be at the station when you arrived to look you over."

"Look me over! Did you think me an imposter? Didn't you believe that I was Jimmy Duval's daughter!"

"Take it easy! I did, but — well, I wanted you and Nick to meet without knowing each other's identity. Instead of helping, guess I put my foot into it. No, I didn't think we had another imposter on our hands."

" 'Another imposter,' Mr. B.D.? Of

course, I know that you mean Philippe. I wish you liked him. I can't bear to have you and . . . and others think him a fraud," Sandra deplored wistfully.

"The 'others' are coming to heel fast. He's getting popular in the neighborhood." Damon glared his bird-of-prey glare. "Are you in love with him?"

"No!" A startling memory of the fervor with which she had responded to the kiss she had thought Philippe's sent the blood in a warm wave to Sandra's hair. She bit her lips to steady them. How could she be so silly! Didn't she know now that it had been but a part of the nightmare of her accident? That he had not been in the house?

"You needn't answer that question." Damon looked white and old and tired as he regarded her. "You are loyal to your friends, aren't you, but remember what I told you about the under dog."

Sandra ignored the reminder. "Loyal? I hope so. Dad used to say that I kept a candle burning in my heart for each friend. Perhaps I do, but — he didn't know that if through disillusionment one goes out, never can I relight it. Horrid disposition to have, isn't it?"

"Horrid only because you are bound to

be hurt. We'll shelve Rousseau for the present; it is evident that you and I see him with different eyes. Let's talk about the races. That won't do either. Of course you are hoping that his horse will win?"

"To be honest, I am. Apart from my friendship for him, suppose the Court decides against Philippe — I don't see how it can with that diary as evidence — but suppose it does? He would have no money. If Iron Man wins this race he would win others; then the gray could be retired for breeding and earn a nice little income for his owner, couldn't he?"

"He could. What made you think of that?"

"Oh, I have been improving my opportunities. I've been taking an Extension Course on the Horse from the old books in the library at Seven Chimneys. They are interesting, but something tells me that most of them are a bit out of date."

Damon's face wrinkled into a smile. His eyes twinkled. "You're an amusing child, Sandra. Something tells you right. You won't find anything in those text-books about ultra-violet-ray glass which Mrs. Pat has put into her stables, nor about the direct ultra-violet-ray treatments given to some of the horses daily. But to return to

Fortune; he must win. To use your argument, suppose the Court decides against the man in possession — I don't see how it can — that black stallion must bring in the money. Not that Nick is thinking of that alone; he is out to show the world that stamina, courage, and a great heart go to the making of a champion as well as to the making of a great man."

"You adore Nicholas Hoyt, don't you?"

"If you weren't confoundedly prejudiced, you would understand why. I love that boy as if he were my own. He is so worth while, so fitted to inherit a big estate. He is like the old aristocrats, the best of them, who believed that privilege carried with it civic responsibility. He's slated to represent this county in the legislature. There is a driving force within him that will keep him going on and up. That's what is needed now. Militant souls who, instead of lambasting every one connected with the government, will get to work and make this country safe for women and children and celebrities! It isn't his losing the money I care so much about; it's the injustice of the thing."

He brushed his handkerchief across his hot forehead. "Here I am steaming up on the subject of the estate fight again. We were talking horse before I switched to Nick and his ambitions. There's no maybe about that Hunt Club course, but Fortune has an 8 to 1 chance with Eddie Sharp up if — if —" His voice thinned to silence as he scowled at the fire.

"Now you've gone Kipling," Sandra teased. As he looked up to regard her sombrely, she regretted: "I'm sorry. Forgive my flippancy. I was trying to cheer you. Tell me the 'if' about Sharp."

Damon's smile had the effect of sunlight dispelling clouds. "No apology needed, my dear. Glad to see you getting back your light heart. You've had me worried these last two days. As I was saying, Eddie is a jock in a thousand, he has an uncanny insight into the mind of his mount; never saw any one to beat him — and I've been about stables and tracks all my life — except Curt Newsome, that boy's a wizard. Slow motion pictures have shown him to be almost faultless. But Sharp is unpredictable."

"Do you mean that he might dope a horse?"

"Where did you pick up the knowledge of that ugly trick, Sandra? In your Extension Course?"

"Sandy to you, Mr. B.D.; it was Dad's

name for me and I love it." She steadied her voice. "I read about it in a newspaper. When you said that Eddie Sharp was unpredictable, I thought of that."

"You thought wrong. That jockey would kill himself before he would tamper with a Thoroughbred. Drink is his Waterloo. Who was it said that he could be a total abstainer, but that he didn't know the first letter of the word temperance? Eddie is like that. Nick will stay down and guard him and watch Fortune's workouts until after the race. If the jock can be kept sober he will ride that horse to a smashing victory."

"Why does Nicholas Hoyt bother with the man? Aren't there other jockeys who could win?"

"Yes, but — hulloa, Nick! Glad you've come. I was succumbing to the anecdotal urge. Sandra's — Sandy's sympathetic attention lured me on."

Nicholas Hoyt looked at the girl who stood with her hand on the back of a chair.

"Ought you to stand? How are you?"

Something deep in his steady eyes quickened Sandra's pulses. It was an effort to answer lightly.

"I'm marvelous, thank you. Behold a

slightly cracked-up, but a wiser, far wiser rider. Catch me dreaming on a horse's back again!"

"Dreams are an extravagant indulgence any way you look at them, aren't they, B.D.?"

Damon's heavy white brows met. "Indulgence! How do you get that way, Nick? Dreams are the source of much of the new thinking, new convictions, new power in the world. They send the adventurous out on uncharted seas, dangerous seas, and it is danger, not security, which develops strength in mind and spirit. No, I wouldn't say that dreaming was an extravagance. I'd list it under the head of a non-taxable necessity. I suppose you young people think that just some of a sixty-five-year-old codger's hokum."

"Mr. Hoyt may speak for himself. I'm not so juvenile as to consider sixty-five old, and I've had that 'uncharted seas' idea myself. But why think of those seas entirely in terms of danger and treacherous reefs and sinister whirlpools? I'm perched on the lookout spying for goodwill ships and treasure islands, and priceless friends, and lovely summer seas with just enough squalls to make me appreciate fair weather."

"Hmp! You're something of a poet, aren't you? I'll wager you get what you are looking for, Sandy. By the way, what does Sandy stand for?"

"Cassandra. Nothing poetic about that. Outrageous, isn't it? Imagine it in a marriage service. 'I, Cassandra, take thee . . .' Could anything be more unglamorous? The bad fairy must have popped the name of her grandmother into Mother's mind when I arrived from playing with the angels. Luckily the good fairy headed off Cassie as a nickname."

Sandra colored as she met Nicholas Hoyt's intent eyes. Did he think her a confirmed chatterbox?

"I like Cassandra; it has character," Damon approved.

Now that you have come to play watchdog, Nick, I'll go out to the stables and pay my respects to Fortune."

"May I go?" Sandra asked eagerly. "I've never seen the inside of the Seven Chimneys stables. Mrs. Pat almost bit my head off the first time I asked if I might visit them."

"Do you mean that you haven't seen Iron Man since you came?"

"Why the third-degree edge to your voice, Mr. Hoyt? I have seen the gray only on the fairway exercising. Cross-my-throat-an'-hope-to-die!"

Nicholas laughed. "You needn't swear to the statement. I believe you. I remember now that Mac Donovan, Mrs. Pat's manager, hates women; he told her once that he would throw up the job if she permitted any skirts in the stables. He wouldn't, but she humors him."

"But he likes her?"

"Likes her! He's off his head about her. I don't mean in love," Nicholas amended. "She put him on his feet when he was down and out, be and his brother Sam. She brought them along when she married Uncle Mark. They would lay down their lives for her. She is worth devotion. She's straight as a string if she did have a brainstorm over Curt Newsome."

"You like her and yet you won't forgive her for that?"

"It isn't a question of forgiveness. Let's not talk about it. Here comes tea. Have that first and then if you're very good we may let you walk to the stables. How about it, Nanny O'Day?"

The chunky little woman in the gray silk gown set the squat silver kettle over the alcohol lamp. Her blue eyes twinkled above her ruddy cheeks which looked like wrinkled winter apples.

"Certain, certain she can go, if she's a good girl and drinks her tea and eats some of those nice little tomato sandwiches I made for her. Will you pour, child?"

Sandra slipped into the chair before the table. "I'd love to. I'm glad that some one in the house has the sense to realize that I am not an invalid if I am one-armed. Sugar, Mr. B.D.?"

"One lump."

Nanny O'Day's glance swept the tray on a tour of inspection before she bustled from the room. Sandra was aware of Nicholas Hoyt's eyes on her hand as it moved among the ravishing silver and fragile china. To dispel an absurd sense of embarrassment, she held it up.

"Anything the matter with it?"

"Nothing. Besides being perfect in shape it looks as if it might do things. Don't you care for rings?"

"Mad about them. I have a few which were my mother's. I haven't worn them since I became a working woman. 'Nice job, secretary.' Remember the day you said that?"

"Do you think I could forget? I . . ."

A spoon tapped out a silver tinkle against a cup. "I'm still here," reminded

Damon. "I . . ."

He stopped speaking to listen to the sound of hurrying feet on the stepping-stones in front of the house. The knocker sounded an imperious summons. Voices. Nanny O'Day's. Another, high and excited as if in argument. A rush through the hall. Emma, the maid, on the threshold, her soft hat slightly awry.

Sandra imagined that she hesitated as she saw her. If she did, it was but for a split second. She clenched her hands on the breast of the cardigan she wore over her black silk uniform. She struggled to control her panting breath as she looked from Damon to Nicholas and back to the elder man.

"I — I didn't know what to do, sir, — I nearly lost my mind when I found it caught in the drawer — so I — I brought it here!"

"Brought what?" the two men demanded in unison.

Sandra sat forward in her chair. Was she awake, or was she dreaming that she was at a play? The situation was too theatrical to be real. Emma produced a creased and crumpled envelope.

"This. It's addressed to you, Mr. Hoyt."

Chapter XIII

For an instant there was no sound in the room save the rattle of the teakettle cover and the slight hiss of steam. Then Nicholas demanded:

"How do you know I'm Hoyt? I've never seen you before."

Color blotched Emma's white face. "I've seen you in the village. Everybody's talking about you and the Kentuckian who's trying to get the property. So when I found this — you see it's addressed to you —"

Nicholas took the envelope. His face darkened redly as he looked at it.

"You said you found this caught in a drawer. What drawer?"

"I hope you won't think I was prying —"

"Great Scott! Stop twiddling the buttons on your jacket and talk, woman!" roared Damon. He glowered from under shaggy brows. "Speak up! Where'd you get it?"

Emma thrust unsteady hands into her pockets. Sandra detected a smoldering fire in her eyes, but her voice was servile as she answered:

"It was this way, sir. Ever since I came to Seven Chimneys I've heard talk about the case to be tried in court; how Mr. Rousseau had a diary that said he was the son they thought had died; how Mr. Hoyt here hadn't a line of writing of that nurse, Anne Pardoe, to test it by. I got awful interested — there isn't much to do in this rotten dull town — an' I thought, suppose I could find a letter somewhere that would help either side, I'd get a reward, wouldn't I? I could throw up the job with the Newsome woman, she's a terror to work for."

"That's enough about your employer," Nicholas Hoyt snapped. "Go on! Where did you get this?" He tapped the letter.

"I told you, sir, I got kinder nutty over the case, hearing so much about it in the servants' hall — Mr. Huckins, the butler, can't talk of much else — I heard there was a secret drawer in that big desk in the library, and every chance I'd get I'd fuss round to see if I could find it."

She looked squarely at Sandra. "You caught me at it, Miss, that time when you were on the steps in front of the bookshelves. You pretended that you hadn't noticed what I was doing, but I guess you had, hadn't you?"

"Yes," Sandra answered.

"Get on with your story," Nicholas Hoyt prodded impatiently. The color had drained from his face.

"I almost went blooey this afternoon when the drawer shot out at me. Then I thought I heard paper crackle. I put my hand way in. That letter was caught in the back; you see how creased and bent it is?" The woman gulped from excitement.

"What is your name?"

"Emma Davis, Mr. Hoyt."

"Why did you bring this letter to me? Why didn't you take it to Mr. Rousseau if you thought it of importance?"

"I didn't know whether it was important or not. It's addressed to you, isn't it, sir?" She was the picture of innocence unjustly accused. "Just because I said I wouldn't mind a reward doesn't mean that I'm dishonest, that I would give that letter to a person it wasn't meant for, does it?"

"My mistake. If it is of importance, you'll get your reward. That will be all. Go out through the kitchen. Tell Mrs. O'Day that I said to give you tea."

"Thank you, sir. I will be glad to get it. I

ran all the way here and I'm dead beat." She paused on the threshold. "You may think I'm fresh, but I hope the letter clinches your hold on the place. That Rousseau fella ain't no gentleman!"

Of what was Nicholas Hoyt thinking, Sandra wondered. He stood by the window looking down at the letter. The bang of a distant door shattered the spell of silence. Damon crossed the room and laid his hand on the younger man's shoulder.

"You should have told her to keep her mouth shut, Nick. What do you make of it?"

"It's addressed in Uncle Mark's writing."

"Open it."

"Wait, please!" Sandra blew out the flame under the kettle and rose. "I'm going. It isn't right that I should hear what is in that letter. I'm Philippe's . . ."

"What?"

The expression in Nicholas Hoyt's eyes was like a grip on her throat. "H — his — I believe in him."

"You're not at Seven Chimneys as his spy, are you?"

"Of course not!"

"Don't choke over it. I told you that you would believe in me, didn't I? I . . ."

Damon tapped impatient fingers on the

window. "Suppose we find out what is in that letter, Nick."

"Right, B.D. I've been stalling. I dreaded to open it. Keep an eye on Miss Duval while I'm reading. She's likely to walk out on us."

How could he smile when perhaps his fortune was at stake? Sandra was tense with excitement and the outcome meant nothing to her. What would it mean to Philippe?

She kept her eyes on Nicholas Hoyt as he pulled two sheets of paper from the envelope. Two letters? His lips tightened as he read, the veins in his forehead stood out like cords. He cleared his throat and looked up.

"One is from Uncle Mark, written the day he died. Remember, don't you, B.D., that I was in Chicago at the time, following up the firm which had been hammering at some of our securities? He had received a letter from Anne Pardoe. She wrote that she hadn't much longer to live and confessed that she had stolen the child. That must have been the letter which troubled him that last day. Here it is."

He flung the letters to the desk and crossed to the window. Hands hard in his pockets, he turned his back and stared out at the riot of color in the perennial border.

Damon picked up the two sheets of paper. Read them. Dropped them to the desk. He backed against the mantel and shook his head.

"Those will about wash up our case, Nick. What will you do?"

Nicholas Hoyt wheeled. His face was white, his usually gray eyes were black.

"Do! Take it on the chin — if I have to. But . . ."

An irresistible force took possession of Sandra. Nerves in her throat she never before had known were there, ached. She said breathlessly:

"Mr. Damon, perhaps I should have told you before, the maid Emma is the woman who applied for the social secretary position just before I did. I'm sure of it. She has dyed her hair since then."

"How do you know?"

Sandra kept her eyes on the elder man's startled face.

"The girl at the switch-board called my attention to her angry eyes that day. I was so excited over my first attempt to secure a position that my mind was like a sensitive film, every little incident was photographed in color."

"Why haven't you told this before?"

Nicholas Hoyt's voice was like an icy wave drenching her, chilling her to the bone.

"Because — I waited —"

"Have you told Rousseau?"

"I have not. I haven't told any one, but now that I have told you, I think it only fair that he should know."

"What will you do now, Nick?" Damon demanded.

Nicholas glanced from one face to the other.

"I think perhaps I'd better keep my program to myself." He thrust the letters into his pocket.

"Still interested to see the stables, Miss Duval?" he inquired as lightly as if the winning or the losing of a fortune were a mere incident in the day's routine.

Had her information about Emma made Nicholas Hoyt again suspicious of her, Sandra asked herself the next morning, as in her brown and white checked sports coat and soft hat she waited in the living room at Stone House for the car which was to take her to Seven Chimneys. Apparently he had been in high spirits while he showed her about the stables. He had been so tenderly thoughtful that some quick fiery stuff in her had flared up each time she had met his eyes. Had he been pretending again? He must have been. Didn't he want her to know how upset he was about those letters?

The questions had been uppermost in her mind during the inspection of the stables; except for an impression of immaculateness and sleek heads and great velvety eyes, she couldn't remember what she had seen. She had been furiously indignant and hurt — yes, she would acknowledge that — at the manner in which he had slammed the door of his mind in her face. It didn't help that Mr. Damon had received the same treatment. Did he think that she would run to Philippe Rousseau with information while a guest in his house?

A car! At the gate. A roadster. Philippe driving. Why had he come for her?

Nanny O'Day bustled in. "It's come, my dear." Was her voice constrained? "The car's come for you. Keep the coat over your poor shoulder; I'll button it close about your throat."

Sandra's eyes filled. She pressed her face against the woman's rosy, wrinkled cheek. "You've been wonderful, Nanny. I can't begin to —"

"There, there, my dear, it's been a joy having you. I sent your riding clothes back by Bridie when she brought the pyjamas, so you have only this small bag. I told her not to let you stir out of your rooms till tomorrow. Now be a good child and do as you're told."

Philippe Rousseau was coming up the path. He must not enter this house for her. "I'll take the bag, Nanny. I'll see you again soon." She was out of the front door before the woman could answer.

"Here I am, Philippe. Why did you come for me?"

"Think I would let any one else drive you home?"

"Don't help me as if I were a centenarian." Sandra shook off his hand on her arm. "I'm fed up on invalidism."

As the roadster started, she waved to the little woman standing in the doorway. Rousseau was intent on manoevering out of the drive whose curves had been planned long before the days of automobiles. Safely on the highway, he turned to her. His dark eyes were drenched in melancholy.

"Are you annoyed that I came for you, Sandra?"

"Of course not; don't go melodramatic, Philippe. I think it would have been in better taste if the chauffeur had come, that's all."

He twisted his dark, clipped moustache with his free hand, his moody eyes on the road ahead. Sandra's conscience pricked. What had made her suddenly aware of Philippe's theatricalness? He was no different from the man she had liked before her accident; then his mannerisms had seemed amusing, now they were irritating. Was it because Nicholas Hoyt's evident suspicion of her was smarting in her mind? He had been suspicious, else why the sudden determination to keep his "program" to himself?

She wrenched her thoughts from him and drew a long breath of the spicy air. Wonderful to be back in the world again; it seemed as if she had been housed for years. After this she would have more sympathy with invalids. What a tragedy to be obliged to sit passively on the sidelines and see life go by. She stole a glance at Rousseau's face. Was he angry?

"Don't be cross this perfect day, Philippe. Look at those trees! The fruit is beginning to show crimson. Summer has gone."

Beyond the colorful orchards, fields, some of them speckled with eruptions of gray rock, rolled away to woods which hoisted scraps of rusty-orange and browny-red that made her think of the gay little sails of Venetian fishing-boats. Scarlet maple flamed among the dark spruces and pines. Silver birches, towering elms, and a white boat-house plunged tops deep into the black mirror of the river. Large houses added the human touch to the panorama, much as the soul behind the eyes of a lovely woman makes them come alive. On the tanbark fairway back of the Seven Chimneys' stables, horses, their backs shining like satin, were being breezed.

"Let's stop by the track, Philippe," Sandra suggested eagerly. "Any chance of seeing Iron Man at work?"

Rousseau glanced at his wrist watch. "Time for him now. I suppose you saw the great Fortune while you were at Stone House? I'm surprised that you have any interest in my horse now."

How like him, Sandra thought, before she protested: "Don't be foolish. Can't a person admire two horses?"

"What did you think of Hoyt's?"

"I'm not sufficiently turf-minded to express an opinion."

"You won't, you mean. Here comes Iron Man."

He stopped the car. Two men perched on the fence turned to look, then whispered to each other.

"Who are they, Philippe?"

"Those railbirds? I don't know. Probably racetrack habitues hanging round to time Iron Man on his workout. He'll walk. Then he'll canter. Then he'll speed."

The gray's back had the sheen of polished pewter in the sunlight. He lifted his fine head and snorted.

"He's magnificent! He looks as if he knew everything there was to know in the world!" Sandra exclaimed.

"Sometimes I think he does. In a race he sets his own time for putting on speed and Piggy Pike lets him have his way. Look! Look!"

Iron Man was a silver streak around the fairway. Every person in sight had a watch in his hand. As the jockey slowed the horse to a stop, Rousseau dropped back into his seat. His eyes burned like coals in his white face.

"He's broken Fortune's record on that course! It's the breaks at last! I suppose you're sorry," he accused bitterly. "Let's go!" He started the car.

"Ever heard of the power of suggestion, Philippe? If you keep on telling me that I am backing Fortune, I may begin to think that I am."

His laugh was as unpleasant as his voice. "If you do, you'll make the mistake of your life. Turf enthusiasts all over the country have their eyes on my horse. He's top choice. Perhaps you're betting on Nick Hoyt's side of the estate case too? I suppose you heard all the latest dope in his favor while you were at Stone House?"

"He's been leading up to this!" The thought blazed through Sandra's mind with a suddenness that caught at her breath. She looked at Rousseau from under the screen of her long lashes. His eyes were intent on the entrance to Seven Chimneys. Why had he asked that question? Did he, could he know of Emma's visit? Of course he didn't. She was disloyal to him to think it. Though still shaken by the intuitive flash, she said evenly:

"I asked no questions about the estate while I was a guest at Stone House, Philippe."

He did not speak again until he had brought the roadster to the door of Seven Chimneys in a spurt of speed. "Here we are. I'm glad to get you out of the irresistible Nick Hoyt's Clutches," he sneered.

Not until she reached her room did Sandra remember that she had decided to tell him of her suspicion of Emma. Why had she forgotten? The question recurred several times during the day. It popped into her mind even while Mrs. Pat was affectionately scolding her for being up and about her flower-fragrant boudoir.

She and Bridie between them had sent her to bed early, and now, braced by downy pillows, she was waiting in the lamp-lighted room for the maid to bring her dinner.

She crinkled her nose at her reflection in the mirror: laughing dark eyes, a slightly tanned face, white shoulders, neck, and arms, one in a sling, dark hair, delicate lace and pale blue georgette against apricot linen pillows.

"They will dramatize your silly accident," she said aloud to the looking-glass girl. She picked up the telephone on the stand beside the bed in response to a ring.

"Sandra Duval speaking." She could feel the color warm her skin. Nicholas Hoyt. Why had he called her? She had better listen instead of wondering. His voice was as clear as if he were in the room; if he were still indignant because she had not before told her suspicions of Emma, he was camouflaging skillfully. She answered:

"How am I? Fine, thank you."

"You look like a million."

Sandra met the startled eyes of the girl in the mirror. "How — how do you know?"

"Your televisibility is grand."

"Wait a minute." Of course it was a joke, but she hastily dropped the phone to drag a blue satin lounge coat over her bare shoulders with one hand. That was better. She picked up the instrument.

"You were saying?"

"Are they taking care of you as well as we — Nanny O'Day did?"

"Care! They are making my life a burden. The doctor was here when I arrived and went into the air when he heard that I had stopped at the fairway to see —"

"Go on, you saw Iron Man sprint, didn't you? Afraid to hurt my feelings? I've heard that he broke Fortune's record on that course. Never mind the horses; what did the Doc say?"

"That my arm could come out of the sling tomorrow. When that happens, I hope every one will forget that I was such a total loss on horseback. Thank you for those gorgeous roses."

"Like 'em?"

"Love them."

"Don't waste your love on flowers.

Bridie has orders to look after you. If you're not a good, obedient girl, B.D. and I will kidnap you and bring you back here. Get that?"

"That threat will keep me toeing the mark."

"Don't you like Stone House?" There was an absurd tinge of anxiety in the question. A little demon of contrariness seized Sandra.

"It's very nice — but . . ."

"But what?"

"I have a single-track heart. I came to Seven Chimneys first. Naturally I am loyal to that."

"Same way about people?"

Sandra remembered her curious suspicion of Philippe Rousseau. "Yes. Until — unless I lose faith in them."

"I understand. Haven't commenced to believe in me yet, have you? I'm waiting," the authoritative voice reminded.

Sandra evaded. "It takes me a long time to make friends. I have seen you so few times . . ."

"Is that it? That's easily corrected. From now on I'll see that that excuse isn't valid. You'll be seeing me."

How could he be so gay and light-hearted with those two letters in his possession? Apparently he wasn't in the least troubled — but shouldn't he know that she had not as yet told Philippe about Emma? She said quickly:

"Mr. Hoyt."

"If Nicholas is too long to pronounce, try Nick."

"Please. Be serious. I want to tell you something."

"Where'd you get the idea that I am not serious? What is it? Shoot."

"I think you ought to know . . . Come in!"

"I wish I could."

"I didn't mean you. Some one knocked. It is Emma with my dinner."

"Hope it's a good one."

"It looks luscious. Essence of tomato, mushrooms under glass. A squab and —"

"What had you to tell me?"

Sandra looked at the maid who was arranging the dishes on a small table. Were her ears pricking with curiosity? She said quickly:

"Thank you for calling. Good-bye."

She placed the instrument on its rack. "That looks delicious, Emma. You and I seem to be meeting constantly lately."

The maid came closer and said under her breath. "Please don't tell any one here that I took those letters to Mr. Hoyt, Miss Duval. I'd be frightened for my life if that butler Huckins found out. I have a hunch he's working tooth and nail for that Rousseau fella."

Chapter XIV

"Two championships, eight blues, six reds, four yellows. Not too bad a collection of ribbons to take in one show. It made the snooty smart set here sit up and take notice. The committee has asked me to stand in the receiving line at the Hunt Ball tomorrow, Curt."

Mrs. Newsome's voice oozed satisfaction as she stood before the fire-place in the living room at Seven Chimneys. The late afternoon sunlight gilded the mimosa trees which framed the great window, streamed in to illumine the gold letters on the heap of rosettes of colored ribbons lying on a table, before it shattered into a pool of light at her feet.

Sandra looked from her tweed-suited employer to the frowning man slumped in a chair. His clothes were of the latest cut and fashion, but the ensemble was mussy.

Curtis Newsome was in a black mood indubitably. Hands in his coat pockets, legs outstretched, a telltale vacancy in his eyes, apparently his thoughts were anywhere but upon his wife at whom he was looking. She made an effort to clear the atmosphere.

"It's grand about the ball, Mrs. Pat. Of course you should be there. Did any one else take so many ribbons at the show?"

The mistress of Seven Chimneys preened. "No. I would have taken another blue had Curtis ridden Rovin' Reddy. The groom who showed him in the five-gaited class made the horse nervous; he cooked him."

"What possible use can a horse have for five gaits," Sandra asked, not because she cared, but one had to say something, one had to act as shock troops to draw fire, when husband and wife returned to the glacial age.

"That's what the Englishmen asked. They have nothing like it over there. What is it, Huckins," she demanded irritably as the butler appeared on the threshold. His eyes seemed to search the room before he answered:

"A note, Madame."

"Who from?" Mrs. Newsome's finger

already was inserted under the flap of the envelope he had given her.

"I do not know, Madame. A man from Stone House brought it."

"What are you waiting for, Huckins?"

"In case you had orders for more places to be set at table, Madame."

"If there is to be a change, you will be told. That's all."

The man backed from sight as soundlessly as he had appeared. Sandra rose and picked up the cape of her rose-color wool suit. Mrs. Newsome, who had been scowling at the note, detained her with an imperative wave of her large, capable hand.

"Don't go. I want you and Curtis to pass judgment on this. The ribbons are not the only victories I've won." She twisted the sheet of paper; her voice was sharp with triumph. "This is from Nicholas Hoyt asking if he may dine here tonight."

Sandra's heart tripped on a beat. During the two weeks which had passed since her return from Stone House she had met Nicholas Hoyt several times on the road; he had stopped her to inquire for her shoulder. The days he had not met her he had called her on the phone. He looked thin, his eyes were hard and strained, but he had made no mention of the estate fight. Each time she had heard his voice she had fought his attraction for her. She would not be a "hound on his trail." Sometimes she felt as if she were struggling in an irresistible current, and like an almost spent swimmer, catching at anything which might hold her back. Mostly she clutched at Philippe Rousseau, clutched, figuratively speaking. Her conscience pricked. She had not as yet told him of her suspicion of Emma.

Had Nicholas adhered to his plan to say nothing about those letters until he faced the claimant to the Hoyt estate in court? Only two persons besides himself, she and Mr. Damon, knew what was in them. Suppose he did not produce them? Would it be her moral duty to tell Philippe about them? No! He was quite capable of managing his side of this fight. Hadn't he a lawyer? She remembered her flash of suspicion the day he had brought her from Stone House, and reiterated with a little shiver, "Quite capable."

Mrs. Newsome's angry voice penetrated her reflections.

"Nick makes no apology for the weeks and months during which he has ignored us. You'd think from that note that he was here yesterday. He begins, 'Dear Pat'; then he writes that Jed Langdon is back from abroad and asks if he and Jed may come to dinner, and ends, 'May I come?' Just like that! Perhaps he thinks that at this late day he may persuade me to back Fortune. I won't; I'm all for Iron Man. If I did what I want to do, I'd send this note back torn into a hundred pieces, but, cheap and showy and common as he thinks me, I hate rowing families, I think they're the lowest form of animal life, and he and I represent the same family, if only by marriage. What shall I do, Curtis? It's up to you. He stopped coming because I married you; you are the one who has been insulted."

Newsome pulled himself up from the chair in which he had been slouched. His fair skin was crimson.

"Why bore Miss Duval with this discussion, Pat?"

"Because it is part of her job to help me make decisions — of a social sort. Well, what shall it be, Curtis?"

"Does Nicholas know that that slick Rousseau, who claims he is Philip Hoyt, is still here?"

His wife grunted derision. "Now I ask you, is there anything that goes on on this estate that he doesn't know? He's the manager, isn't he?"

"Say, listen, Pat, pipe down! I've nothing against Mr. Nicholas; he's a grand fella. I liked him when I rode for his uncle's stables. He treated me as if I was his own kind, even if I was a professional jock. Tell him to come on; it's the only sporting thing to do when he waves the white flag. Can't you see his hand in that Hunt Ball invitation you're so set up about? He's the big noise in this town. He probably said to his set, 'Lay off Mrs. Pat! Count her in!' — and you were invited."

"If I thought that, I wouldn't go to the ball!"

"Oh, yeah? You know wild horses wouldn't keep you away. Of course you'll go. Of course you'll have Nicholas Hoyt here. If you ask me, I'll say he is the one to do the forgiving after the way you've backed up the man who is trying to steal his jack — to say nothing of taking Rousseau's horse, which, with Hoyt's Fortune, will make the race competing for that twenty-five grand day after tomorrow."

His wife watched him as he left the room. The pitiless sun intensified the crow's-feet at the corners of her troubled eyes as she appealed to Sandra.

"What do you say?"

"I think there will be an explosion of

red-hot sparks when Nicholas Hoyt and Philippe Rousseau get together, but I agree with Mr. Newsome, the sporting thing to do is to send word to Stone House that you will be delighted to see him."

"Sure you'd say 'delighted'?"

"Or words to that effect."

"Here's Philippe!" Mrs. Newsome's voice and eyes were spiced with malice as she announced: "Your *cousin* Nicholas dines with us tonight."

Did the hand with which he held a lighter to his cigarette shake? It was a second only before he laughed:

"The heir and the Pretender. Which is which?"

Would Nicholas Hoyt come early to make his peace with Mrs. Pat, or would he come late to avoid the possibility of reproaches? Sandra's thoughts were on the dramatic potentialities of the meeting as, two hours later, she slowly descended the stairs. She paused a moment before the Chippendale mirror to note if the quivery sensation, which had persisted since she had heard the contents of his note, were visible in her appearance. No, her red lips were steady, her dark eyes gave no evidence of turmoil within. She lingered to adjust the ragged chrysanthemums, as golden as her satin frock, in a tall vase on the console. For some unknown reason she balked at entering that room. What use stalling? Hadn't she learned yet that the best procedure when one dreaded a thing was to get it behind one as soon as possible?

She stopped on the threshold of the library, her surprised eyes on the picture above the mantel. The too, too fleshly coryphée had given place to a portrait in a massive gold frame, the portrait of a young man in pink coat, soft yellow waistcoat, white breeches, white stock and tie. A polished boot-top was visible, one hand was in his pocket, the other held a whip. A Master of Fox Hounds, Nicholas Hoyt. No mistaking the extraordinary clearness of the gray eyes. A much younger, gayer Nicholas Hoyt, with a more sensitive mouth, than the man whom she had seen breaking the black stallion, yet a man already showing those essential qualities of firmness and responsibility which go to make up a good M.F.H.

Mrs. Pat must have had the pictures changed when she decided to welcome the original of this one. She was a good sport, no half way measure with her, Sandra thought as she entered the library. Nicholas Hoyt was not there. Estelle Carter, for once ahead of time, was perched on the arm of a chair which faced the door. Had she dressed early that she might not miss the comedy of his entrance? Her slim body, in a black sequined frock, glinted like a lithe Harlequin with every movement. Her cigarette holder, sandals, and sheer handkerchief matched the jade of her earrings. Jed Langdon and Curtis Newsome were bending over the puzzle table. Across the room Mrs. Pat, in a deep horizon-blue chiffon, magical in its slenderizing effect, was chatting with Philippe Rousseau.

Sandra was aware of electricity in the atmosphere. After an instant of hesitation she joined the two men.

"Welcome back, Mr. Langdon! You two have the air of dark and dour conspiracy in spite of your apparent absorption. Something is about to happen to somebody. I —"

"Mr. Nicholas Hoyt." The butler's voice, a trifle more suave, a trifle more impressive than usual, interrupted her gay prediction.

There was a slight hush like the instant which precedes the bursting of a shell — then Mrs. Newsome took a step forward; her chin quivered like a hurt child's. Nicholas met her with outstretched hand.

"It was mighty nice of you to let me come, Pat."

The color, which had darkened his face as he greeted his hostess, faded as Philippe Rousseau said easily:

"How are you, Nick?"

Apparently he had decided to ignore his ejection from Stone House on the day of the accident. He could be counted on for surperb confidence. He had had the sense not to offer his hand, Sandra approved, as she watched the two. Nicholas Hoyt's eyes were blazing; she could see the muscles of his jaw twitch, but his good manners held.

"How are you!" he responded with a faint touch of warmth before he turned toward Estelle Carter. She exhaled a long breath of smoke and laughed.

"Looks like a good party! Enter the rightful interrogation point — heir. What a man! You certainly know the dramatic value of a late entrance, Nick." She flung her arm about his neck and kissed him squarely on the mouth. "Priceless boy! It's a lifetime since I've seen you!"

Sandra's world whirled and steadied. She knew the woman's kiss meant nothing, knew that probably she had seen Nicholas Hoyt every day, but it made her furious.

How could he stand there smiling down at her? Did he love her? Except for the fact that his color had deepened, apparently it was an every-day occurrence for him to be kissed. Thank heaven she had seen the demonstration! She would no longer have to fight his attraction; probably that had been nothing but a feverish hang-over from her fall, anyway. How she hated his type! He removed the clinging arm.

"Can't take the credit for that dramatic entrance, Estelle. Jed and I arrived twenty minutes ago; I had hoped to have a heart-to-heart with Mrs. Pat before the rest of you came down. Bud and Buddy were the real directors of my late appearance in person. They were lying in wait outside. In their exuberance they planted four great paws on my, until then, immaculate shirt-front. I had to go back to Stone House to change. Better keep those dogs shut up after dark, Curt."

Curtis Newsome's sensitive lips twitched, his eyes glowed with fervent admiration at the friendliness of Nicholas Hoyt's smile and voice, at his tactful assumption that he would be the one to give orders, not his wife.

Mrs. Pat's despotism did not admit of authority contrary to her own. She promptly caught up the reins of management.

"I'll see that it doesn't happen again. You know every one here, don't you, Nick? Miss Duval has been your guest, so you may have caught the idea that she's a treasure. She ought to be secretary for some hundred thousand dollar a year man, she has executive ability and then some."

"Executive ability — and how! A girl who can manage to come a cropper at the door of a rich, good-looking bachelor. . . ." Estelle Carter ended the sentence with a laugh.

The suggestion had been made so lightly that resentment seemed out of place, yet Sandra felt the prick of malice in the words. She protested gaily:

"Please don't discuss me. I feel like — like a germ which has been isolated for observation under a microscope."

Philippe Rousseau slipped his arm in hers. "If you are, you're a rare and precious germ. Come out on the terrace until dinner is announced. You and I are outlanders at this — family reunion."

His smoldering eyes betrayed the blandness of his voice. Unless she wished to precipitate a scene she had better go with him, Sandra decided. Once outside on the shadowy terrace above the pool, he resented:

"Nicholas Hoyt didn't look at me when I spoke to him — I, who was ready to overlook his rotten treatment the day you were hurt! He's a fool! I could be generous to him — but, after that, do you think I will be when . . . when all this comes to me?"

He nodded toward the dusky shapes of the stables with their winking lights. A middle-aged moon was rising among fleeces of cloud. A drift of dance music from a distant radio floated past on the scented breeze which set little noises creaking in the shutters, whipped white ribbons on the surface of the dark river. To Sandra the world seemed unreal in the dim light and the man beside her the most unreal thing in it. Had he by any chance heard of those letters?

"Are you so sure that it will come to you?"

He squared his shoulders, looked down at her as one might at a foolish but very dear child.

"I am. The proofs that I am the son of Mark Hoyt are incontestable. Only three days now before the date set for the hearing. They have been trying to find some papers, letters of my mother's they claim Mark Hoyt had."

"Your mother!"

"My foster-mother; not surprising that I should think of her as the real thing, is it? Remember, I didn't know the truth about her until she was dying and gave me her diary and an old letter of Mark Hoyt's. They won't be able to disprove that little book."

He caught her hands. "Do you wonder that I want all this which is rightfully mine? What a home! What a home in which to live, to which to bring a wife! Sandra — the moment I am acknowledged the heir —"

"Sorry to interrupt, Miss Duval, but it has been several minutes since Huckins announced dinner," Nicholas Hoyt suggested from the French window.

For all the notice he took of Philippe, the claimant to the Hoyt fortune might have been a flagstone in the terrace. There was an unpleasant glint in Rousseau's eyes. Sandra hurriedly slipped her hand within his arm.

"Come, Philippe. Mrs. Pat is a forgiving soul, but lateness at dinner is the one thing she won't stand for. Unless we want to be sent to our rooms without anything to eat, we had better go in."

Nicholas Hoyt stood aside for them to enter the dining room. Sandra gazed up at him defiantly as she passed. Did he believe that laughter-veiled insinuation of Estelle's that her accident had been planned to excite his interest? Conceited as he may have been made by pursuing females, he couldn't be so brainless as to think that. In case he did, she would make it her life work from this minute on to smash the supposition.

She was uncomfortably aware of him as she sat beside him at dinner. The table decorations were blue and red, tall blue tapers in silver sticks, bachelor buttons and red roses in a massive bowl.

"Are the red and blue flowers to celebrate the victories?" Nicholas Hoyt inquired of his hostess.

There was a quiver of excitement in Mrs. Pat's coarse, hearty laugh. She was evidently bubbling with happiness. Had his return contributed to her joy over winning the ribbons, or was it entirely the change in her husband? Curtis Newsome was in one of his gay moods; there was a hint of you're-the-only-woman-in-my-life in his voice when he spoke to his wife, a devil-may-care challenge in his blue eyes. Sandra caught herself hoping that he would draw her within the circle of his charm. Ridiculous, of course; just the same, her eyes were attracted to him as to a magnet. It was with difficulty that she dragged her attention back to Mrs. Pat's answer to Nicholas Hoyt's question.

"That was Sandra's idea, Nick. To use the colors of the ribbons we won. I wanted to have yellow also, but she thought it would spoil the effect. Ben Damon certainly handed me something when he found her. She is sure she will like it here in the winter."

"The winter! I can't see you spending a winter here, Pat. Week-ends as usual to keep an eye on the stables, but not the winter. You'll blow out with the first snow flake."

"Wait and see, Nick. You'll be surprised. Except for National Horse Show week, we'll be here, won't we, Curt?"

Curtis Newsome's gaiety went out like a candle-flame in a puff of wind. Estelle Carter bent eagerly toward him. Sandra never before had seen her so forgetful of an audience.

"We? Not a chance. If you stay you'll stay alone."

His wife opened her lips in an angry retort, closed them tight, before she snapped at the waitress who had filled the water glass too full.

"Clumsy! Huckins, where'd you get this greenhorn?" she demanded of the butler who was preparing to serve *champignons sous cloche*. "Where's that new girl Emma? She knew her business. Has she left?"

"No, Madame. It is Emma's day off," Huckins explained in a low voice, and proceeded about his business with a face of Oriental impassivity.

"Caught in the act," Nicholas Hoyt accused Sandra.

She confided in a whisper. "I don't like little-neck clams. I always hide them in the ice."

"Why not leave them in their shells?"

"Why advertise my plebeian lack of taste?"

"That's a characteristic of yours, isn't it?"

"What?"

"Burying things you don't like in ice? That's what you have been doing to me tonight."

Sandra's eyes were on the roll she was crumbling. Was her avoidance of him so evident? He must think her ungrateful after his kindness at the time of her accident. Her father would be amazed at her attitude. He had counted ingratitude, disloyalty, and unreliability the three cardinal sins. She looked up and smiled.

"What an imagination! Are you a fictioneer as well as a banker and a horse-trainer? Do you think I have forgotten how kind you were to me at Stone House?"

"I hope so. I don't want gratitude — from you. Shoulder all right?"

"You should know. I have answered that question either in person or over the phone every day during the last two weeks."

"Answer it again."

"It is quite all right, thank you. You are rather a persistent person, aren't you?"

"I mean to be in a certain matter. I couldn't get here, I had to hear your voice, so —"

"Oh, Nick!" Jed Langdon interrupted. "Persuade Miss Duval to enter the Ladies' Race which is scheduled for the charity events. Her shoulder is okay, they tell me. You're a stout-hearted lad. Tackle her. Curtis says that he has talked himself hoarse arguing."

"Useless," Sandra declared gaily. "The last Ladies' Race I entered was a mess. One horse fell down; a girl lost her stirrups and fell off; three cut a flag; one bolted into the parked cars; and one cried when she stuck at the water jump. Woman's place may not be in the home, but from that exhibition I am convinced that it isn't on the race-course. I'm off Ladies' Races for life, thank you."

Nicholas Hoyt laughed. "It would take a stouter-hearted lad than I to combat that decision, Jed, even if I wanted to. I don't. Miss Duval is right not to attempt it after her fall. We took great care of her at Stone House, even got a wireless through to the ghost not to moan in the underground passage while she was there. You didn't hear any strange sounds, did you, Miss Duval?"

Sandra shook her head. Her voice wouldn't come. A vivid flashback of the thing she had seen at the pool had paralyzed it. Something drew her eyes to the butler. He was rigid, staring at Nicholas Hoyt. As if suddenly aware of her glance, he straightened like a marionette which has been jerked into action and began to move about the table.

Philippe Rousseau drained his glass. "I hate that rotten supernatural stuff. When I take possession of Stone House, I'll make a clean sweep of it, fill in the underground passage, and burn that portrait with the peep-hole eyes." There was a suggestion of hoarseness in his angry declaration.

Curtis Newsome rose half-way from his chair. "Say listen, Rousseau! Counting your chickens before they hatch, aren't you?"

" 'Happy days are here again,' " trilled Estelle Carter. Her light snatch of song cleared the air to a degree. Unable to refrain from tormenting, she asked:

"What else will you do when you become lord of this vast estate, Philippe? Tell us; we are all agog."

Rousseau's eyes flamed dangerously, but he smiled; he had himself in hand again. "What else? I'm all set to retain my cousin Nicholas as manager of the estate — if he will stay."

Crimson with anger, Nicholas started to reply, but remained silent as Huckins murmured:

"Excuse me, sir," and tenderly removed the glass bell from the plate of delectable mushrooms before him.

Chapter XV

A few hours later Sandra slipped into vivid green pyjamas. As she pulled on the lavishly embroidered coat, she smiled at the picture of her father.

"Your daughter is getting thrifty, Jimmy Duval; she is saving her evening frock. She knows that there won't be more French gowns until she makes a fortune. Oh, come on Fortune! Come on!" The two dogs dozing before the low fire sprang to their feet.

"I'm not talking to you, darlings. Your foolish Sandy is getting caught in the American gold-rush, that's all. She was appealing to the little god who spins the money wheel. Go to sleep."

"I wonder if I ever will have even a small fortune again?" she reflected, as she deposited a cushioned stool on the balcony on which the long French window opened. "It gives one a ticklish feeling to realize that there is little money, no near relatives behind one."

She rested her elbows on top of the intricate iron railing, the ends of which were crowned with boxes packed with blossoming plants. She propped her chin in one pink palm and looked up at the starry sky. Worlds upon worlds above her. Would the riddle of the meaning of their existence ever be solved; would rocket ships ever shoot their way through airless and heatless space to the moon or to red Mars? If only she could live to see it. Scientists had made some progress. They claimed to have heard the hum of a planet. Gorgeous night! The air was freighted with the scent of heliotrope and petunias. It was so still that the beat and rhythm of the earth seemed to shake her body; the movement of unseen creeping, hopping, fluttering things purred a faint accompaniment.

What a balcony! What a balcony on which to sit and dream! She could see the dim outline of hills, the ebony gleam of the river; could look down upon the garden which the lighted windows of the music room at the end of the loggia were patching with gold. Never in her travels over the world had her heart snuggled down as it had here. She adored the house and its surroundings. She loved the mellow old church in the village with its candles, which the Protestant clergyman was not afraid to use. She felt there, as she had felt in rich, hushed, incense-steeped churches abroad, the surety of the Everlasting Arms. How did people live through terror and sorrow without a belief in a Divine Power to which to cling? She had her father to thank for that comfort. He had asserted that it was as much her right to know the treasures of the spiritual world as of the intellectual and material worlds. All he could do was to show her the way to them; the choice as to what they would mean in her life was hers.

Would she love this place as much when snow covered hills and fields and the river was drab ice? Would Mrs. Pat spend the winter here, or would her husband's protest change her plans? Protest! It had been an ultimatum. How out of character for Estelle Carter to show her triumph so plainly. Curtis Newsome had pointedly avoided her during the remainder of the evening and had been noticeably tender to his wife. Nicholas Hoyt had taken Estelle on at backgammon. Had he, after seeing them together but an hour, perceived the battle of wills being waged between the two? Pity he hadn't taken a hand in the game before. Why had he not come to Seven Chimneys during the last two weeks? Too busy socially? "Gladys," "Blanche," — how many more girls had phoned him for a date?

He had been furious at Philippe Rousseau's proposition that he remain as manager of the estate. Had he been about to hurl a refusal when Huckins had obsequiously removed the glass bell from the plate before him? Had she not seen the butler stiffen at the word "shock" — he had reacted to Nicholas' intimation about the ghost in the underground passage; she had not imagined it — she would have suspected that he had been trying to avert a crisis.

Why did Estelle take such delight in tormenting Philippe? He had deserved it tonight. What a breach of good taste to tell what he intended to do with an estate not yet his, and then to pile Ossa on Pelion by offering to retain Nicholas Hoyt as manager. How had be dared? At times she was passionately sorry for him. If he were Mark Hoyt's son — hadn't Nicholas proof that he was, in his possession — it must hurt intolerably to have to fight to establish his claim, must be maddening to be doubted. She should be more friendly to him — he had told her once that she was the only person upon whose loyalty he could count — but could she be? The doubt of him she had felt the day he had brought her from Stone House persisted in pricking at her consciousness like a splinter in a finger.

Lucky that her fall had not been more serious. Her shoulder was as good as new; the accident had left no trace. Hadn't it? Estelle's feline suggestion that it had been staged to happen on Nicholas Hoyt's property irritated like a bunch of nettles whenever she thought of the man. The fall would be a lesson to her not to dream while riding.

The crisp air throbbed and quivered with music. Was Curtis Newscme playing? Sandra leaned over the railing. The shadow of a figure crossed one of the oblongs of golden light cast by the windows of the music room. Was he pacing the floor as he played? Another shadow! A woman's! Who was with him? The room was his castle and no one entered unless invited. Even Mrs. Pat respected his orders much as she resented them. No matter who it was, it was none of her business. If she didn't watch out, she would go small-town minded.

He was playing Puccini's Cavaradossi. The lachrymose aria sobbed through the scented stillness. Poor boy. There was no doubt but he was quite mad about Estelle; it was incredible that she could be seriously interested in a one-time professional jockey. How would it end? End! The complication would go on and on, gathering electricity like a thunder cloud, till finally it exploded and blew another marriage to smithereens.

Some one would be horribly hurt — Mrs. Pat, of course; neither Curtis nor Estelle was of the stuff of which martyrs are made. That reminded her — she must ask again for the list of guests to be invited to high tea after the race. A late invitation, but the hostess knew that her friends — most of them — would come without one. The caterer had been given his orders weeks ago. The servants were to have the afternoon off; they would be back only in time to serve. It would not do to wait until morning; Mrs. Pat would be furiously irritable; she was always on the rampage until noon. She would be at her desk now. The croon of the violin still drifted from the music room; Curtis Newsome had not yet come upstairs.

The dogs stretched, yawned, and languidly pulled themselves to their feet as Sandra returned to the boudoir. She dropped to her knees to hug their sleek heads.

"Darlings! I'm never lonely when I have you! Love Sandy, Bud and Buddy?"

They raised expectant eyes as they snuggled their cold noses into her neck. She shook her head at them.

"Greedy things! You don't love me for myself alone. I know what you want." She took two pieces of candy from a silver box. "Here you are. When you are stout and bulging with the middle-age spread, don't reproach me for having helped ruin your youthful figures."

She threw a kiss to them before she closed the door of the boudoir behind her. No sound of the violin. She had better hurry or Curtis Newsome would be coming upstairs.

Her wide pyjama trousers flapped about her feet as she raced along the hall. She rapped at her employer's door.

"Come in!"

She had closed it behind her before she realized that Mrs. Pat was not at her desk in the stiffly modernistic room. She was on the chaise longue, which was a false note among the cones and tubings of the black and silver furnishings. Its mass of lacy pillows made a background for her yellow hair and the pale blue lace of the negligee which left her beautiful shoulders and arms bare. In that feminine garb the woman's tremendous and inflexible energy seemed in abeyance. A smile stiffened on her lips; her eyes darkened.

"You! I thought it was . . ." Bitter disappointment choked off the sentence.

It was evident whom she had expected. As if she were oblivious of the electricity in the atmosphere, Sandra explained:

"Sorry to disturb you, but I came for the list of extra guests for Race-Day tea; I must phone the invitations early tomorrow. I knew that with the buyer coming to look at Rovin' Reddy's filly, superintending the moving of Iron Man and his entourage to the race-track in the morning — I can't see you letting some one else do it even if the gray is only your stable guest — you wouldn't have a moment in which to think of such an unexciting thing as a party." Not too bad, she congratulated herself.

"The list is on the desk." As a hint to her secretary that she was dismissed, Mrs. Newsome turned the pages of the Breeders' Magazine. Even Sandra's ears burned with resentment. She was being slapped because she was not some one else. Mrs. Pat had been snippy before but never like this.

As she crossed the room with the slip of paper in her hand, she tried to think of something casual to say, something which would give the impression that she was departing with all sails set. She owed that to herself, but her mind wouldn't work.

Mrs. Newsome swung her feet from the chaise longue and stood up.

"Run down to the music room, Miss Duval, and tell my husband that I want to see him at once."

Miss Duval! She hadn't called her secretary that since her return from Stone House.

"And if that Carter woman is with him, tell her — tell her. . . ." Her voice grated in a sob. "Don't tell her anything!" Fury burned away tears. "I suppose my friends are whispering, 'Why does Pat keep her here?,' that they're laughing in their sleeves." She stalked toward Sandra like a tigress approaching her kill.

"Do you think I'll admit I'm licked by sending her off? They'd laugh more then, wouldn't they? That's what they'd all think, isn't it, that I was licked? Well, I'm not —

yet. Go tell Mr. Newsome I'm waiting for him."

Her lips were drawn in a bitter line, her eyes had contracted till they looked like beads. Sandra's heart ached for her. Wasn't it hard enough to be intolerably hurt without having the effect so unbecoming?

She made an inconsequential reply before she left the room and pelted down the stairs. Poor Mrs. Pat. Of course her job was to do what her employer asked, but, sorry as she was for her, she wasn't keen to round up a reluctant husband.

She crossed the terrace, ran along the loggia. By supreme effort of will she kept her eyes from the hedge at the end of the garden. Even had the "thing" she had seen been a combination of mist and imagination, she didn't intend to see it again.

The music had stopped. Perhaps she would butt in upon an impassioned tete-a-tete. Why couldn't Mrs. Pat send some one else on this sort of errand? Absurd to send her when the house was honeycombed with telephones; but she remembered now, there wasn't one in the music room. She could hear a voice as she approached the door which was partly open. Was Curtis Newsome talking to the other shadow?

"Say listen, I've said it before, I'll say it

again, nix on the divorce stuff. What cause have I to ask it? No one doped me into marriage. I may have been only a jock, but I've got self-respect. Don't! Keep away! I've had all of that I can bear and —"

Sandra rapped smartly. It was none of her business, but she could not endure that tortured voice another second. Perhaps she should go and allow the two to fight it out — but. . . .

She swallowed her heart as she looked up into the haggard face of Curtis Newsome who had pulled open the door.

"You, Miss Duval! Come in!"

There was relief in his voice, a lessening of the strain in his eyes. He was glad that she had come. Very well then, her cue was to enter.

As she stepped into the softly lighted room, Estelle Carter, leaning against the grand piano, laughed.

"See who's here! Another secretary gone blooey about you, Curt. You certainly are the great lover."

"Estelle!" There was hurt amazement in the man's protest.

Sandra silenced him with an imperative motion of her hand. Her heart still stung and smarted with the memory of Mrs. Pat's passionate outburst.

"Are you suggesting that I want another woman's husband, Mrs. Carter?" she asked lightly. "Not good enough for me, thank you. I have an old-fashioned mind. Never have been able to convince myself that a man who would be untrue to his first wife would be true to his second."

"The snow-maiden doesn't believe in divorce!" Estelle's tone added straw to the fire.

"Of course I believe in divorce," Sandra flared, "for justifiable cause."

"Justifiable cause! That has the genuine pre-war tang. Perhaps Miss Duval has come with a message from her — *your* boss, Curt. I will wait outside until she goes."

Sandra bit her lips on a caustic retort. It was time she remembered that she was a paid employee and that she had not been engaged to do battle for Mrs. Pat in her matrimonial tangle. She waited until Estelle Carter had closed the French window behind her before she said as evenly as the throbbing pulse in her throat would permit:

"I'm sorry, Mr. Newsome, but I had to come. Your wife wants you at once."

"What for? Good gosh, can't she let me out of her sight for a minute?" His boyish blue eyes looked enormous; there was no trace of the gay host of the dinner table. Evidently the storm she had interrupted still raged within him.

"Know what it feels like to be trailed and watched every minute, Miss Duval? Sometimes I wish I had the courage to end it. I'm sunk! I'm ab-so-lutely sunk!"

The broken admission of defeat twisted Sandra's heart unbearably. She never before had seen a man cry. Man! He wasn't a man; he was a boy. She laid her hand on his sleeve.

"I wish I could help."

"I know that it is against the rules, Curt, to enter your bailiwick without permission, but . . ."

Nicholas Hoyt! What would he think to find her alone here with her employer's husband? That another secretary had fallen in love with the one-time jockey? With a choking breath Newsome straightened. Only thing for her to do was to face the music. Sandra turned.

"Miss Duval!" For an instant Nicholas Hoyt's expression registered savage surprise; then he adjusted a mask of polite indifference.

"Sorry. Didn't know that I was butting in on a special musicale."

Newsome cleared his voice and sheepishly brushed the betraying moisture from his lashes. "That's all right, Mr. Nicholas. Miss Duval came in just as I was finishing that aria of Puccini's. It always gets my goat, and — well, I went cuckoo, that's all. It's what Pat calls my musical temperament, I guess."

Nicholas Hoyt's silence and expression infuriated Sandra; her eyes blazed a challenge to doubt her words. "You were not butting in and it was not a special musicale. I came with a message from Mrs. Pat."

"Don't apologize."

"I'm not apologizing! I — I am explaining!" She resisted a violent urge to add, "Darn you!" and stalked from the room.

Why hadn't she stayed and fought it out with him, she demanded of herself, as she ran along the loggia and across the terrace; she was in fighting trim. Why hadn't she blazed at him as she had at Estelle, made him understand that she was not carrying on a clandestine flirtation with the husband of her employer? How like her to act first and think afterwards. Why worry? If Nicholas Hoyt had a hateful, suspicious mind, why care what he thought?

Between speed and resentment she was breathless when she reached the living room. Silly to get so excited — she was actually trembling. One of the dogs met her at the threshold. She must have left her door unlatched. With her hand on his collar she crossed to the mimosa framed window. Perhaps a glimpse of the garden would cool her anger. How lovely the pool was in the pale moonlight. Would Estelle return to the music room? Was Mrs. Pat in her laces still waiting and longing for a husband — who did not *want* to come? The mere thought was heart-twisting.

What was that white — she shrank back. The dog, who had been looking out, wrenched away from her, crouched on his haunches, stretched his nose toward the ceiling, and howled. Sandra stood in numbed, powerless terror. The wail rose, quavered, dwindled to a whimper.

Did he see something outside? The thing she had seen? A dull, overpowering dread of the great house settled like a leaden weight on her heart. In the tense silence which followed, the high note seemed to echo through the corridors of her mind.

How could she be so silly! Just showed how the talk of ghosts and the memory of that — that thing she had imagined at the pool had wrecked her common sense. A door clanging! The grille to the terrace. Footsteps! Who was coming? Some one in a hurry. She leaned forward that she might see the hall. She clutched the dog's collar. Philippe! He was ghastly. Had he seen the white thing? He was tearing upstairs.

She waited tense and still. The dog whimpered deep in his throat. At last! The house was quiet. She stole from the room. Shaking with a chill, made up of anger at her fright and fear which would persist, she pushed the dog ahead and charged up the stairs.

Safe in her boudoir, she leaned against the door she had closed behind her. Her breath came raggedly. She appealed to the picture of her father.

"How could I live if I didn't have you to talk to, Jimmy Duval? Am I a poor sport or just plain foolish? If you had seen the ghastly thing . . ."

The sentence trailed off in a long drawn "Oh-o-o." To her excited fancy her father's dear face seemed to wrinkle into a smile, his eyes to blaze with delighted laughter. She had seen him look like that when he had gleefully told the tale of the Three Musketeers of Melton and the Stone House ghost.

Eyes still on his, Sandra sank to the floor and sat back on her heels. Did he — he couldn't — he did — mean that the thing was a hoax? It was amazing. It was incredible — but of course he knew. Why hadn't she thought the incident through to a solution instead of hysterically shoving it from her mind every time it poked its spectral self in? What an easy mark! What an unbelievably easy mark she had been! Who was behind the trick? Why? She had seen the apparition the night she had arrived at Seven Chimneys — as she had gone up, Jed Langdon had come down the stairs, he had been startled by her face — tonight he had returned and the horrid thing had appeared again.

She put her arms about the neck of the dog who had been uneasily nuzzling her hair. She shook with nervous laughter as she said aloud:

"Your Sandy may be plain dumb, Jimmy Duval — but from now on, watch her, that's all, just watch her!"

Chapter XVI

In that moment when he had discovered Sandra's head so near Curtis Newsome's, her hand upon his arm, Nicholas Hoyt's hope and faith and illusions went down. Now he absentmindedly pulled his pipe from the pocket of his dinner jacket and as absentmindedly lighted it. He leaned against the piano, moodily regarding the man who, with unsteady hands, was returning the violin to its shabby case. He had come to help him. Lot of help he needed! What the dickens was there about that fair-haired boy which fascinated women? First, Mrs. Pat, almost old enough to be his mother — the late secretary — hard-boiled Estelle Carter — and now Sandra.

"What's that, Mr. Nicholas?"

Had a throb of intolerable pain forced a sound through his clenched lips?

"I didn't speak. Cut out that 'Mr.,' Curt,

we are sort of in-laws now, you know. I started to explain that as I was walking and smoking outside with Langdon I heard the wail of your violin. Sounded like a soul in torment. Couldn't stand it. Hoped that I might help. Sorry I butted in on your party. My mistake."

"It wasn't a party. You got us wrong. I'll bet I haven't said a hundred words to Miss Duval since the day at the paddock when you told me not to let on who you were. You sure had her fooled; she thought you were a trainer all right. She's a swell kid. Of course she isn't a kid, but she seems kind of fresh and young. She brought a hurry-up call from Pat; I was worked up by the music and — and other things; there was something in her voice that — well, I cracked-up just like I was a little fella, and she was sorry for me. That's all there was to it."

A load dropped from Nicholas' heart. He could eliminate Curt from Sandra's stag line. Would she ever forgive him for his suspicion? Had he lost the ground he had gained with her since her fall? The fact that she had told him her suspicion of Emma had buoyed him through the last anxious weeks. She had told him and not Philippe! In her heart she must believe in his cause.

She had been frosty enough before dinner. Had Estelle's laughter-cloaked insinuation about the accident been responsible, or had she expected that long before this he would have declared the two letters the maid had brought him? She had been excessively friendly with Rousseau tonight. Too friendly. She had overdone it a trifle. If she — he must keep her out of his mind — that was a joke. As if he could!

What a confounded tangle life was. Could he help Newsome along the rough road he was traveling without seeming intrusive, he, who would bitterly resent interference in his own affairs? Where did Curt stand in regard to Rousseau? Perhaps his present mood was a heaven-sent opportunity to find out whether he were with or against the man in possession.

He looked at the blowing shadows the fire cast on the paneled walls. Dame Fortune had given her wheel a fantastic whirl when she had tossed Curtis Newsome from the stables to be lord of this beautiful room. His eyes focussed sharply on a bit of betraying black glitter on the floor at his feet. Ladies in sequined frocks shouldn't make late visits in gentlemen's music rooms unless the sequins were riveted on. Estelle, of course. Why couldn't she let the boy alone? He was doing his best to play the game.

"What did you think of Rousseau's noble offer to keep his poor relation on as manager, Curt?"

Nicholas' abrupt question shattered the pulsing quiet. Newsome straddled a chair and took its back into his embrace as if he welcomed any diversion from his own troubled thoughts.

"Good gosh, I almost pushed his face in. How can Pat put up with him? She's been pretty sore at you, but —"

"She doubtless thinks it is a sporting proposition to give the long-lost son every opportunity to prove his claim. Where do you stand, Curt? Do you believe Philippe Rousseau's story?"

Newsome abandoned the chair in such haste that it toppled to the floor.

"Believe it! Of course I don't. Say, listen, it's a frame-up. I'll bet Pat doesn't believe in him either. How can she? But you never can tell about women. If you ask me, his place is in the movies. With his slushy line, he'd have the ladies in swooning heaps at his feet and a pile of fan mail with the sky the limit."

"If she doesn't believe in him, why welcome him at Seven Chimneys as her guest?"

"You know she's good-hearted, but you know too that she's got a rotten temper, and when you stopped coming here she went fighting mad. Having him and especially that Thoroughbred of his here to run against Fortune was her meat. Wait a minute," he implored, as Nicholas opened his lips. "Don't think I blame you. Your uncle's widow pulled a bone when she married his jock —"

"Forget it! Want to help me, Curt?"

Eagerness routed despair from Newsome's eyes. "Sure thing. Give me something to do. When I'm not practicing, I feel like a pet poodle with a bow on his collar. Sometimes when a longing for horses comes over me so strong that it seems as if I can't stand it, I think I'll chuck music and go back to jockeying and be on my own again. I've thought of it so much that I've kept my weight down to ride Iron Man in some of his workouts. How can I help?"

Nicholas glanced at the French window which opened on the garden. He lowered his voice. "Damon, Langdon, and I have a feeling that the people on Rousseau's payroll are not all in the stable."

Newsome ran his fingers through his fair hair as he intently regarded the semi-circle he was outlining on the polished floor with the toe of his slim patent-leather shoe.

"Meaning?"

"That there may be a servant or two at Seven Chimneys who will retire on a fat pension if the estate comes to him."

"Got 'em spotted?"

"Nothing more than suspicion as yet."

"I get you. Haven't thought that the suspects may be interested in your stables instead of the estate, have you? Haven't forgotten that you have a probable winner in the Charity Races?"

"I have not. I am sure of the loyalty of every one on my place. Rousseau has been there several times, but every breath he has drawn has been watched. Huckins the butler —"

"Huckins!" Curtis Newsome whistled — a long, low whistle which sounded for all the world like a policeman's signal in a gangster talkie. "Huckins! There's something phoney about Huckins. What's he staying here for? Pat treats him like the dickens. She looks after his ordering so sharp that he has no chance for graft. He's been here longer than any other butler has stuck it out. He came just before Rousseau showed up. I'll bet he's here on some crooked deal about the races. There's a lot of jack at stake."

"You're raving, Curt. What harm could that butler do?" Nicholas knew quite well what he could do, but he wanted Newsome's reaction to the man.

"How do you know he's always been a butler? If he can't dope your horse and make winning sure and lay everything he has on Fortune, he might put a fast one over on Eddie Sharp — and make a swell job of it too — put him out of the running, and lay his money on Iron Man. Ever thought of that? How do you know he isn't Rousseau's man? Suppose Sharp disappeared at the last minute? Who would ride Fortune? That jock knows every thought the black stallion has before he has it, and those he hasn't he ought to have, he whispers to him. Oh, yeah! What could Huckins do!"

"He won't get anywhere with my jockey. There is only one way he can put him out of the running, and Sharp has sworn to me that he won't take a drink before the race. I trust him."

"I've heard that one before. You've got more confidence in your jock than I have." He glanced at the watch on his wrist. "I'd better get a move on. Got so interested I forgot Pat sent Miss Duval for me." He went livid — the surface evidence with him, Nicholas remembered, of inner turmoil; he had seen him look like that as he rode to the post. "She doesn't trust me too much. Good gosh, life is an in-and-out all right; guess I'm kind of hopelessly lost in it."

"You'll pull through, Curt, just as you have in races when you thought you hadn't a prayer. Don't think I'm posing as a saint — the Lord knows I'm human enough — if I say that the things a — a gentleman doesn't do are worth all the self-denial they may cost. A Thoroughbred isn't judged by his winnings; he's rated by the fight he puts up against strong odds. There are great losers on rolls of honor, injured horses who have gamely run the last heat never knowing that they were beaten. But you know all that, I didn't come here to preach, Curt, I came to help."

There was a curious light in Curtis Newsome's blue eyes. He laughed — his gay, rollicking laugh.

"You weren't preaching, you were just telling me — you and — Miss Duval. She said a mouthful too. I've always thought you the real thing in gentlemen, Mr. Nicholas. Course, I never can be like you, but from now on I ride straight — if I find I can't — well . . ." He shrugged. "Lock up here, will you? Good-night and — thanks!" His furtive glance at the French window betrayed his reason for haste.

Nicholas' face still burned with embarrassment from his attempt to give the boy something stable to cling to in his emotional turmoil. He wouldn't have blamed Curt had he walked out on him. He gazed thoughtfully at the door to the loggia which he had closed with a bang behind him. Had he been afraid that if he were left alone Estelle might return? Did the woman really care for him, or was she trying to show her power?

Curious the power one person sometimes has over another — power of attraction, power of influence. Wasn't that what kept the world going? His instant attraction to Sandra, her — well, he had better face it — her instant aversion to him. He had started off on the wrong foot the day he had met her at the station. That fool deception had been B.D.'s suggestion. Why pass the buck to B.D.? He had fallen in with it readily enough. He need not have kept it up that day at the paddock.

Why stand here conjecturing? He had better lock up and get back to Stone House. He picked up the black sequin and dropped it into his pocket; there it would tell no tale to Mrs. Pat or the servants. Before he could lock the French window, Estelle Carter pushed it open, closed it, and backed up against it.

"Well, what are you going to do?" Her face was colorless; her painted lips were defiantly curved.

Nicholas smiled. "Looks as if I would be obliged to treat you rough, drag you away from the window so that I can lock it."

"Don't bluff. You know what I mean. I saw you pick up the sequin, saw you look at it as you held it in your hand. What are you going to do about — Curt and me? Tell Mrs. Pat?"

"I have a hunch that Curt is capable of managing his own affairs without help from any one."

"If he doesn't need help, how about me? You know that he is sick of his marriage; Mrs. Pat bribed him into it. If he were happy, I'd let him alone. He isn't. He has a right to be happy."

"I'm surprised at you, Estelle. That 'right to be happy and darn the consequences' is a hangover from the departed jazz age. Never expected you to be even slightly old-fashioned."

"Trying to laugh me out of it, aren't

you? It can't be done, Nick. Curt and I were made for each other. I have money enough for us both. We like the same things. The woman he married —"

"Don't forget that you are a guest of that same woman."

"Suppose I am? I didn't invite myself. When I met her abroad and she found that I had grown up in this one-horse village, Mrs. Pat begged me to come. I — remembering you, Nick dearest —"

"That's side-splitting, Estelle. Why make me the goat? You had forgotten that I was in the world. Don't touch my tie!"

Estelle rubbed her wrist. "You needn't have grabbed me like that; I don't care about your old tie, only wanted to straighten it. You're the original cave man." She exhaled a long breath of smoke and looked at him from eyes which glinted like green glass between blackened lashes. "I may have forgotten you, perhaps — but not your uncle's fortune. Ask Miss Duval if it isn't a lure; she's hedging until the rightful heir is acclaimed before she pins her flower on a coat lapel. If you ask me, she's laying her money on Rousseau, he's an exciting person. She spends every moment with him she can snitch from her job."

Nicholas Hoyt's laugh was a triumph of will over fury. "I'm willing to concede the Peerless Pretender many fascinating qualities. Hear the clock? Midnight. The servants will be here to dust, or whatever they do in the early morning, before I get this room locked." He opened the door to the loggia. As she hesitated, he suggested grimly:

"Shall I have to put you out?"

"I'm going." She looked back from the threshold. "You really should see Philippe and the lovely Sandra together when they think they are unobserved. A fiery southerner leaves a cold-blooded northerner like you at the post, Nick."

He heard her malicious laughter like the tinkle of ice against glass as she ran along the loggia.

Chapter XVII

Jed Langdon paused in his restless pacing of the living room floor at Stone House. He faced Nicholas Hoyt who, back to the mantel, was filling his pipe.

"Of course, you've got an explanation coming to you, Nick. Haven't had time to go into it before, and in all its ramifications the story of my hurry-up trip to England needs time. When Sandra Duval told me that first night at dinner that her father had been the victim of a forger — of a forger at the same time that Rousseau was doing the devoted-friend act, get that — my mind spun like a Dervish doing his stuff. At last! At last I had something to work on! The breaks were with me. I would be able to drive a ten cylinder truck through that diary of Anne Pardoe's. I must have gone white with excitement for Miss Duval asked me what was wrong. I muttered something about a bad heart — I with the constitution of an ox — getting to France to consult a specialist, and bolted from the room to phone for passage on any ship sailing the next day for London."

"Go on! Don't stop there, Jed. B.D. and I suspected that you had gone on estate-fight business. We've nobly refrained from asking questions. We'll crack-up if we don't know soon the result of your trip." Nicholas Hoyt's voice was strained.

Langdon perched on one corner of the table desk and thrust his hands hard into his coat pockets.

"Boy! Result! There ain't no such animal."

"What do you mean?" Damon, in a deep-red cushioned chair, matched his broad-tipped fingers and glared from under bristling white brows as he growled the question.

"I mean that I found the bank on which the cheques had been drawn, all right; told my story to the proper official, to be assured suavely that the forger of Duval's name was at the moment cozily ensconced behind bars. He made a sly reference or two to our slowness in convicting our man on this side of the big pond in contrast to the English method, and bowed me out."

Nicholas drew a long breath. "Now we can laugh that off! What do you think of the letters the maid found in the secret drawer, Jed?"

"If I hadn't somewhat lost confidence in my judgment, I would say that we haven't a prayer if they are presented in court."

"Then why go through the strain of appearing? Why not send them to Rousseau's attorney, wind the thing up, and take our medicine?" demanded Damon testily.

"We'll keep the Kentuckian hopping over the hot coals of suspense as long as we can. We've got to get some satisfaction out of the fight. Ever thought how easy it would be to drop those letters into the fire, Nick? They'd burn with a lovely light."

"Cut out wise-cracking, Jed. I wish you had been here when the Emma person brought them. She didn't ring the bell with me. Her valedictory just as she left the room: 'That Rousseau fella ain't no gentleman,' was out of character with her voice and manner which preceded it. After she had gone, Miss Duval told us that she was sure that she was the woman who had applied to B.D. for the secretarial position just before she did."

"For Pete's sake! Why hadn't she told you before?"

"Sorry for her, imagined her in such desperate need of a job that she would take anything. As she was satisfactory in her work, considered it no business of hers."

"Had Miss Duval told Rousseau her suspicions?"

"She had not — then."

"Who hired Emma for Seven Chimneys?"

"Either the housekeeper or Hutchins."

Damon sat forward in his chair. "The woman seemed honest enough when she brought the letters, made no secret of the fact that she hoped for a reward. I wonder — if we should have given it to her at the time, Nick? She may go to Rousseau."

"If she does, she'll only tell him what he will know the day the case comes to trial, B.D."

"I used to be a fairly good sleuth but this mix-up is getting too complicated for me. I've had one blinding flash of light though. Have you boys ever thought that Huckins, the butler, might be Raoul Rousseau, the father of Philippe?"

Jed Langdon came up standing. "You engaged Huckins for the Seven Chimneys' job yourself, didn't you, B.D.? You've got his *dossier,* haven't you? He's butlered for years, hasn't he?"

"Ask Nick. I was away when the man applied for the job and he interviewed him."

"His references were O.K.," Nicholas reassured.

"If you think my suggestion so wild, Jed, perhaps you can give us information as to what became of the man Anne Pardoe married," Damon challenged.

"We've had him looked up. He started his married life as a gray sheep and got blacker and blacker. Used to disappear for years at a time, leaving his wife and boy to manage the plantation and the horses. That part of Philippe's yarn is well authenticated. The tricky Raoul would reappear when he was on his uppers, repent, reform until he had been fed and decently clothed, then off he would go again."

"Is he still living?"

"Philippe says that had he been alive he would have appeared when his wife died to claim what he could of her estate."

"That sounds reasonable. I guess it squelches my blinding light about Huckins. But I still wonder why he stays in this country place and puts up with Mrs. Pat's rages if he hasn't an axe to grind. Do they let him into Stone House stables, Nick?"

"No one from outside this place has been there during the last two weeks, B.D."

"Fortune has already gone to the track paddock, of course?"

"Yes, with Ping Pong and Parsons and the swipes and one boy. I'm going back again before dinner. Hated like the dickens to leave. The thrill of the place got into my blood. Applications for stalls and the entries for stakes have been record-breaking. Wouldn't have left had not Mrs. Pat asked last night if she might come and see the young Thoroughbreds. I took it that she was loosing the dove of peace, so said: 'Of course. Come on. Bring any one you like.' "

Langdon crossed to the lattice window. "Speaking of angels — here they are. Mrs. Pat, Curt, Estelle on foot, and the Pretender in his roadster. He had the nerve to come!"

In the stir of arrival and greeting, Nicholas avoided speaking directly to Rousseau. Mrs. Pat sank into a chair with an abandon which wrenched a toll of creaks from its internal organs. She stretched out heavily shod feet. Her rough brown tweeds were in character with her manner. Estelle Carter, in a white sports suit, held her cigarette up to Nicholas Hoyt for a light.

"Greetings, dearest boy!"

Nicholas was aware of the cryptic challenge in her eyes. "Will you help me?" they were asking.

He laughed. "Estelle, I would as soon expect to see the Statue of Liberty without her torch as to see you without your cigarette."

With a shrug she went to the piano. Curtis Newsome prowled from book-shelf to book-shelf, apparently engrossed in reading the titles of the classics, best-sellers of yesteryear, last minute fiction, recent publications of science, countless books on American history, and volumes upon the horse with which they were crowded. Rousseau was gazing at the riot of color in the garden border. Was he remembering the day of Sandra's accident when he had been forcibly ejected from this very room? Sandra! Where was she? Had he so angered her last night that she had refused to come? Nicholas tried to keep his voice casual as he inquired:

"Where is Miss Duval, Pat?"

"She said that she would come along later — if she came at all. She had work to finish. Perhaps she is resting for the Hunt Ball tonight, though she's always so full of pep that I never think of her being tired. I guess perhaps the real reason is she's mad at me. She's a touchy kid; didn't like the way I spoke to her. Well, Nick, tea first or the stable?"

"That's up to you."

"Then I say tea. I'm dead to the world. And just as if there wasn't enough going on this week, some imbecile tucks in a Hunt Ball. I don't know if I'll go. I've been on my feet every minute since I got up at seven this morning when Mac Donovan shouted outside my window:

" 'The filly's come, Mrs. Pat, an' the mare's doin' fine!' How-do, Nanny O'Day! I'm dying for tea."

"Sure then an' this is a good place to come to keep from dyin', ma'am."

The chunky little woman in the gray gown gave orders to a flaxen-haired, rosy-cheeked maid with the air of a general manning walls for a defense. Damon brought Mrs. Pat her tea and Jed Langdon offered two Sheffield trays of sandwiches.

"I don't know anything about antiques, Nick, but your Great-great-grandmother Hoyt's silver tea-set starts wheels of envy whizzing every time I see it, and usually I don't give a tinker's dam for such things. Can't beat your mushroom sandwiches, Nanny O'Day! I pay out hundreds of dollars for service each week but I can't get anything like them. Life is just one fight after another and I'm getting sick of it — the fighting I mean. Stop prowling, Curt, bring the cream. If you won't ride for me, at least you can see that I don't die of thirst."

Estelle Carter ran her fingers lightly over the keys of the piano. "Are you trying to turn Curtis Newsome, the violinist, into a jockey again? If you are — well, professional jocks are quite without the circle of *my* young life."

Mrs. Pat's eyes widened suddenly; dull color darkened her face. She opened her lips as if in acrimonious retort, snapped them shut. Nicholas wondered at her unusual self-control. He had looked for, if not a profane, at least a fierce outburst. He wondered more as she said smoothly:

"I was speaking of riding my show-horses, Estelle. So jockeys are out of the picture with you. Remember that, Curt, if ever you are tempted to get back on your own."

Newsome's sensitive face went beet-red; his lips were set in a straight line as he approached the tea-table. With an apologetic laugh, Rousseau turned from his contemplation of the garden border.

"Tea already! Can I help? I was so absorbed in memories that I forgot my manners. The garden brought back the stories my foster-mother used to tell of bringing young Philip Hoyt from Seven Chimneys to call upon his grandfather. I little thought as I listened to her that I was that boy."

Nicholas felt as if all the blood in his body had charged into his face; the tumult left his brain light. The nerve, the colossal nerve of Rousseau to come into this house and talk of his grandfather, before his claim had been proved! But it would be proved, wouldn't it, when the letters which the maid had found were produced? An arm slipped within his and pressed with a light warning. Had his fury been so evident? Damon's shaggy head loomed above his shoulder. He had come in time to prevent an explosion. His voice was suave — suave for him — as he sympathized:

"I don't wonder Stone House gets you, Philippe — you won't mind if I don't call you Philip yet, will you? I suppose your mother — beg pardon, foster-mother — also told you the weird history of the picture of the Puritan and . . ." He stopped to light a cigarette.

Nicholas watched Rousseau's eyes go wary. Did he suspect a trap? He was on his guard.

"Have a heart!" Mrs. Pat interrupted irascibly. "Don't set the Stone House ghost to walking! I hate it! It gives me the shivers! That yarn has been handed down so long that of course every one believes it. I'll bet you do yourself, Nicholas."

"It has its points; at least it serves to keep curious sight-seers away after dark, now that they have found the river entrance to the underground passage. We found the door broken above the bolt the other day."

"The underground passage!" Mrs. Pat's startled exclamation brought all eyes to her face. Her laugh was forced. "Sounds as if I never had heard of it before, doesn't it. I was thinking what a hiding place it might make for gangsters and bootleggers. Better have it walled up, Nick."

"After the races I will."

"Or I will," cut in Philippe Rousseau. "As I said before, Nick, you've been too easy. When this house comes to me, I'll see that no stranger steps foot in it. I'll not stand for trespassers anywhere on my estate. As for the Stone House ghost, I'll lay that if I never do anything else in my life." His voice shook, his eyes burned like black coals.

Nicholas wondered if a person's heart could break from pain. The thought that the cockily assured man might be master here instead of himself hurt intolerably. His tongue felt thick as he answered:

"Yes? You've said before that this house would be yours. Hate to discourage you, Rousseau, but have you ever heard that little adage about the slip between the cup and the lip?"

"Oh, for the love of Mike, stop fighting you two! I get enough of that at home." Mrs. Pat cut into an atmosphere charged with electric currents of anger. "You ought to have the dogs here, Nicholas; they would keep prowlers away. Take 'em, they're not crazy about me, and if Bud and Buddy do like a person, their playful charge of welcome would knock him down. Did you hear one of them howl last night? If that happens again, they'll go back to the stables even if I lose my priceless secretary. It's unlucky; it's a sign of —"

"Cut it out, Pat, you're shivering," Curtis Newsome interrupted. "You may be a swell horse woman, but you're as superstitious as they make 'em. You cross your fingers at a race, you knock on wood, don't you now?" He laid his hand on her shoulder; his tone of affectionate raillery brought a mist to his wife's eyes.

"Perhaps I do, perhaps I'm a dumbbell that way, but I don't like a howling dog. You can have Bud and Buddy, Nick, but you may have to take Sandra with them — they are her shadows."

"That wouldn't be too hard," chuckled Damon. "How do you feel about the big race, Mrs. Pat?"

"That Nick and Philippe have it on ice between them. Up Five is the only one of the big circuit horses they have to fear, and he scuffed skin off one of his fore legs Saturday — nothing serious, but it may be enough to withdraw him. Curt has been riding Iron Man in some of his workouts. I wish he could be up at the race. I forgot, the jock has to be a pro. He might lose a friend if he rode again," Mrs. Pat reminded, with a crudity which flooded her husband's face with color. His reply was to spread out his sensitive hands.

"I'll cut out even workouts from now on. Riding stiffens my fingers for the violin."

"You care more for your old music than for anything else in the world, that's the real answer. Oh, come on, what's the use! Let's go see the horses."

As they left the house, twilight was drawing a violet veil over hills and fields. At the gate Rousseau stopped.

"As I've seen the Stone House youngsters, I'll go back to the paddock. My trainer is a bunch of nerves before a race and he'll have the men from Seven Chimneys Mrs. Pat loaned me strung on wires."

"But you'll be back for dinner? You're going to the Hunt Ball, aren't you, Philippe?"

"Certainly, I'll be back, Mrs. Pat. With the track only five miles away it doesn't take long to make the trip." He flicked a glance at Nicholas Hoyt, before he added: "I'm taking Miss Duval to the ball. Do you think I'd miss it?"

When Nicholas returned to the living room, it seemed hours — though the old clock in the hall assured him that but five minutes had passed — since Mrs. Newsome and her husband had left. Poor Pat. She had been so unlike her usual breezy self. It was quite apparent that her thoughts were anywhere but upon the horses she was viewing. She had appeared as if working out a problem. Was the financial statement of the Seven Chimneys' stables going red? It wouldn't be surprising in this year when any business which had not gone deep crimson was faintly pink.

He stood with his arm on the mantel looking at the gleaming Georgian silver on the tea-table. Would that go with everything else if Rousseau were legally proclaimed Philip Hoyt? In forty-eight hours he himself would appear in court to fight — fight, that was a joke with those two letters the maid had found. The estate would go to Rousseau. Had Estelle been right? Was Sandra hedging until the rightful heir was acclaimed before she pinned her flower on a coat lapel? How could he believe it for a moment? If Sandra married Rousseau, it would be for love, not money. Estelle had jeered at the cold-blooded northerner. He cold-blooded, when every pulse and nerve in him throbbed at the mere sound of Sandra's voice? When he had to thrust his hands hard into his pockets to keep from seizing her, and kissing her tempting, headily tempting lips? If it were cold-blooded to love with such concentration, heaven help the men she called "fiery."

He counted the strokes of the old clock. Six! No time to go to the track again if he were to get to Seven Chimneys in time for dinner. Of course Fortune was safe with Parsons and his own men. Perhaps it would be better if he kept away. Fortune vs. Iron Man. The man in possession vs. claimant. Hoyt against Rousseau. Race. Estate. Girl. All worth fighting for, but in the last analysis nothing so important as Sandra.

Chapter XVIII

"Why aren't you coming to Stone House?" Philippe Rousseau had demanded of Sandra as she stood on the terrace at Seven Chimneys with her arms crossed on the top of a white bamboo chair.

She shifted her attention from the high, smoothly clipped hedge at the end of the garden to the windows above her. Curious that the two in the middle should have the shades drawn.

"What were you saying, Philippe?"

"Do you never listen when I speak? I asked why you were not going to Stone House for tea?"

"You forget that I am a working girl. I can't play all the time. I have things to do."

"Come along. I'm driving over. I shan't stay more than ten minutes; then I'll go back to the track paddock. I'll drop you here on the way."

"I don't wonder you are going back; the wonder is that you could leave at all. I saw the horses start this morning. I'll never forget the thrill of it. To see priceless Iron Man starting off with that funny goat boy-friend he has picked up since he came here. It was like a circus cavalcade. Grooms, swipes, exercise boys, water and fodder for the stallion, and everywhere your colors, orange and black. Mrs. Pat doesn't do things by halves when she backs a proposition. I'm still tingling from the excitement of watching that departure."

"You don't have to tell me. I'm getting the vibration. But come on to Stone House. I shall need you there to offset the ice in the atmosphere when my cousin Nicholas sees me."

"Why go, if you think yourself unwelcome?"

"To stay away might be construed by him to mean that I had doubt as to the outcome of the fight, mightn't it? Doubt! Only two days more and then . . . Come on to Stone House and back me up."

"Can't. Must work. I haven't a fortune in the offing."

"Yes, you have." Rousseau caught her hands and drew her from behind the chair. "You'll share everything I have, Sandy."

"Don't call me that. It's a very special name, for those . . ."

Some one coughed discreetly. Emma was standing beside one of the huge box trees. Had she come from behind it? Rousseau's face darkened.

"What is it?" he demanded.

"Mrs. Newsome sent me to find you, sir, to tell you that she is starting for Stone House."

"All right. I'm coming. I'll be seeing you, Miss Duval."

Without a backward glance he hurriedly crossed the terrace and entered the house. Curious that suddenly he should have gone formal, Sandra thought.

"Sorry to interrupt, Miss."

The maid's tone was civil but her eyes shot little darts of hate. Why? Because Sandra Duval had procured the job she herself had wanted?

"Interrupting seems to be the best thing you do, Emma. Popping up like a jack-in-the-box is getting to be your speciality, isn't it?"

In spite of something within her urging, "Hurry! Hurry! Hurry!" Sandra crossed the terrace and entered the house with an excellent imitation of indifference. In the hall she obeyed the voice of the prompter and flew up the stairs. In her boudoir she looked at the turquoise and silver clock ticking away the minutes. Half after four. How long before it would be dark enough for her to begin the search for the habitat of the phantom of the pool?

Because of the plan she had in mind, she had appeared coolly aloof when Mrs. Pat had asked her to join the Stone House tea-party. She had hoped that her employer would think her still annoyed because of the cavalier treatment she had received last night when she had asked for the guest list for the Race-Day tea. It had been difficult for her to maintain her hurt manner as she never harbored a grievance — it rolled off her mind with the ease of a glycerine tear down the cheek of a movie star — never, except with Nicholas Hoyt. Curious how he could stir her resentment.

Last night, for instance, why hadn't she laughed when he had appeared as she was sympathetically patting the arm of Curtis Newsome, why hadn't she treated the situation lightly? She was already seething with anger, that was the answer. Perhaps she had been preachy to the Carter woman, but, even at the cost of being rated a back number, one had to fight for one's convictions occasionally. Lucky Mrs. Pat had not been the visitor; her secretary would have been hard put to it to explain why she was attempting to comfort her husband. Had Estelle returned to the music room last night after Nicholas Hoyt's departure? What would he do if Philippe Rousseau proved to be the missing son? If! He must be. Didn't the letters Emma had found prove it? She couldn't see Nicholas remaining as manager of the estate. His eyes had been black with fury when Philippe had proposed it. She had held her breath, expecting a clash; then Huckins' voice had gumshoed into the situation and the incident had slipped away into the limbo of averted crises.

What had he thought when she had not appeared at Stone House this afternoon for tea? If — it was a mammoth if — he had thought of her at all, had he wondered if she had stayed away because of his suspicion of her last night? His eyes had been savage, the remembrance of them caught at her breath: they had picked up her heart as a magnet might steel and held it quivering. That sentimental comparison must have come straight out of a story of the romantic nineties; just the same, it had happened, it had been a terrifying sensation. Nicholas Hoyt must never suspect it.

He might think that she had joined the pack of hounds which kept his telephone ringing.

Why, why, was she standing in the middle of her room thinking about him instead of getting busy? She had not too much time as it was; Mrs. Pat and her guests might cut the tea-party short.

She caught up a pocket flash; if dusk came on as quickly as she hoped, she might need it. The sight of its elaborate monogram, S.D., brought back the Christmas in Rome when her father had given it to her. The drawing room of the apartment in which they were living had been fragrant and colorful with blossoms which they had bought at the flower market in front of the sunken boar fountain at the Spanish Steps. They had lingered to watch an animated group of red-frocked students, terribly in earnest over something, before ascending to the old church with its rich altars, its candles and incense, to hear the nuns sing at sunset. A perfect Christmas eve. Life had seemed one long party then, but now — well, it might not be a party, but it was stimulating and thrilling.

Outside her door she stopped to listen. The house was sepulchrally quiet. Usually at this time one could hear the tinkle of spoons on china, voices, laughter; could sniff the aroma of tea and coffee. This afternoon there was no sound, no scent. So much the better for her plan.

She stole along the hall, holding her breath at every creak of a board under her feet. Now she was in the corridor of the main house the rooms of which were devoted to guests. Mrs. Pat's suite was in the opposite wing from hers. She visualized the tall clipped hedge at the end of the garden. The apparition had appeared against that. She would try the door in the middle of the corridor.

She tapped gently. How could she expect to hear with the sound as of rushing water in her ears? She tapped again. No answer. Softly, cautiously, she turned the knob. Pitch-dark and uncannily still. This must be the room with shades drawn she had noticed when talking with Philippe. She slipped in, closed and locked the door. Darn the key! Did it have to squeak?

Better not use her flashlight yet. She peered into the dusk. Shapes suggested, not revealed. Chairs with enticing contours. A table with something high on it. A pictureless expanse of white wall. She cautiously snapped on the flashlight in her hand. Wall! It was a silver sheet. The mound on the table was a moving picture projector!

In spite of the fact that it was what she had expected to find, little chills coasted down Sandra's spine and crawled up with icy feelers. Spooky! Just plain spooky! Suppose it were, she rallied herself, she couldn't stand here shivering. She had better get busy before the party returned from Stone House.

She set her flash so that the ceiling threw back the illumination. Lucky she knew how to work this projector; taking moving pictures had been one of her father's greatest pleasures. During his last year when they had settled in London, he had been vastly entertained by living over his adventures as portrayed on the screen.

She picked up the tin case on the table. Empty. There was a film in the projector! Was the machine connected with electricity? She turned off her flash. Cautiously pressed a knob. A figure sprang out on the silver sheet! A shrouded figure with a skeleton hand!

Hideous thing! Sandra shivered, clenched her teeth, and set the film in motion. The skeleton hand waved, faded out, reappeared, waved again. She shut off the current. The room was black.

"S-stop s-shivering," she scolded herself. "S-stop s-shivering! You know now that it is nothing but a f-film, don't you?" Her mind steadied, but the icy merry-pranks still tobogganed down her spine.

"S-so far so g-good," she told herself. "That goes for this room, but does it prove that the picture would reach the hedge?" In the dark she crept to the window, cautiously moved the shade. The garden was quite dark. Mrs. Pat would not yet have returned from Stone House. At this hour the servants would be on the other side of the wing. This was her chance.

She tiptoed back to the table, snapped on her flashlight and carefully began to wind up the film. It wouldn't do to try the picture against the hedge. If she experimented with the light only, a person seeing it would think it came from a window. She counted every turn of the roll. She must put it back and leave it as she had found it. She listened. Not a sound in the house.

The film was out! It seemed as if she had been years unwinding it. She pressed the button. A square of light on the screen! She turned the projector toward the window. In an instant she had snapped up the shade.

The light struck the hedge. Not in the middle where she had seen the spectre! Too bad! At the corner! Was she seeing things? Two white faces! Was that a man and a woman? Close together? They stared at the house as if fascinated. Their eyes glittered in the glare. Emma! Emma the maid! And Philippe!

In an instant they had disappeared. Sandra couldn't remember whether she jerked down the shade first or tore across the room and snapped off the light. Her heart was pounding unendurably. She must get that film back. Quick! Philippe might investigate the source of the light. She forced her fingers to steadiness. Counted every turn of the reel. Suppose he came? He was suspicious of every one these last days of suspense. What should she say to him? It was in! If only she could get out of the corridor without being seen. She stole to the door.

Emma and Philippe! The words kept going round and round in her mind. Emma and Philippe! He had said that he was going to the track! Camouflage. An excuse for returning to Seven Chimneys. Had the woman told him of the letters she had found? Was she trying to get money from him as well as from Nicholas Hoyt?

Double-crosser! Gold-digger!

She steathily turned the key. Listened at a crack. Silence. The house was eerily still. She closed the door softly behind her. Started to run.

" 'Walk — don't run — to the nearest exit,' " she told herself, and giggled nervously as the warning she had seen on countless theatre programs flashed into her mind. She forced herself to walk slowly.

Emma and Philippe! Allies? Perhaps Nicholas Hoyt had not come across with a reward and the maid was selling her knowledge of the letters to the claimant to the estate. Whatever the explanation, Nicholas Hoyt must know. There had been an inexplicable something in the situation revealed by the projector light which had snuffed out the candle she had kept lighted for Philippe in her heart. Her belief in him had gone. Where? Why? She wouldn't dare phone the information she had acquired. She must go to Stone House — but not before Mrs. Pat had left there.

What was that sound? Some one in the corridor? Philippe? Emma? They must not find her here. They might suspect that she had thrown the light, that she had seen them. She tucked her flashlight inside her blouse. What a bulge! She pulled it out.

She flew down the stairs. Where had she better go? The library. She pushed the flashlight on top of a row of books. The puzzle table. Praise be to Allah for the puzzle!

She slipped into a chair and began to poke among the fantastically jig-sawed bits of wood. The loggia grille clanging! She would recognize that sound anywhere. Who was coming?

For an instant she glanced up at the portrait of the M.F.H. The eyes looked down into hers as if probing her soul. Even in paint and canvas the man's vitality persisted. She must get to the original of the portrait quickly. How?

Footsteps on the tiled floor of the hall! Sandra attempted to fit a piece of clear blue sky into the middle of a fleecy cloud. Some one was crossing the rug behind her! Who? She hummed airily:

> "The hounds are on the trail,
> The hounds are on the trail."

A hand fell on her shoulder. Her heart missed a beat but she went on:

> "Heigh o the derry oh,
> The hounds are on the trail."

She looked up. Philippe Rousseau was frowning down at her with the tinge of suspicion in his eyes which was becoming chronic. She protested theatrically:

"You shouldn't interrupt a coloratura soprano in the midst of an aria, Philippe. Aren't you back from the track early?" She glanced at her wrist watch. "But it isn't early. I must have been working at this old puzzle for the last half hour. Did you find Iron Man all right?"

She rose. Why didn't he speak? Had he in some way found out that it was she who had turned the betraying light on the hedge? If he didn't say something soon she would scream. He gripped her shoulder.

"Sandra, have you . . ." He shot an oblique glance at the stairs which descended from the musicians' gallery. Huckins had stopped half way down.

Sandra swallowed hard. Had he come from the upper hall? How long had he been within hearing? Had he seen her dash across the room? Perhaps he was in league with Philippe too? No. Emma had seemed afraid of him. His manner was servile, but the hateful, secretive smile lurked about his pinched lips.

"Sorry to disturb you, Mr. Rousseau, but they've been phoning for you from the track for the last half hour. I tried this room at once, but Miss Duval, working here on the puzzle, said she didn't know where you were, and I've been all over the place since."

"What's happened now!" The words trailed behind Rousseau as he hurried to the hall.

Sandra's eyes followed him, then returned to the butler. He knew that she had not been here an half hour ago. Why had he said it? Had he seen her come out of the room upstairs? Did he think the knowledge would give him a sinister hold on her? The thought set her heart beating in her throat. In spite of the tumult it was kicking up, she managed a cool smile.

"These are hectic days for Thoroughbred owners, aren't they, Huckins?"

The butler laid his hand on the heap of puzzle fragments and leaned nearer.

"They'll be hectic days for some others if they don't stop prying into things that aren't their business, Miss," he warned.

What suspicion was back of those dark, impenetrable eyes? What code of life? Was it just fussy curiosity, or was the man in some one's pay? If he knew that she had found the projector, what would he do? All the more reason now for her to get the knowledge of what she had discovered to Nicholas Hoyt. She must go to Stone House at once. She said as lightly as she could with every pulse hammering:

"How you dramatize life, Huckins! It must be a lot of fun to feel of colossal importance, to think in terms of mystery and —"

"Oh, here you are; Sandra!" Mrs. Pat spoke from the threshold. She was colorless, her eyes were set in dark rings. "Come up with me, will you? I want to talk over the gown I'll wear to the ball. That maid of mine is a total loss when it comes to clothes."

"I'll never make the Seven Chimneys to Stone House hop now," Sandra thought, even as she agreed cordially:

"Of course I'll come, Mrs. Pat. I know just the gown you should wear to reduce the bright young things at the ball to speechless envy."

Chapter XIX

" 'The gods provide the thread once the web is started.' "

That favorite axiom of her father's slipped into Sandra's thoughts as she dressed for the ball. To be sure the thread was supposed to be provided for weaving, but wouldn't it apply to unraveling as well? She had the end of a thread to a mystery in her fingers. If she kept pulling and following, it must get her somewhere. She would manage to tell Nicholas Hoyt that she had seen Philippe and Emma together. Perhaps her discovery amounted to nothing, perhaps he knew already. Even if he did, her responsibility was not lessened. Only two days now before the matter of the right to the estate was settled. What would Nicholas do if . . ."

"Forget it for tonight," she told her reflection, as she noted the tiny pucker between the mirrored girl's brows. "You eat, sleep, and work with that question at the back of your mind."

Remembering Mr. Damon's instructions, "You will be expected to dress as a daughter of the house should — and it is some house to dress up to," she had made a special trip to town for a gown.

"To Sandra with love from Sandra," she said aloud as she approved the frock she had presented to herself. "You shimmer like a frosted Christmas card, gal."

She thoughtfully regarded a diamond bracelet in its velvet case. It was more beautiful than any one of the three Estelle Carter wore. Her godmother had given it to her on her twenty-first birthday. She had not worn it since she came to Seven Chimneys; it had seemed too costly for a social secretary. But tonight — why not enjoy it? No one would credit her with wearing real jewels, and she adored the sparkle.

She snapped it on her bare arm. It was a perfect touch for her gown. She had chosen white for the festivity because it would make a better background for a pink sleeve than would color. "What a blow if no pink sleeve slipped about you this evening. It might happen; you are a mere social secretary, you know, and Mr. Damon warned you that the residents were snooty in regard to Mrs. Newsome's household," she reminded the looking-glass girl.

"Nice job, secretary!"

She turned sharply away from the mirror as the trainer's curt comment broke in on her thoughts as clearly as if his voice had shattered the silence of the room. Couldn't she forget him and his fight to retain his inheritance for a moment? It looked as if she were being drawn into the maze. Would she have an opportunity tonight to tell him what she had discovered? She must make one. Tomorrow would be race day. He would have no thought tomorrow for anything but Fortune.

She went slowly down the stairs. Still absorbed in her problem, she entered the softly lighted library. Back to the mantel under the portrait of himself stood Nicholas Hoyt. His long-tail pink coat, expanse of white shirt and waistcoat above black trousers made him look even taller than he was.

"Haven't you dash and sparkle enough in yourself without adding to the slaughter by wearing that corking gown?" he asked.

There was laughter in his eyes, a buoyant

note in his voice which ran along Sandra's nerves like quicksilver, an underlying firmness which made her feel thrillingly alive. "Forgive me for last night, Sandra. I — I — well, I nearly lost my mind when I saw you with Curt Newsome."

"It was a spot-light situation, wasn't it? Don't apologize." She mimicked his words to a tone. He laughed and put one hand into his pocket.

"I'm not apologizing. I'm — I'm explaining." He had out-mimicked her. "You will forgive me, won't you?"

His voice was grave enough now — too grave — its vibrant depth was maddeningly disturbing. She hurried up reserves to barricade herself — from what, she wondered, even as she parleyed theatrically:

"I will consult the stars. If the signs and portents are propitious — I have been reading up on astrology — I will be magnanimous and forgive you."

He caught her hands tight in one of his. "Do you know, sometimes I think you are a worldly-wise woman, Cassandra; at other times I think you are just a lovely kid."

Her eyes reproached him from between sweeping, sooty lashes. "How archaic! Be modern. What you are trying to say is, I take it, 'Is your assumed sophistication an immaturity defense?' "

His grip tightened. "Ever heard that children shouldn't play with matches, beautiful? Wear my colors tomorrow, will you?"

He opened his free hand. On the palm lay a gorgeous diamond and emerald clip. Green and white! The Stone House colors. With difficulty Sandra dragged her fascinated gaze from the sparkling jewels.

"Of course not, in that form!"

"Why the horror? I didn't steal it; I had it made for you. I shall have a little pocket money even if I lose the estate."

"How — how can you jest about it when you have . . ." Her question was a whisper.

He looked quickly about the room. "Those letters? You've heard about that chap Nero who fiddled when Rome was burning, haven't you? Why cast gloom on Mrs. Pat's party?"

He slipped the clip into his waistcoat pocket. "We'll let that ride for the present; I should have finessed. Drive to the ball with me, will you?"

Something from his darkly intent eyes plunged into her heart. Quiveringly responsive to his nearness, she thrust back the frightened thought that her soul was being drawn into his. She warned herself:

"Don't let go! Don't! Hang on to

Philippe. If you turn him down now, he will be sure that you saw him by the hedge."

She said aloud: "Sorry, but I'm going to the ball with Philippe Rousseau."

"So he informed me, but only over my dead body you'll go with him."

"How thrilling! Will the papers have a spot marked X where the body was found?"

"Any horse that can run the last nine furlongs in twelve seconds, as that gray did last week in the practice run, is going to have things pretty much to himself tomorrow." The coarse, exultant voice drifted in from the hall.

Sandra was bending over the puzzle table when Mrs. Newsome, in a backless black frock which glittered with an artistic design of brilliants, entered the library with Damon in conventional evening clothes and Jed Langdon in hunt pink. From under her lashes she could see Nicholas Hoyt standing, straight and uncompromising, with his hands clasped behind his back. He reminded:

"Still championing your guest horse, Pat? Hate to take the joy out of life, but Iron Man wasn't the only oyster in that stew; I feel bound to remind you that Fortune was away slowest in a field of seven runners and that Sharp had him in front in fifteen strides — after that — well, you know what happened."

"You needn't remind me what happened, but it won't happen again! You sure look like a million in that rig, Nick; doesn't he, Mr. Damon?"

"He does. In my sombre black I feel like a scene-shifter caught on the stage as the curtain goes up on an exotic review. I hope that you won't entirely neglect me for these gay young blades, Sandy?"

Sandra crossed the room to him.

"Don't be foolish, Mr. B.D. Just as if you didn't know that you go up five points every time I see you. Observe that I am getting my mind geared to run on stock quotations; I understand that almost every man I meet tonight will be a broker. I mean to be a riot."

He shook his head. "I also notice that you are picking up our Americanisms. Don't lose all your old-fashioned flavor, my dear."

"Not necessarily old-fashioned, Mr. B.D., the flavor of Dad and his friends." Sandra bit her lips to steady them. "Wait, let me help!"

She crossed swiftly to Mrs. Newsome

who, struggling with a long court earring which had become twisted, was jerking her head with the impatience of a racer under restraint.

"I don't know why I wear the pesky things, I, who loathe doodads," she fumed. "Curt likes them — but would he put on a tail-coat tonight like Nick's to please me? He would not; he's wearing hunt clothes. I don't know why I'm going to this ball either."

"Keep your head still just a minute. You are as restless and twitchy as one of your blue-ribbon horses. There — I have it! It's all right now."

Mrs. Pat shook her earrings violently. "That's better. Thanks, Sandra. I hope the Lord lets you stay with me as long as I have to do the social act."

"I believe you are developing nerves," Nicholas teased. "I never have seen you like this before. Anything wrong?" There was no hint of laughter in the curt question.

"Of course there's nothing wrong. I — I — well, I've got a lot at stake."

Did he suspect, as she herself suspected from her manner, that Mrs. Pat was plunging heavily on this race, Sandra wondered.

"Buck up, Pat. Less than twenty-four hours to wait before we know whether you have been entertaining a champion or I own one."

One would not suspect from Nicholas Hoyt's laughing voice that in less than twenty-four hours after the race he would be in court defending his inheritance. Never before had she seen him so debonair. Weren't his high spirits slightly premature? Wasn't he overdoing the "Nero" act? Suppose he lost? The blow would be so much harder. Not that it mattered to her which way the Court decided, Sandra assured herself; it was only that his light-heartedness on the eve of a crisis made her shiver. Mrs. Pat responded gamely to his mood.

"I wish I were as sure of heaven as I am that Iron Man will clip Fortune's best time." Her laugh of triumph broke in the middle. She pointed.

"Well, look who's here!"

Philippe Rousseau, in pink evening dress differing a little in cut from that worn by Nicholas Hoyt, stopped on the threshold. His face was white with anger; his eyes smoldered at the hint of ridicule in the voice of his hostess. Even with that scene at the hedge fresh in her mind, Sandra's tender heart smarted for him. After all, he had a right to get any information he could to help his case. How could Mrs. Pat be so raw? She smiled a welcome.

"At last, Philippe. I began to think that I might be obliged to drive myself to the ball."

The color came back to his face. "As I had the regalia of my own Hunt Club here, I decided to wear it. Hope that I haven't infringed on the social code of this neighborhood, Mrs. Pat?"

"Course you haven't. Have you forgotten that I'm to be in the receiving line tonight? Guess I'm important enough to take any one I like," Mrs. Newsome boasted, with a none too tactful emphasis on "any one." "Why doesn't Curt come? Here he is!"

She cast a swift, suspicious look at the hall behind him as her husband entered. His hair and skin seemed fairer in contrast to the pink of his hunt coat. He was in one of his gay moods. His white teeth flashed in an engaging smile; his blue eyes widened as he looked about.

"Good gosh, am I late? You're not waiting for me, are you? I was at the stables. Mac Donovan had just returned from the track. He had Iron Man on his mind, wanted to make sure that the men he had sent with the gray were on the job. Gathered from what he said that you motored over there after you left Stone House this afternoon, Pat. You shouldn't have done it. Some day you'll snap if you keep such a pace."

"Nonsense, Curt, I'm strong as a horse. What did Mac say?"

"He said to tell you that he had talked with Sam and everything was O.K. What's in that message to turn you chalky?"

Unbecoming color patched his wife's face. "Don't be foolish, Curt. As Iron Man had been in my stable, I wanted to be sure that everything possible had been done for his comfort and security. You may bet your life that I'll never again take in another person's horse, too much responsibility. The Thoroughbred was on my nerves and Mac knew it. If he says everything is O.K., it is O.K."

"I'll bet it is. Say, Pat, you look swell! I like all that rhinestone stuff. You'll put their eyes out tonight."

"Dinner is served, Madame," Huckins announced suavely at the door. Sandra had a terrified suspicion that his eyes rested upon her for an instant.

Mrs. Newsome started forward and

paused. "Where's Estelle?" she demanded brusquely.

"Mrs. Carter passed me on the stairs as I came down. She was in riding breeches and a dark pull-over. Perhaps she had been at the stables too," suggested Philippe Rousseau suavely.

Mrs. Newsome's suspicious eyes flew to her husband. He looked steadily back at her and laughed.

"Perhaps she had, but you know Mac Donovan, Pat; can you see him or one of the men left in charge of the stables permitting any skirt but you inside his bailiwick without the boss's orders? Let's eat." He slipped his arm within his wife's. "Can ceremony. Don't wait for Estelle, she's always late. Come on. I'm starving."

Mrs. Pat smiled radiantly and caught Rousseau's arm.

"Come on, Philippe!"

Rousseau looked back at Sandra before, with a shrug, he allowed himself to be swept on to the hall. Langdon said thoughtfully:

"Ain't Huckins grand?"

"Grand and slightly saturnine. He gives me the creeps." Sandra was conscious of the strain in her voice. Time was flying and she had not yet told Nicholas Hoyt about

Emma and Philippe. If she made a point of detaining him now, they might suspect her reason for doing it. Would she have to wait until the ball?

She turned the question over and over in her mind during dinner. It was still uppermost in her thoughts as salad was being served, Japanese persimmons with their crimson skins opened like pointed petals, Frenchily and delectably dressed, flanked by blended cheeses in puffy white balls. Philippe Rousseau, who had been taciturn during dinner, frowned at Emma, the waitress, as she stopped behind his chair.

"Long distance call, sir."

With a murmured apology to his hostess he left the room. The eyes of Damon and Jed Langdon met across the silver bowl of crimson carnations in the middle of the refectory table which glistened with crystal in the candlelight. It was a mere glance but Sandra caught it. What did it mean? What did they know?

Later, in the library, she resolutely attempted to keep her eyes from the shelf where she had left her flashlight. She must retrieve it. What a perfect background the rich paneling was for the pink coats of the men, the sparkle of Mrs. Pat's jewels, Estelle Carter's ice-green gown. The face of Emma, who was passing the coffee, was like a clear-cut cameo against its darkness. Strange that the room should have given her such an eerie feeling the first time she entered it. Philippe had not returned to finish his dinner. Why? It had been the second phone call within a short time; the first one from the track apparently had been upsetting. Ordinarily she would think nothing of it, even if she noticed it, but these were critical days. Where was he?

As if conjured by her thoughts, Philippe Rousseau entered. He was in street clothes. His face was colorless but his manner was jaunty.

"Sorry, Mrs. Pat, to pass up the ball but my lawyer phoned that he must see me at once." A self-conscious smile tugged at the corners of his lips as he explained. Had his late moodiness been swept away by good news, or was he putting up a bluff?

Sandra glanced surreptitiously at Nicholas Hoyt. Had he noticed Philippe's evident exultation? If he had, the fact was not apparent. He was laughingly arguing with Jed Langdon and Mr. Damon. He had been on the crest of the wave during dinner. Had that fact contributed to Philippe's moroseness? Rousseau came to her.

"It hurts to cut out this evening with you, Sandra, — but — only a comparatively few hours now and — well, you'll be the first to hear the news of my victory." He caught her hands and pressed his lips to them before he added, "dearest!"

"For the love of Mike, Emma, what's the matter with you? That cream pitcher just missed my dress."

Mrs. Newsome's anger, aimed at the waitress, recorded but faintly on Sandra's mind. She was thankful that Emma's casualty had diverted attention from Rousseau's theatrical exit. Had every one in the room heard that absurd endearment? Had Nick Hoyt and Jed Langdon and Mr. Damon? They were looking up at the M.F.H. Had they turned their backs to save her embarrassment when Philippe had gone sentimental?

"Well, that seems to be that." Curtis Newsome's laugh broke the silence. "Come over here and help a fella, will you, Miss Duval? You're a demon at this puzzle stuff. I've found the scraps of two boy friends for the girl in the picture and I thought there was but one."

"Two to one is the other way round in this house," snapped Mrs. Pat as Estelle Carter strolled toward him. "Oh, lay off that puzzle, Curt! I promised to be at the ball early. Better come with me, Sandra, now that Philippe has walked out on you. He must have a heavy date to break one with you. Coming in the big car with us, Nick? You ought to be there early too."

This was Nicholas Hoyt's cue to again ask her to go with him. Would he, or had his threat to let her depart with Philippe only over his dead body been merely a desire to thwart, in every way possible, the man he considered a fake? Sandra felt her face grow warm as involuntarily her eyes sought his.

Estelle Carter snuggled close to Hoyt. "Nick is taking me, aren't you, Nicholas? We arranged it this afternoon, didn't we — *dearest?*"

The last word was a perfect imitation of Philippe Rousseau's impassioned voice. That and the sight of the woman leaning against Nicholas Hoyt sent a devastating surge of fury over Sandra. She clenched her hands to keep them out of that near-gold hair, from jerking that silly head till the teeth rattled. First Curtis Newsome, now Nick! Her nails cut into her hands. Anger ebbed, a wave of faintness set her shaking. Horrible! What had happened to her? Was she really Sandra Duval? She was a stranger to herself.

Nicholas Hoyt removed the hand from his arm. "As I have told you before, Estelle, your amazing talent for dramatizing the simplest situations is wasted in this village. With your imagination you should be at a scenario desk. Can't drive you over; duty calls. Take your guests along without me, Pat. I — I want to look in on Sharp before I go to the ball. He is a bunch of nerves the night before a race. I'm taking him to the track myself in the morning."

"Better keep away from him tonight, Nick. He'll be better alone."

Sandra sensed the strain of anxiety in Mrs. Pat's voice. Curious, she never before had heard that tone nor seen that apprehension in her eyes, and she had seen her in many moods. Had Nicholas Hoyt noticed it? Evidently not. He was smiling.

"Alone! No chance of Eddie's being alone. I will have to yank the swipes and exercise boys and the man in charge of the stables out of the jockey's room by the scruff of their necks. They will pile in there to listen to the radio race-prophesies for tomorrow."

"I'll bet they will. Are you coming with

us, Estelle, or must you be personally conducted?"

"Thank you, Mrs. Pat, but I never go in a crowd. I'll phone a friend to call for me."

Curtis Newsome took an impetuous step after her, stopped, and turned to his wife.

"Come on, Pat, get your wrap. Let's get going!"

Humiliation swept over Sandra in a sickening wave as she left the room. That very humiliation dated her, that and her rage at Estelle, set her back years. Mr. Damon was right, she was old-fashioned. Had Nicholas Hoyt assumed that she was looking at him expectantly; had he imagined the hound look in her eyes when he had so easily slipped out of his invitation to her? Didn't it prove that her suspicion a few moments ago that he would do anything to combat Philippe Rousseau was right? All his kindness to her had been planned for that. It was maddening, maddening, maddening! She wouldn't try now to tell him about Emma and Philippe. He could find out for himself.

Chapter XX

Sandra's heart still smarted as hours later she went up the stairway at Seven Chimneys, weariness in every step. Perhaps it wasn't her heart, perhaps it was her mind which writhed whenever she pictured herself standing in the library waiting — *waiting,* that was the unendurable fact — for Nicholas Hoyt to ask her to drive to the ball with him. His cool refusal to escort the Carter woman had helped a little. Why had she asked him to take her? To rouse Curtis Newsome's jealousy? If so, she had succeeded; he had hardly spoken on the way to the Club House.

Thank heaven, she had been able to ignore Nicholas Hoyt coolly when he had come into the hall as she was starting, though her pulses had thrummed when he had laid her wrap over her shoulders with disturbing care. Had he touched her bare shoulder with his lips before he had whispered, "Sandra — please," or had she imagined it? If imagination had sent that swift flame through her, what would reality do? Better not think of it. Care! A lot he cared. That was just his line. Was it his line also to present diamond clips of the Stone House colors to his girl friends? She had not had much opportunity to think of that episode during the evening.

Her lips relaxed in a gratified smile. No wonder she was tired — she had not danced for months, and tonight there had been no lack of pink sleeves about her, her dances had been cut into with flattering frequency, no thanks to either of the men who had stepped out after their apparent eagerness to drive her to the ball.

"Bridie!" she exclaimed, as from the threshold of the boudoir she regarded the rusty-haired woman sitting stiffly upright in an apricot colored chair. Bud and Buddy stood like sentinels on each side of her, their cars pricked to attention, their tails wagging a welcome. She closed the door.

"Bridie! Why are you waiting here? Don't you know that it is almost morning?"

The woman rose and took Sandra's

white velvet coat. "Sure an' why wouldn't I know, Miss; I'm not deaf. Haven't I been hearin' the cock at Stone House a-bustin' his throat answerin' the crow of one here at Seven Chimneys? I couldn't find the dogs early an' I hunted round till I got 'em. Set down, Miss, and I'll take off yer shoes while ye eat them nice little sandwiches I put on the dresser for ye. I'll bet yer feet are tired."

Sandra dropped to the bench in front of the *poudreuse* and extended a silver sandaled foot. She bit into a round of bread and tomato and mayonnaise. The dogs with heads tilted watched her hungrily.

"Tired isn't the word; my feet feel as flat as a duck's. This sandwich is luscious! And a glass of milk too! What a dear you are!"

"Sure an' I thought ye'd be hungry whin ye got here, wid the gintlemen all askin' ye to dance. I'll bet ye had a lot of beaux." The woman eagerly encouraged confidences as she gently massaged a slim foot.

"I wasn't too unpopular. Your hands are like magic, Bridie, they take out all the ache. It was a marvelous ball. Lovely ladies in gorgeous frocks; a tropical setting of palms and ferns and shrubs in every conceivable shade of green for a background; men in hunt pink, men in sombre black; and through it all the beat and throb and croon of music, music that pulled your heart up into your throat and held it there beating in time to the rhythm. It was heavenly!

" 'Good night, Sweet-heart, till we meet tomorrow,
Good night, Sweet-heart, sleep will banish sorrow.
Good night, Sweet-heart, good night,' "

she sang softly.

"That's kinder sad an' yet liltin', Miss, almost makes my feet go." Bridie held out a soft rose négligée. "Sure an' I'll bet ye sing like a bird. You an' Mister Nicholas ought to do some duets together. You've heard him sing, haven't ye?"

"Never." Smoldering resentment blazed up in the word.

"Is that so? An' him so fond of singin'! I guess it's worry about the family fortune what's checked him up. He ain't like he was; he used to be such a gayhearted lad. My, an' wasn't his uncle crazy about him! Sure an' when he told me tonight to get them dogs up here if it took me all night —"

"Mr. Nicholas told you!"

"Lord love ye, now I've done it!"

"Bridie, what did Mr. Nicholas tell you?"

"Well, sure, Miss, now I've gone so fur I might as well be hung fer a sheep as a lamb. Ever since the first week ye come, he's been kinder watchin' yer."

"Watching *me?*"

"I guess I'd oughter say, watchin' over yer, Miss. Mister Nicholas has me call him every night after I get Bud and Buddy up here. See thim two dogs prick up their ears! They know we're talking about 'em."

"He does? Is he afraid that some one will run away with me? Or — perhaps he is afraid I will run away with something."

"I guess it ain't that last; he was terrible excited when he talked to me tonight to find out if the dogs were here. There, I shouldn't have told ye that. Forget it, Miss. Wouldn't ye like me to give yer hair a good brushin'?"

"I'd love it." Sandra smiled at the faded eyes regarding her from the mirror. "But you ought to be in bed. You will be dead to the world in the morning."

"Sure an' there won't be much doin' tomorrow inside the house; it's today now though, ain't it, an' the races this afternoon. When the clock strikes three the big horses will be off. It's a grand sight, I'm tellin' yer. Ye're goin' of course."

"Going! A police squad couldn't keep me away. I'm all of a tingle. I never have been in the midst of race preparations before. I suppose the Stone House outfit has gone?"

"Sure, Miss. But that's a small stable; Mister Nicholas won't send so many people; Mrs. Newsome has done the handsome thing by Mr. Rousseau's horse. Fortune's a great stallion though. I remember when he was a little thing Mister Mark Hoyt said he'd be a champeen. There, don't that shine like satin?" She held up a strand of dark hair that had the bluish sheen of a raven's wing.

"It is marvelous, Bridie. You make me think of Mother Goose.

" 'Old woman, old woman, whither
so high
I'm off to brush cobwebs out of the sky.'

"You have brushed the sleep cobwebs from my brain." Sandra rose and stretched lazily. "I will read until I get dozy."

"Excuse my sayin' so, Miss, but that's a

beautiful bracelet. It sparkles like cut glass."

Laughter twitched at Sandra's lips. Cut glass must be Bridie's acme of brilliance. "I like it too. It was a present from some one I love."

"I guess there's plenty of folks love yer, Miss. Anything more I kin do for ye?"

"Nothing, and thank you for everything. Don't disturb me in the morning. My work for tomorrow is done and I may sleep late. I want to look grand for the races."

"Sure an' ye'll look g-grand anyway, but ye'd better get all the sleep ye can. I don't hold much with readin'. Readin'll fill yer head up with thinkin' again."

Sandra stood in the middle of her room until Bridie closed the door behind her. She didn't need "readin' " to fill her mind with thoughts. Anger and humiliation at Nicholas Hoyt's change of mind when he discovered that Philippe was not taking her to the ball still pricked unendurably. She had learned one thing tonight, that deep within her lurked fiercely elemental forces of fury of which she never would have believed herself possessed.

With an impatient exclamation at her impotence against the memory, she crossed to the window and looked out upon an indigo world flooded with soft opaline light. A few stars blinked sleepily; one bolder and bigger than the others tossed on the rippling surface of the river like a jewel glittering on the bosom of a woman's sombre gown. Where the world slipped away into the east the horizon was faintly luminous. The moon, like a piece of a broken silver plate, was sinking westward. The stables twinkled with topaz lights. This was the dawn of the day of the great race. How could one sleep?

Somewhere a cock crowed lustily, and faintly from the distance another answered. Almost day! Why stand here nursing her grievance? She would read. She picked up books on the table, shook her head and dropped them. She couldn't keep her mind on fiction or biography with the world in which she was living vibrating with the excitement of an estate contest and a horse race.

That gave her an idea. She would slip down to the library, retrieve her flashlight, and get the modern book on Thoroughbreds she had noticed. It would help her watch tomorrow's — no today's — race more intelligently.

She opened her door a crack. The house seemed quiet. She flung the négligée in a rose-colored heap on the chaise longue — she wouldn't go out of her room in that — slipped into the pale blue velvet pyjamas she had worn at Stone House. Stone House. Bridie had said that Nicholas Hoyt had been watching her since she had come to Seven Chimneys. What had he thought when her eyes had flown to his as if she were waiting for him to insist upon driving her to the ball? Half way across the room she stopped. Should she take Bud and Buddy? What had he had in his mind when he had told Bridie to be sure that the dogs were in her room?

"Oh, lay off Nicholas Hoyt, Sandy!" she admonished aloud, and laughed at her perfect imitation of Mrs. Pat's slangy irritation. B.D. was right — she was picking up Americanisms fast. Why not, when they were so crisply effective?

She whistled softly to the dogs, opened her door and listened. A tomblike silence prevailed. The halls were dark. Mrs. Pat was an illogical spender. Millions for the stables, not a penny for extra light, might have been her paraphrase. Sandra crossed the hall to the stairs with the two dogs like a bodyguard beside her.

She descended cautiously. It would be awkward, to say the least, to rouse the household by tumbling the entire length. Never before had she realized the number of stairs from one hall to another; at a guess she would say there were a thousand or two — tonight. She held tight to the rail. She had heard of Stygian darkness. This must be the brand. What a noise the dogs made on the tiled floor. To her excited fancy, their toe-nails sounded as loud as the tap-tap of the Legionnaires' canes on asphalt roads as they had paraded one Armistice Day.

Except for that click, how still, how eerily still the house was! It was not the silence which caught at her breath; it was a vague sense that some malevolent influence abroad in the night was stalking her.

She ran the last few steps, stopped in startled surprise on the threshold of the library. It was dimly lighted! The colors in the portrait of the M.F.H. glowed like jewels. Light fell also on a sleek black head, on a face by the desk. Philippe Rousseau was staring at the door. Something sinister and blue and shiny glinted in his hand.

"Come out of the dark, whoever you are!" he warned with deadly quietness.

His low voice echoed through the still room in wisps of sound. Even if these were the crime-thirties, he would not fire,

Sandra reassured herself. Why was he in the library at this hour? Why was he at the desk? Emma had told him of the secret drawer, that was the answer.

She wished that her lips were not so dry and stiff; he might think that she was frightened. Frightened! She, with Bud and Buddy as a bodyguard? The rumble in their throats was a protection in itself. Head up, stiff lips smiling, she stepped within the glow cast by the light above the portrait.

"Well, see who's here!" Her whisper was gay, if guarded.

"Sandra!" Rousseau's face was colorless; his menacing hand slid into his coat pocket. "What are you doing here?" he demanded in a voice as repressed as her own.

She backed up to the shelves, reached behind her for the flashlight. She mounted the steps. Threw the spot of light along the titles of books. THOROUGHBREDS. That was the one she wanted.

The dogs crouched at the foot of the steps, their eyes on the man by the desk. She wasn't in the least afraid, Sandra reminded Sandra again; excessive dancing earlier in the evening was responsible for the sudden all-goneness where her knees should be. They trembled like the proverbial aspen in a breeze. She sat down suddenly on a step.

"What am I doing here? Can't you see? I couldn't sleep. It is so long since I have stepped out socially that the excitement set my mind whirling like a mechanical top. I came for a book on horses which I discovered here yesterday. Now that I have accounted for my prowling, it is your turn Philippe. Why are you here?"

He started toward her. Bud and Buddy rose as one, with the sound as of far away thunder in their throats; the hair along their backs ruffed. He stopped. There was a hint of brutality in his low laugh.

"Nice fellas. Those dogs will go out with some of the other junk when I take possession. Meanwhile —"

"Meanwhile you were about to explain what you are doing in the library at this ungodly hour. I thought you were in the city."

"Did you think of me, Sandra?" The dogs stalked forward. He checked his eager approach. "I did go to the city but I came back early. That second call was from the track again. I didn't want any one to know it."

The lines had deepened about his

mouth, his eyes were haggard. Sandra forgot Emma, forgot her suspicion of him in interest in his horse.

"What has happened, Philippe?"

"Iron Man got a scratch just above one of his hoofs. They've washed it out and applied an antiseptic, but the leg is beginning to swell a trifle. When my trainer called the second time he told the maid long distance. The news of the gray's condition must not get out. I shouldn't have told you, Sandra, but I'm terribly worried. Luck's against me."

"The persecution complex again." Sandra was instantly ashamed of the thought. She said warmly:

"I'm sorry, Philippe, terribly sorry. Perhaps you are taking it too hard." Suddenly she remembered his gesture when she had appeared on the threshold; followed the memory of him standing by the hedge with Emma. A warning doubt of this last story pricked at her mind. She asked lightly:

"Why the racketeer touch?"

"Racketeer! — Oh, you mean the gun? There have been so many hold-ups lately that I have picked up the habit of carrying one; besides, I don't trust Huckins."

"Huckins!" Sandra converted a contemptuous sniff into a faint cough. Did

Philippe suspect that she had linked the butler up with him? Was he trying to switch her from that train of thought? Better let him think her dumb.

"I agree with you; there is something queer about Huckins. All for preparedness, aren't you?" She stifled a yawn. "I have my book. I'm going up." She backed down the steps. "Come, Bud and Buddy."

"Wait a minute. I'm going too."

"Put out the light," she whispered. "Mrs. Pat has views as to economy on electric bills."

Dawn was creeping in at the windows; a pale cold light sifted through the gloom as Rousseau joined her in the hall. He moved stiffly. He answered the question in her eyes in a whisper:

"Stiff working over Iron Man so long. Been living too soft. It did me up. Feel ninety years old."

Sandra sent the reluctant dogs ahead. At the top of the stairs Rousseau caught her hand. She allowed him to draw her nearer; he must not suspect that she doubted him.

"Sandra. Tomorrow —"

"What was that? I thought I heard something!" They listened. "My nerves broadcasting. There won't be a tomorrow for me if Mrs. Pat sees us now. Goodnight,

Philippe." The light from the room shone on him as she opened the boudoir door. He was as colorless as she felt. She pushed the dogs, who seemed inclined to follow him, into the room ahead of her, closed the door and leaned against it.

"That seems to be that," she said softly. Apparently she had played her part well. Philippe Rousseau did not suspect that she had been behind that projector this afternoon. He and Emma! The picture the light had revealed flashed with cinematic clarity. She should have told Nicholas Hoyt what she had seen; terribly small of her to withhold such information because her feelings had been hurt.

Back again on the old treadmill of thought. She looked at the clock. No use going to bed, she couldn't sleep. She flung herself on the chaise longue, adjusted the light, opened the book she had taken from the library shelf. Unseeing eyes on the dogs stretched back to back on the rug, her thoughts whirled on.

After all, why should she tell Nicholas Hoyt, why should she care whether or not he kept the estate? Why should she care what happened to a man who cast her off as casually as he had last night? The memory of his indifference stung unendurably. Had she shown so plainly that she hoped he would insist upon taking her to the ball? Hoped! Why not be honest? She had longed to have him catch her hands tight in his, hear him say, "Only over my dead body you'll go with him!"

The mere thought of his voice set her heart throbbing. Why? She leaned back and covered her eyes with her hands. Was it love? She liked men tremendously. Once she had thought herself in love, but it had not been like this; her breath had not caught at the man's look, she had not longed for his arms to close about her as she longed for Nick's now. Had jealousy been back of her rage when Estelle Carter had nestled up to him in the library? She had gone savage then, she, Sandra Duval, had touched the depths. So this was love! It was as if the outer shell which had cramped and stifled her heart had been peeled off, leaving something quiveringly sensitive to one voice, one pair of eyes. She made a bitter little face. If this were love — and it was, she admitted it — it was the most distracting experience of her life.

Her hands dropped from her eyes. Only five minutes gone since she had entered the room. Had she been facing a revaluation of her feeling for Nicholas Hoyt for only five minutes? It seemed as if she had been living in this emotional chaos for a lifetime. Having reached this world-shaking conclusion, what good would it do her? In spite of his caressing voice — the memory of it caught at her heart — she was just one more girl to him. Why, why had she let herself care?

She was only making it harder by thinking; she must put him out of her mind. Reading always closed the door on problems for her. Resolutely she opened the book in her lap. THOROUGHBREDS. Mark Hoyt's name was on the title page, also the date when he had acquired it. It must have been a short time before he died.

She snuggled down into the pillows. A letter dropped to her lap. Pale mauve. Curious. She picked it up. Registered. The sender must have thought it of great importance. It was addressed to Mark Hoyt. What was that pencilled line?

"Nick must see this at once."

She swung her feet to the floor and sat up straight and rigid. The postmark was blurred, but she could make out Ky. Kentucky! Kentucky! The one-time nurse had been living in Kentucky! Yes, there was the return address. A. P. Rousseau. The letter had been opened. Should she read it? No! No! She must get it to Nick. How had it come in the book? She looked at the date on the title page. It must have been on the desk, perhaps Mark Hoyt had dropped it when he had fallen forward, perhaps this very book had been under his head. In the excitement of discovering him dead, the book with the letter in it had been swept aside.

She sprang up. Never mind how it had come there. She must get it to Nick. Philippe was suspicious of undercurrents. Wasn't the automatic proof of it? Perhaps he suspected that a letter had been sent to Mark Hoyt by his mother. Tonight he had seen her take that book from the library. What should she do?

She looked at her father's picture. If only he were here to tell her. His eyes were not smiling now. She could almost hear him say:

"Steady, Sandy, steady!"

The thought quieted her excitement. She would take the letter to Stone House now, it wasn't safe here a moment. Even if Nick already had started with Eddie Sharp for the track, Nanny O'Day would guard it with her life. She must get away. There were too many in this house who would be keen to get it, Philippe, Emma, Huckins, she was sure of Huckins. She pinned the envelope to the inside of her pyjama jacket. She couldn't stop to change. She kicked off her sandals, pulled on a pair of walking shoes. She slipped into her checked coat, thrust her flashlight into the pocket. She looked at the book — the date on the title page meant such a lot — but, safer to leave it here.

At the slightly opened door she listened. The dogs thrust their noses at the crack. She pushed them back.

"Go! Go to bed, Bud and Buddy!"

Their aggrieved manner brought a little gust of laughter to her lips. "You look at if you were about to burst into tears," she whispered to them.

Lucky that love and excitement had not numbed her sense of humor. She patted the head of each dog apologetically before she softly closed the French windows and shut them out on the balconies. Come what might, she must be on her own. A girl on her own! The phrase she had read so often while abroad, which had seemed to open a new world. Her life at Seven Chimneys had indeed been a new world, a more rushing, noisy world than that she had left, more real, more vibrant.

Step by cautious step she went down the stairs, turning her head at the faintest sound, stopping at a creak in the wainscotting, hearing her heart beating like a tom-tom in the silence. Perhaps she should have waited until morning to take the letter. No! No! Suppose, suppose anything happened to her in the night — people had been known not to wake up — Nick might never see it.

The hall filled with a chill gray light. No sound in the house. What was that? She stood motionless, barely breathing. A vine tapping. It made her think of a pale spirit from another world begging admittance to warmth and luxury. Lucky she had found out the truth about the phantom by the pool or she might imagine that that was drifting by.

She tiptoed through the hall. The grille to the loggia was locked! If only the key wouldn't squeak! What was that? Icy fingers seemed to clutch her throat. No sound but the thump! thump! of her heart and the eerie tap! tap! of the vine. Something grim about the silence. She hurried up reserves of courage. One moment of hesitation bred a dozen chances of being stopped. The door opened at last! How could she have let it clang? It would rouse the sleepers.

She stole across the terrace — why hadn't she worn a dark coat — how keen and fragrant the air! Was that soft pink light dawn?

She flitted along the garden path, past the still, dark pool. Day was coming over the hills. An awakening murmur stirred the air. Shadows were thinning. The high, exultant song of a bird broke in the middle. Was the singer being pulled back into a warm nest by a sleepy mate? Faint footsteps crossing the terrace? Was some one following? Had she been seen on the garden path? Had her light coat betrayed her? She shrank into the shadow of a hedge. Held her hand over her heart to muffle its loud throb. No sound. Had the footsteps stopped when she stopped? She must go on.

It seemed hours before she reached the road she had followed the day Happy Landing had flung her over his head. It was the shortest way to Stone House. Once out of sight of the windows of Seven Chimneys she ran; past grass meadows; open fields; the rise crowned by the in-and-out; by post and rail fences; stone walls; patches of woodland; the pasture with the water-hole.

"Faster! Faster!" she lashed herself, and thought of the Red Queen and Alice. Her throat was dry, her breath pumped in ragged gusts. Was that a shout behind her, or was imagination playing tricks again?

Fear lent wings to her feet. She must, she must get to Stone House. Evidently she was not in sight of the person following yet. If she could get around the next turn without being seen, the letter would be safe. If — there wasn't such a word! There couldn't be such a word for her now! Did lungs burst from overexertion? She would sprint every day after this to keep fit. Around the bend! No stir at the stables. Had Nick gone? Nanny O'Day? The side door of the house was open!

She cautiously closed it behind her and leaned against it panting. Her heart must stop thumping; her breath must stop tearing up from her lungs soon. She tried to call. Her voice wouldn't come. Had her legs gone back on her that she could not move? The demon on her trail would find her. Where should she go? The secret panel!

She forced herself forward, half stumbled through the hall. A clock striking! Five! Was Nanny O'Day still asleep? If so, why the open door? No time to hunt for her. She must disappear.

The panel slid open at her touch. She sprang into the darkness. Lucky she had her flash. It was not in her pocket! Gone? It wouldn't help if her pursuers picked that evidence up on the road. She fumbled for the panel and pulled it forward. The lock clicked. She had not meant to close it! A million icy chills skittered through her body. Locked in! Without a light! She tried to push the panel open. It would not move!

Chapter XXI

Nicholas Hoyt had started after Sandra as she followed Mrs. Newsome from the library. Immediately a hand lightly pressed each of his arms. B.D. and Jed Langdon were reminding him that there would be no ball for him. Did they think he had so soon forgotten the decision made in the moment they had stood looking up at the portrait of the M.F.H.? Not likely.

It was a mean break that Sandra should leave the room thinking him a quitter, after that impassioned "dearest!" of Philippe Rousseau's which he had heard and hated. Her eyes had flashed to his when Mrs. Pat had suggested that she drive to the Club House with her, and then Estelle bad butted in. What had been her idea? He wouldn't make a date with her if she were the only woman in the world.

After his brag to Sandra that she would

go to the ball with Rousseau only over his dead body, he had stood like a dummy when his chance to take her had come. He squared his shoulders. His defection must go without explanation for twenty-four hours; then he would tell her that he loved her.

"Step on it, Nick!" Jed Langdon's low voice broke into his reflections. "Get back to Stone House and change and hang around with an eye out for Sharp. B.D. and I will show ourselves at the ball; then I'll start on Rousseau's trail. He has some deviltry up his sleeve tonight, I'll bet a hat."

Nicholas listened for voices in the hall. At least he could go to the car with Sandra. He agreed absentmindedly:

"Don't worry about Eddie Sharp. I'll sit beside his bed all night if I have to. He won't double cross me, you needn't worry, I wish that I were as sure of the loyalty of all my friends as I am of his. Here they come!"

He was at the foot of the stairs as Sandra reached the lowest step. He took her velvet coat with its deep white fox cuffs from her arm and held it. In a surge of love and desperation he touched her bare shoulder with his lips. For an instant she hesitated; then she slipped into the coat. As he adjusted the collar, he pleaded:

"Sandra. Please . . ."

She twisted free and joined Damon and Langdon whom Huckins had been assisting into their coats. "You two men are coming with us, aren't you? I would so hate being the odd woman."

"Yours to command, Sandy," the older man responded gallantly.

Mrs. Newsome called over her shoulder: "Coming with us after all, Nick?"

"Sorry, I can't."

Langdon turned and closed one eye expressively. "Bye-bye, Nick. Don't sympathize with him, Miss Duval. He'll join us later."

"I! Sympathize with Mr. Nicholas Hoyt! Where did you get that fantastic idea, Mr. Langdon?"

If there was such a thing as bitter honey, Sandra's voice was it, Nicholas thought savagely, as he watched the three, arm in arm, follow Mrs. Pat to the door. Jed needn't look so like a grinning idiot.

"Got a light, Mr. — Nicholas?" Curtis Newsome asked. "That will be all, Huckins," he added with an unwonted show of authority and a tinge of his wife's dictatorial manner.

The butler bent his head obsequiously. "Very good, sir. Anything I can do for you, Mr. Hoyt?"

"Nothing — wait a minute — where are the dogs, Huckins?"

"Mr. Rousseau gave orders that they were to be sent to the stables, sir."

"Good gosh! How long since Rousseau has been giving orders and having them obeyed around here, Huckins?"

The butler glanced at Nicholas, coughed a deprecating little cough.

"I thought as how the madame would want her guest's wishes carried out, Mr. Newsome. You see, the dogs don't like the new heir — I beg pardon, Mr. Hoyt, in the servants' hall we've got in the habit of speaking of Mr. Rousseau as the lost son — and he's afraid of them."

"Say listen, if during the next twenty-four hours he gives you orders, don't obey them. Get that straight, Huckins?"

"Yes, Mr. Newsome."

"All right then, get out!"

With an apologetic look at Nicholas and another cough, the butler departed.

Newsome shrugged. "Pat will give me the dickens for barging in on her business, but that flunkey gets my goat. There's the French horn! She'll be swearing mad if I keep her waiting — I suppose she thinks I'm hanging around for Estelle," he interpolated bitterly. "I'm not; I waited to warn you to keep your eye peeled for Rousseau. He hasn't gone to New York tonight to see his lawyer. Mac Donovan told me in confidence that something was wrong with Iron Man. Look out for your hoss."

"I will, Curt. Get going. There's the horn again."

"Coming!" Newsome shouted. "What I really came back to say was, I — I — have sort of a hunch that something's going cockeyed soon, and if there is any blooming thing I can do to help — anything — I'm with you. Get me?"

Nicholas laid his hand affectionately on his shoulder and walked with him toward the door. "I get you, Curt — and thanks."

"Coming!" Newsome shouted again in response to another summons, not so musical this time, and charged down the steps.

Nicholas turned and thoughtfully regarded the door through which Huckins had departed. Should he ring for the butler and find out just what the servants were saying about Philippe Rousseau's claim? No. He was not ready for that yet.

Had there been a motive in Rousseau's

order to have the dogs shut up tonight, or was the man really afraid of them, he wondered, as he sent his roadster at a clipping pace toward Stone House. If he had motored to town, what difference did it make to him where they were? One never knew what was lying in wait around the next corner. When dressing tonight, he had determined to drive Sandra to the ball, and here he was, not taking her but going home himself. Sometime she would wear that jeweled clip. He wouldn't give up until she was the wife of another man. He was crazy to get that possibility on his mind! He needed to concentrate his thoughts on Rousseau's tactics. So far his reputation in the turf world was spotless — but . . .

He went directly to the telephone in the library when he reached Stone House. It took several minutes to get the housekeeper's room at Seven Chimneys and several more to get in touch with Bridie to tell her that the dogs were shut up, that she was to find them and take them to Sandra's room. He paced restlessly as far as the length of the cord would permit. He was impatient to change, to locate Sharp, but he must talk to the maid first. There she was!

She responded soothingly to his instructions:

"Sure, Mister Nicholas. I'll get Bud an' Buddy. Don't ye worry. I'm goin'. Good-bye!"

That took a load from his mind. It had been evident to him from the first time he had seen them together that Rousseau was quite mad about Sandra. Her safety had been his first thought. He wouldn't trust the Kentuckian as far as he could see him where a lovely girl was concerned. The defendants of Mark Hoyt's will had learned that much about the claimant's past record.

What had been his idea in having the dogs shut up? Suppose, in spite of whatever evidence the defense might produce — that was a joke; what had they to produce but two letters which would hand the estate over to the claimant, Nicholas reflected, as he changed to tweeds. He'd better cut out that line of thought, he had no time to spend being a calamity-howler now, it was his job to locate Sharp and stay with him.

As he strode along the path patterned with flags, he looked up at the sky. What a night! The one-eyed moon smirked gallantly in the star-powdered sky. Little mists floated like wisps of silvery gauze above the shimmering river. Somewhere a frog croaked and quickly the shrill tremolo of a tree toad answered. The leaves above his head stirred with a sound like rippling water; the late perennials shook out a lovely perfume. From a hill where burned the lonely red light of a camper's fire came the faint, eerie hoot of an owl. In a nearby field one cow-bell tinkled.

"What a night!" he said again. The air was spicy with the fragrance of evergreens. Far, far to the north, quivering pinkish white rays shot toward the zenith of the heavens. The Northern Lights. Was some one showing them to Sandra? Was her lovely head tipped back near some man's shoulder? Her eyes would be as deep and dark as . . .

"Cut it out! You have all you can take care of tonight without getting Sandra on your mind," Nicholas warned himself as he pulled open the stable door.

"Oh, Sharp!"

No answer to his call. He looked into the tack room; usually the jockey would be found tipped back in a chair with his head against the wall. No one there. The place seemed uncannily empty; a mouse was nibbling behind the plaster; vague shadows flickered on the wall as the jet-black stable cat, crouching on the window-sill, waved her plumy tail and narrowed her sphinx eyes to glittering emerald slits. The clock ticked monotonously. An apple plumped to the ground outside.

Apprehension without cause, a certainty of disaster without evidence chilled Nicholas to the bone as he stood on the threshold. Rage at the trick his nerves were playing started the blood surging through his veins again. Of course the jock had turned in early to be steady for tomorrow. He went on to the stall room. No one here either. What the dickens did the men mean by leaving the place deserted?

Curtain Call floundered to his perfect feet and thrust his head over the gate. He drew his nose up and down his master's gray waistcoat. Nicholas rubbed his ears.

"Love me now, don't you, old fella?"

The colt snuffled and rolled unfathomable brown eyes toward a barrel. Other sleek shining heads appeared above other gates as Nicholas passed with a hand full of apples. His eyes were on the two empty stalls as Curtain Call daintily picked the last tid-bit from his hand. Fortune and his stable-mate were bedded down at the race-course paddock tonight. Would the black stallion come home tomorrow a winner?

"Sure, Mr. Hoyt, you must have crept in." A red-faced, cross-eyed groom sent his voice ahead of him as he hurried forward.

"Crept! I could have broken in and walked off with a colt and no one would have been the wiser. Who's on duty tonight, Bond?"

"I am. Parsons, a couple of grooms, and a boy have gone to the track. Wasn't them your orders? I could have sworn that no one could come in without me hearin' them."

"You're not here alone?"

"Just the exercise boys, the swipes, an' me. We were up in Sharp's quarters listenin' to some hayseed talkin' about the chances of the racin' tomorrow over his radio. You'd a bust laughin' if you'd heard it, Mr. Hoyt."

"You men know better than to be in the jockey's room tonight. He ought to be asleep."

"Asleep! Sharp! He ain't here. You sent fer him yourself, sir."

Nicholas' heart stopped, plunged into a thundering beat. He forced his voice to steadiness.

"What do you mean, Bond? I didn't send for Sharp."

The man's face went purple, his eyes locked.

"Well, what d'y know about that! Some one's pulled a dirty trick, Mr. Hoyt!" He burst into frightened, uncontrolled laughter.

"Shut up, Bond, the others will hear you. Come out of here. You are making the colts nervous."

Back in the room hung with saddles and harnesses, with its cases of silver cups and gold-lettered rosettes, Nicholas Hoyt commanded:

"Tell me all you know about this thing, and tell it quick." He glanced at the clock ticking ponderously. "Ten! Every minute counts. Sit down, you're shaking."

Bond sank to a chair and clenched his trembling hands. "Why shouldn't I be shakin' from shock, sir?" He gulped. "It was this way: I was lookin' at a scratch on Curtain Call's ankle — don't worry, 'tain't hardly skin deep — when Eddie Sharp come along an' said as how you'd sent for him to join you at the Hunt Club rooms this evenin', that you wanted him with you tonight."

"Did he say who 'phoned?"

"I asked him that right off. I haven't liked the way that butler from the big place has been hangin' round here. He —"

"Don't waste time! Who 'phoned?"

"Sharp said it was Mr. Langdon."

"Langdon! Was he sure?"

"He seemed sure enough. When I said as how even if 'twas him he'd better wait for orders direct from you, he says, 'Isn't Mr. Langdon the boss's lawyer? An' didn't Mr. Nicholas tell me he was the doctor an' to take orders from him? I couldn't say nothin' but 'yes' to that an' off he went."

"How long ago?"

"I'd say an hour at a guess."

"How did he go?"

"One of the boys drove him in his own fliv. He took his silks in a suitcase."

"Which boy?"

"I don't know sir. Want me to see if the car's back?"

"Yes. But don't talk. Understand?"

"Sure, I get you, sir."

"Come to the house; I'll be in the library telephoning."

The heavens were shimmering with pale colored lights as Nicholas left the stables.

"Colder tomorrow and fair — ought to give us a good track, but Fortune is good under any track conditions," he thought.

He resisted the urge to pace the floor of the library as he waited for his call to go through; he forced himself into a chair in front of the desk. His roaming eyes stopped at the portrait of the Puritan. The great idea Jed had worked out of frightening the truth out of Rousseau by having the phantom, who "walked when treachery was afoot," appear at stated intervals hadn't been worth the film it was printed on. It had been a kid trick at best. The only time they had used it they had frightened Sandra almost to death. When Jed had told him that he believed she had seen their "movie" — as he called it — they had agreed not to try it again. They weren't out to frighten women and children.

"Hulloa! Hulloa! That you, Jed? Nick speaking. Any one near? Keep your voice low. They've shanghaied Sharp!"

The wire faithfully recorded Langdon's gasp of horror. "What do you mean, shanghaied?"

"Some one, using your name, told him I wanted him at the Club."

"Where is he now?"

"Be your age, Jed! If I knew, would I stop to 'phone you?"

"Keep your shirt on, old man. Where are you?"

"Stone House."

"I'll burn up the road getting there. Shall I bring B.D.?"

"No. Leave him to look after Sandra."

"Sandra! She doesn't need him. She has a stag line a mile long. I'll be with you!"

Nicholas replaced the instrument with a bang. Why couldn't he have been with Sandra tonight? That would do for that! He had better keep his mind on the problem of Eddie Sharp. Where was he? Who had him? He sprang to his feet as Bond entered the room. The man's crossed eyes were ludicrously terrified.

"Well! Well! Don't stand there like a dummy! Found the boy?"

"Just come, sir."

"What about it?"

"He says that he drove to the side entrance of the Club, as he was told, and that —"

"If you gulp again, Bond, I'll, I'll — Go on! Go on!"

"Sure I'm tellin' it as fast as the words'll come, Mr. Hoyt. The boy said —"

"That he drove to the side entrance. I know that. What next?"

"You scare the words out of my mind, sir, your face is terrible. He said, when Sharp jumped out of the car, a couple of fellas with hats pulled low over their eyes — the way you sees 'em in the movies — stepped up, linked their arms in his an' says:

" 'Here you are, Eddie.' "

"Then what?"

"Our jock says, 'What's the big idea . . . ?'

"One of the fellas cut in: 'We'll explain — your boss wants you.' They walked toward the Club House an' one of them turned and called to the boy in the fliv: 'Don't wait!' "

"And he didn't wait!"

Bond shifted uneasily at Nicholas' sombre laugh. "I don't know as it has anything to do with our jock's goin', Mr. Hoyt, but as I was comin' from the stables I remembered that that man Huckins 'phoned Sharp."

"When?"

"I'd say it was about fifteen minutes before the other one called. As Eddie came away from the 'phone, he says:

" 'That butler at the big house was asking for a tip on the races. He must take me for a sucker.' "

"So Huckins 'phoned!"

"What'll I do next, sir?"

"Go back and stand guard at the stables. You realize, don't you, that this settles the question of the winner tomorrow? Fortune is beaten without Sharp in the saddle." The crossed eyes stared at Nicholas blankly as he added:

"Who has the most interest in seeing my horse lose, Bond? Answer that, and we'll know where to look for Eddie Sharp."

Chapter XXII

On hands and knees Sandra crept up the dark stairs behind the panel at Stone House. She would wait an hour perhaps and then she would shout and pound for release.

She crouched on the top stair and leaned her head against the wall. Her heart was quieting down and she could breathe without feeling as if she were pumping fire up from her lungs. Plenty of air. It crept through cracks somewhere; it wailed and shrieked like radio static which always made her think of the cries of witches as they whipped up their broomstick steeds. If only there wouldn't be any mice! She could bear anything but mice. Was the man, who had been shouting behind her, trying to pick up her trail? Had a man shouted? Had footsteps followed? Locked in. In her zeal to help Nicholas Hoyt she had landed in a mess.

Suppose she had to stay here all day? Cheerful thought! Even so, what was one day out of a lifetime? She wouldn't smother and she wouldn't starve, thanks to Bridie's sandwiches — but — she would miss the race; the big horses would start on the stroke of three! Oh, she couldn't! She wouldn't! She must get out! She must! How like her to plunge into this *impasse*. It was amusing — she might as well think of that side — that she, who had known of the Hoyt family only as it had figured in her father's reminiscences until a few weeks ago, really had no connection with it now, should be in jeopardy because of it.

No connection with it? That was not true. Didn't she love Nick? Love him! Something had flown from his eyes to her that day by the paddock. It had come with a sense of shock, she hadn't known what it was. The thought of him set her pulses throbbing, made her wildly eager for the feel of his arms, she had loved them without knowing it the night he had carried her upstairs at Stone House. It would be heaven if he cared, agony if he were indifferent. It was so like her to love like that. She, who had been disdainful of matrimony. But Nicholas Hoyt would not be like many of the husbands she had seen; even if he ceased to love a woman — it would be the woman's fault if he did — his self-respect, self-respect and decency and loyalty, would keep him true, through struggle and endurance, sunshine and shadow, dreams shattered and visions realized, sickness and health, new lives coming and lives passing, gorgeously happy days and dull days — all of which she had learned from observation could be summed up in the one word, marriage.

She tried to force him out of her mind. What use loving him? Hadn't he sidestepped taking her to the ball last night? Was it last night — it seemed months ago. If he had not taken her, he had not taken any one else, for he had not been there. "Where's Nick?" — if she had heard that inquiry once she had heard it fifty times. Conjecture had buzzed through the Club House, but no one could answer the question. Mrs. Pat, looking white and old, had admitted her surprise at his absence.

Estelle Carter had arrived with a ruddy-faced, vacant-eyed man who was the impregnable bachelor of the hunting-set. She had danced with one white arm about his neck. Later Sandra had seen her with Curtis Newsome in the shadow of a cypress near the garden fountain. His hands had been clenched behind him while she pretended to adjust his tie. Adjusting ties seemed her specialty. He was such a boy, a boy sensitive to the humiliations his wife heaped on him when enraged. Was Estelle really in love with him? Estelle, with her wealth, her social background? Incredible as it seemed, such attraction happened occasionally. She had tried her wiles on Nicholas Hoyt last night. Had she wanted to hurt Curtis Newsome? Whether she had or not she had succeeded in making Sandra Duval jealous. She burned now with the memory. Silly to have been so excited over it. If rumor were true, up to now Estelle had picked lovers up and dropped them, with no more conscience than a lady hawk snitching chickens in a poultry yard. How would this infatuation end?

She couldn't keep her mind on them; they faded into shadows; only Nick seemed real. The thought of him brought the sense of the worthwhileness of life which swept through her whenever he looked at her, and he had looked at her as if he cared last night — she ought to know; she had had some experience with men. Always happy ones for her — for the men too, she hoped; she had let them know before it was too late that what she felt for them was merely friendship.

The nearest she had come to love was the man she had met that spring in Seville, the Stanford University graduate with whom she had looked out from the bell tower of La Giralda over the city with its fertile plains and the shining Guadalquivir flowing half around it. Her liking for him had reached fever heat that morning, but later, when he had gluttonously revelled in a bull fight which had brought the chic world out *en masse* but which had turned her sick with horror, it had dropped to zero, and even though she told herself that most men would have been like that, she never went out with him again.

That vignette of the past had been like a magic carpet; it had transported her from the dark stairs behind the panel into the world of light and color and sound. How long ought she to wait before she pounded for release? She had no way to tell the passing of time. Could she hear the old clock in the hall when it struck the hour? She must listen carefully.

Lucky the air was fresh. Evidently it seeped in under the crack of the door which closed off the underground passage. Sometime she meant to explore the river.

She loved all waterways. Brooks and streams spelled romance to her, and in spite of the age in which she lived, she was incurably romantic. She could remember as if it were yesterday the hours she had spent punting on the Thames with the Oxford man. They had discussed every subject in the world; nothing had been too profound for their youthful courage to tackle nor their supreme confidence to settle as they glided along in the shade of majestically drooping willows and under arched bridges.

That was the summer the Harvard boy had gazed adoringly at her over the table at the charming thatched tea house across the road from Sulgrave Manor. She could see the blue and pink, pale yellow and lilac perennial bordered path as plainly as if she were on it, could smell the flower fragrance through which stung the spicy scent of lavender.

Color always had been meat and drink to her and now in memory it was irradiating this dark place. April in Holland, miles and miles of tulip fields, orderly patches of red and yellow, white and pink and purple; Egypt and a deep blue sky with the Great Pyramid rising, that heavenly pinkish gray, above golden sands.

Color everywhere.

Had it been in Marrakech where gaily blossoming vines had flung themselves from the top of a high wall across a narrow street to the roofs and lacy iron balconies of the houses opposite? Of course not; that had been in Seville.

She was dull to have mixed those two. Dull! She was sleepy, tired too, after her race to Stone House on top of hours of dancing. What a yawn! Not surprising that she was heavy-eyed. She had not slept a minute last night, she, who usually put in eight hours of dreamless sleep. The clock! Chiming the quarter hour!

She had been here fifteen minutes! It had seemed a lifetime. She would wait thirty more before she battered at the panel. By that time the person in pursuit of her — had some one been pursuing her, or had those shouts been but a figment of her inflamed imagination — would have given up the hunt.

Perhaps if she closed her eyes the time would go more quickly; with her feet braced against one wall and her shoulders against another, she was fairly comfortable. The letter was safe over her heart. What was in it? Was Philippe an imposter? He had waited until after Mark Hoyt's death before trying for the great estate. It had been done before. Hadn't he said that a recent *cause celebre* had had thirteen "rightful heirs" fighting for a fortune? Had he gotten his idea of claiming the Hoyt estate from that?

Another yawn like the last one would dislocate her jaw. Where had she been in her travels? Curious, her thoughts were all loose ends, she couldn't seem to tie them together. She had been walking along that narrow street in Seville. It had been in a garden there that she had heard a stringed orchestra playing:

> "Good night, Sweet-heart, till we
> meet tomorrow.
> Good night, Sweet-heart, sleep will
> banish sorrow.
> Good night . . ."

No, that had been at the ball. The music, and the lights among the palms strung like luminous, creamy pearls on a glistening chain, had caught at her throat, but not as had the lights along the water front of New York as the ship upon which she was returning without her father approached the country her ancestors had fought and died for. They had glimmered and shone with rainbow colors as she had seen — them — through . . . a . . . blinding . . . mist . . . of . . . If she yawned like that . . . again . . . the top . . . of her head . . . would split. . . .

Rap! Rap! Rap!

Sandra forced up heavy lids.

Rap! Rap! Rap!

Nothing but that spooky vine against the library window. There it was again — what was she doing here at this time of night? Pitch dark — she had come to —

Rap! Rap! Rap!

The sound again! She wasn't in the library! The witches? They didn't rap; they shrieked. She was dreaming to the sound of raps.

Memory surged over her in a life-giving tide. Her mind went ice-clear. She had been asleep! Trapped behind the panel at Stone House. Sandra Duval trapped! For how long? She had no idea of the time. The situation wasn't real; it was something straight out of an Edgar Allan Poe story.

She jumped up as if yanked erect by invisible cords. Ooch! Her feet prickled intolerably.

Rap! Rap! Rap!

The sound which had wakened her! Her breath caught. Where was it coming from?

"Hi! Hi-i-i!"

The hollow call rose, fell to a groan, and reached a new high. Sandra shivered. No static about that! Was it the Stone House ghost? Silly! Hadn't she pricked that spooky bubble? But nothing could be too fantastic to believe after the experiences of the early morning. Was it still morning? If only she knew the time.

"Hi! Let me o-u-t!"

Ghost! The call was real; she was not hearing it in a nightmare. It came from the underground passage. If she remembered correctly, the door at the foot of the stairs had been bolted the day she had investigated the region behind the panel. She wasn't sorry for that! Who was shouting? Friend or foe? Sounded like a movie caption. She set her teeth in her lips to suppress an hysterical ripple. A sense of humor was all right in its place but this was the time for thought. The captive might shout his head off where he was and no one would hear him, while she could easily make herself heard now. She would at least parley with the door bolted on her side.

Stiffly, on hands and knees, she backed

down the steps, repeating under her breath her father's counsel:

"Remember, Sandy, that the future holds nothing that your unconquerable soul, your faith, your trust cannot meet."

She held her breath as she reached the door. No sound on the other side. Had the person fainted? She put her lips close to the crack and whispered:

"Who's there?"

Not even a creak. Had that muffled voice been part of her dream? Fortified by the feel of the bolt under her hand, she repeated softly:

"Who's there?"

The door shook like a rat in the jaws of a vicious cat.

"For the love of Mike, open the door! I've got to get out!"

A man! That settled it. He could stay where he was. There was not room for both of them on her side of the door. Thank heaven for the bolt!

Fists pounded. "Let me out! I gotta get out!" The last word was a sob. "I've gotta ride in that race!"

Sharp! Eddie Sharp here on race day! What did it mean?

"Stop pounding, Sharp! Sandra Duval speaking. I can't pull the bolt unless you stop. It's com-ing! It's stuck! Wait! Wait! You can't help by shaking. It's mov-ing! There!"

The door creaked opened. She could see nothing. She could hear hard breathing. Why didn't the man speak? Suppose — suppose it were not . . . She reached out. Her hand touched cloth.

"You are Sharp, aren't you?"

"I'm Sharp, Miss. For the love of Mike! I can't see! 'Where am I? I heard a door open. Have I gone blind?"

"No, no! It's pitch dark here. You're in the underground passage at Stone House. At the foot of the steps which lead to the little room behind the portrait. I'm shut in too."

"Who shut you in, Miss? What difference does it make about you? I gotta get out! Understand? Mr. Nicholas is depending on me to ride Fortune! What time is it? I gotta get out." His voice broke in a harsh sob.

"I don't know the time, Sharp. I want to get out too. Do you think I mean to miss the race? That tricky secret panel locked me in. Feel your way up the stairs. Hear my grand five-year plan! We'll shout through the eyes of the old Puritan. You knew they were peepholes, didn't you?"

Chatter! Chatter! Chatter! How she was chattering to keep up her courage! And Sharp's too. Suppose no one should hear them? Something uncommonly like a hand of steel squeezed her heart. What time was it? Perhaps every member of the household would be at the track! She must get out. The King of France act again. She had rushed to Nicholas Hoyt, thinking him here. Now every nerve, every inch of her was pushing her back to Seven Chimneys with that precious letter. He would go there after the races. The person who had kidnaped Eddie Sharp might come back here. Then what chance would she have of getting to Nicholas?

She could hear the jockey's heavy breathing as he felt his way up on hands and knees. She crawled across the landing. It was not safe to stand; she might pitch down the stairs to the panel. She looked up to where she thought the portrait would be.

"Sharp! Sharp! See that crack of light? Nothing but canvas over the opening which used to be a window. We'll pull the picture from the frame. I'll jump down into the room. You come after me. Can you see? Can you feel? The canvas is tacked in. I've pulled out one tack. Ooch!

That hurt! Found one, Eddie? Found one?"

"Sure, Miss. Here's another! Can't reach the top ones."

"Pull the picture down! It's coming! Coming! Easy! Don't bend it! Keep it straight! We've got it!"

The portrait slipped free from the frame with a suddenness which upset the balance of the two tugging at it. Light streamed in through the opening. It set the diamonds in Sandra's bracelet sparkling, revealed the streaks of dust on the blue velvet pyjamas, the spider-like eyes in the blood-streaked face of the jockey. The girl shivered. What had happened to him? Treachery, of course; some one had tried to prevent his riding Fortune. The fiend would have the disappointment of his life. Sharp was sound and sober. He would ride!

"What next, Miss? We've gotta hurry!"

She stuck her head through the opening. The charming old living room was basking in the sunshine pouring through the diamond panes of the window. It must be noon at least. No time to lose.

"I will back through the frame, Eddie. Grip my hands till I wriggle them, then let go."

"I'll hold you tight, Miss. Hustle! Mr.

Nicholas must be thinking I've double-crossed him. Steady!"

"Let go!"

She dropped. The jockey's feet shot through the opening. She was pulling at his arm as he landed.

"Come on! We . . ."

The clock in the hall drew a long wheezing breath and struck. Sharp stared at Sandra.

"One! Two! Three!"

"Three! Three! Is the clock running backward?" From the threshold she stared incredulously at the ancient timepiece. Sharp licked dry lips.

"Three, Miss! Then I've been shut up all night! Three! The race is on. Who's riding Fortune?"

"Three! *Three!* The horses must be at the post! They're lunging forward this minute! Can't you hear the thunder of their hoofs, Sharp? Shout! Shout! Fortune will hear you. He must! Come on, Fortune!"

"Come on, Fortune! Come on, boy! Come *on!*"

Sandra's voice cracked on a high note. The jockey's broke on a sob of excitement. His spider-like eyes bulged.

"Folks hearing would think we'd gone

crazy, Miss, an' I guess we have."

"Crazy! I should say we had. How do we know but they are holding the big race waiting for you? Don't wait! Get to the track! Quick!"

In the hall she stopped as if galvanized. Her terrified eyes stared at the side door. She clutched the jockey's arm, whispered:

"The knob moved! Some one's waiting to pounce! Watch it!"

Chapter XXIII

Bright skies and a fast track. During the morning the unreserved seaters had thronged the highways: they had come by automobile, by air, by bus, behind plodding horses, on foot, by train, and in boats on the river. Some carried folding chairs, some toted step-ladders. Small boys by the shrill score on bicycles crowded toward the enclosure. A few trees commanding a view of the grounds bent almost double from the weight of daring spectators.

A day made for racing, and he with a horse bound to win and no jock to ride him, Nicholas Hoyt thought bitterly, as he looked from the Club House porch out upon the laughing, jostling crowd. The panorama throbbed in his blood like the muted beat of oncoming drums; for an instant he forgot his problem.

It was a stirring show, a show with

time-honored embellishments, with a glittering present and a glamorous past close behind it. Through it ran the tradition of years. It was a show in which business and barter, art and science, good and bad, beauty and the beast, waxing careers and waning careers, professional racing folk, confidential touts, trainers and stable owners, smartly dressed bookmakers with their no less smartly dressed womankind, touched elbows. A group of blind veterans with their interpreter were being guided to their seats; a few crippled ex-service men were being carried.

The grandstand habitués were pouring in, already the seats were filling. The front row boxes were filled with leaders in society, business and public life. A roar of applause greeted the arrival of a heavyweight boxing champion. In the brilliant September sunshine, women in the latest, swankest fashions, women in costumes of pre-depression vintage in reds, greens, blues, purples, blacks, and browns shifted and shimmered into a gay kaleidoscope of color on the green lawns about the brown oval of the perfectly groomed track. Already dense tiers of spectators lined the rails; the huge parking area was black with cars. On the back stretch the stand for the accommodation of stable hands and their friends was filled. The enclosure rustled with exciting sounds: music drifting from the band, an automobile horn sounding for right of way, voices broadcast by amplifiers, hawkers shouting, flags flapping, the musical fanfare of a four-in-hand horn, the jingle of a silver harness. A gorgeous spectacle!

Nicholas clenched his fists in his pockets. The time before the race was shortening, and no Sharp. He had been so sure that he would appear that he had made no attempt to secure another jockey to ride Fortune. Even if the man had been sobering up after a drinking bout, be would be better on the black horse than a stranger.

"Hi, Nick!"

He wheeled in answer to Jed Langdon's hoarse whisper.

"Found Sharp?"

"No."

Langdon's face was colorless; his eyes looked as if they had been rubbed into their sockets with a dirty finger; the knuckles of the hand which gripped the strap of his binoculars were white. Nicholas spoke to Curtis Newsome who was with him.

"Heard what happened, Curt? Isn't it the limit? Instead of shadowing Rousseau, Jed was out with me all night trying to round up that jock. We found his suitcase with his silks hidden in the shrubs here. Didn't dare call in the police; a mere rumor of his disappearance would play heck with the odds. We've found out that Rousseau returned to Seven Chimneys in the early morning; apparently he shot for town when he left after dinner. Now, I've got to find some one to ride Fortune. I won't withdraw him. That's what the demon who shanghaied Eddie Sharp is waiting for."

"Let me ride him."

"You, Curt! You've cut out jockeying."

"Not for you, if you'll have me."

Nicholas felt as if the world had stopped, as if all sound had hushed awaiting his answer; he could feel Langdon tense as a fiddle string behind him. Curt Newsome up on Fortune! Even if he were a stranger to the stallion, his superb riding would take him through. A thought gave him pause:

"You'll have to go pro again. No gentlemen jockeys in this race. What will your wife —"

"Say listen, Mr. Nicholas, I ask you, have

I got to ask permission of — of any one? Am I a man or a tame cat? Will you take me or won't you?"

Nicholas flung his arm about the slender shoulders. "Come on! I'll go change the entry."

Langdon relaxed with a sigh of relief. "All set for the shift. I had a session with the stewards. Curt's weight is right to an ounce. They're so hot over the disappearance of your jock that they feel justified in making any concession. Only awaiting your O.K., Nick. Sharp's silks will fit Curt. Hustle and put it through. Somehow a rumor has got around; enthusiasm for Fortune is waning."

Not until he was on his way to the paddock with all arrangements made for Curtis Newsome to ride his entry did Nicholas Hoyt draw a long breath. With Curt up his horse had a chance. He had watched Fortune's exercise gallop under wraps in the morning; the black horse had seemed fit and ready. It wasn't losing the honor or the money he cared so much about, but it was being licked by Rousseau. Rousseau was at the bottom of the disappearance of Sharp he would bet his last dollar. Anger hurled into his thoughts solution after solution of the mystery of the jockey's disappearance only to have reason kick them out. He would pin the guilt on Rousseau, and then Sandra . . .

Sandra! He plunged his hands back into his pockets. Even with his anxiety about the missing jockey it had taken all his mental control to keep the information Huckins had volunteered in the back of his mind. He had been cross-examining the butler. In answering questions as to his activities, the man had said that he had seen Mr. Rousseau and Miss Duval going up the stairs at Seven Chimneys in the early morning. The girl had been whispering. She must have come from the ball some time before, she wasn't in evening dress, she had been in blue velvet pyjamas. Questioned as to how he knew that, he had answered that as she had opened the door, light had shone upon her. Huckins had explained that he had come home a few minutes earlier and, as was his custom when he came in, had gone over the lower part of the house.

Sandra and Rousseau! He couldn't believe it. Didn't the girl's instinct warn her that even if the man were Mark Hoyt's son, he was a bad egg? She would be in Mrs. Pat's box this afternoon. After the great race, no matter what the outcome, he would . . .

A professional racing man, in checkered suit and brilliant tie, white topper, and matching spats, caught him by the elbow.

"Hi, Hoyt! Meet the girl friend. Hoyt owns Fortune, one of the best fancied in the field, next to Iron Man — Five Up comes third in the betting, Remote Control fourth," he explained to the highly perfumed, sloe-eyed, diamond besprinkled woman with him. "Say, I hear that because the Thoroughbreds failed to round into form, scratches have cut the original entrants to a field of six. What do you know about it?"

"Nothing. Sorry, got to break away."

Nicholas escaped into the milling crowd. Men slapped him on the back; neighbors tried to buttonhole him; his tailor begged for a tip; the head waiter at one of his town clubs eyed him wistfully. He pushed his way through the infield, crowded with the men and women who had come to see the horses as much as the show, jockeys, breeders, stall-walking trainers shaking hands, stablemen and plutocrats exchanging tips and studying the form sheets. Photographers were jumping around like grasshoppers; men were putting numbers up on boards; radio announcers, in the midst of crowds bigger than those about the favorites or the sellers' windows, were talking into microphones which broadcast over an extensive hook-up.

He stopped in the paddock to watch the entourage of Iron Man who was carrying most of the money. Trainers and grooms, wearing neckties of orange and black — if they wore ties at all — were busy with bandages, with orange and black blankets, with buckets and bottles painted in Rousseau's colors. A stable boy, trying to look indifferent but succeeding only in appearing about to burst with importance, rode by on a lead pony. The air was heavy with the odor of saddlery and sawdust. Breeders were craning their necks for a glimpse of Iron Man's shoes. The gray stallion might have been cast in metal from flowing mane to billowy tail as he stood gazing into space with unfathomable eyes. Suddenly he stamped a fore foot; ropes of muscles corded into a network on his sleek legs; he rolled his wild eyes as if considering the spot in the front row of eager spectators into which to let a hoof fly with the most devastating effect.

Nicholas ran a practiced eye over him. Curt had said that Donovan had intimated there was something wrong with the gray. The horse looked fit to him. He caught a glimpse of Rousseau in the background. His skin was pasty. It wasn't half so pasty as it would be when the race was over and he was accused of abducting Sharp, Nicholas thought furiously, as he moved on.

Curtis Newsome, in the green and white of Stone House stables, was listening to Parsons' instructions when Nicholas arrived. His face was the color of old ivory; there was a set to the boy's jaw Nicholas never had seen before. The crowd gathered was almost as great as that about Iron Man. The black stallion snorted and glared. He reared, thrashed, and kicked a board loose from the wall.

"Gentle little critter, ain't he?" commented a trainer, and the crowd burst into a nervous guffaw.

"A horse has got to know his stuff on this course, or turn back at the stall gate," a man in the front row of spectators observed to his companion.

"Oh, yeah? So has a jock. I heard that the fella up on this baby's never been on his back before."

"Referrin' to Curt? Say, he don't ride just for exercise. You'll be surprised."

Apparently Newsome heard the comments for he linked his arm in Hoyt's and turned his back on the crowd.

"Don't you worry, Mr. Nicholas, if we seem to get away slowest. It'll take me a second or two to understand Fortune; then watch us say good-bye to the field. Got that paper safe, Jed?"

Langdon patted the breast of his smart coat. "Right here, Curt, but forget about that. Get me?"

Newsome laughed shortly. "I'll forget, all right, after I get started. Did you — did you tell Pat?"

Langdon wheeled to greet Damon who hurried up eager-eyed and breathless.

"Wanted to be sure you were all set before I join Mrs. Pat in her box," he puffed.

Curtis Newsome turned to Nicholas. "I guess Jed told her, all right. He heard me, but he doesn't want me to know what she said. She won't forgive me for riding for you when she's backing Iron Man, but it seemed the only square deal to me. I'll never dare go home if we win."

His twisted grin hurt Nicholas. "Curt, it isn't too late —"

"Too late! It's a year too late."

A stable-boy in orange and black sweater thrust a note into Newsome's hand and vanished. The jockey looked up at Nicholas with haggard eyes before he untwisted it.

"Pat's telling me where I get off, I guess."

His already white face went livid as he read the written words. He thrust the paper into Nicholas' hand.

"That was all I needed." His reckless blue eyes flamed as he brought his whip up in salute.

"To — the ladies! They get me comin' and goin'. God bless 'em!"

The bitter sarcasm of the last sentence was drowned in the call:

"Mount your jockeys!"

Parsons, the trainer led out Fortune.

"Look out that this horse isn't crowded at the start, Curt," he whispered.

The bugle sounded Boots and Saddles.

Curtis Newsome twitched his cap to a cocky angle and mounted. "Good luck to your hoss, Mr. Nicholas. You're a grand fella," he leaned over to whisper.

There was deviltry in Fortune's flashing eyes, deviltry in his thrashing hoof. Nicholas' blood chilled. Would his rider be thrown before the race began? He scowled at the hastily scribbled words on the paper which Curt had forced into his hand:

"If you enter this race as a jockey, it's all over.

E."

"Estelle has done her darndest to help Curt lose the race; why, why can't she let the boy alone?" Nicholas growled, and tore the note to bits.

A hostler in scarlet coat and white breeches led Iron Man at the head of the parade to the post. A cheer rent the air. The three-year-olds following pranced and curveted and snorted, shifting the red, green, orange, blue, purple, white and black of the jockeys' silks into a new pattern with every move. The starter in his stand leaned against the rail, ready to press the electrical contact which would ring a gong to start the field away.

A couple of bad actors, unstrung by the track band, reared and backed and refused to enter the stalls. Fortune caught fire and put on a show. He made a futile attempt to unseat his rider. Curtis Newsome gave him his head while he plunged at assistant starters and terrified stable-boys. The other riders relaxed and waited.

Jed Langdon caught Nicholas' arm. "My eye, what a jock! Get Curt, Nick, get him? That boy's letting Fortune wind up to *n*th pitch, while the others are letting their mounts cool off."

Nicholas nodded. His voice couldn't get through his tight throat. Langdon's fingers bit into his arm. "There he goes! Your hoss has decided to be good. He's in!"

They watched breathlessly as the assistant starters went from horse to horse to make sure that all were ready.

"There goes the tape! The bell!"

Langdon capered with excitement; the crowd in the grandstand and boxes surged to their feet; the jockeys whooped; colors flashed; the field, sleek coats glimmering, plunged forward in the sun. A voice through a microphone shouted:

"They're off!"

Loud speakers, scattered through grandstand, club house, betting ring, and paddock, took up the cry:

"They're off!"

Nicholas raised his binoculars in ice-cold hands. Iron Man was looking good. Five Up, the third choice, was running with head covered; the rangy roan was being smoothly handled. Fortune was lying out behind Remote Control, and then came two others. Corking jockey that he was, would Curt understand the black horse? Nicholas felt his teeth chattering with excitement as the loud speakers boomed:

"They're rounding the first turn, Five Up leading! Iron Man second! Remote Control third! Fortune fourth!"

Curt had told him that he would be slow getting away, Nicholas reassured himself.

"Back stretch, Five Up by two lengths!" the raucous voices shouted. "On the far turn, Five Up tiring! Iron Man going to the front! Remote Control moves up! Fortune moves up! Iron Man leads! Fortune moves up!"

The crowd went crazy, shouted themselves hoarse as they recognized the black horse's jockey.

"That's Newsome!" "That's Newsome!" "It's Curt Newsome!" The words surged about the enclosure in wild acclaim. One shrill boyish voice peaked all others.

"Step on the gas, Curt! Step on the gas!"

Nicholas could hear nothing but the pounding of his heart, the thunder of flashing hoofs, but he could see Fortune. The black was hanging on to Remote Control's heels as the field swung on the turn. He was on the inside! How easily he ran! Great effortless strides. He was coming up! He was coming up! Curt hadn't used the bat once — was he saving his horse for the last rush? He could just see the jockey's livid, grim face bent low over the horse's neck.

Down the back stretch! Was Iron Man gaining? He was! Was Remote Control tiring? Curt was talking to Fortune!

A roar went up from thirty thousand throats.

"Here they come!" "Fortune moving up!" "Fortune passes Remote Control!" The crowd went wild. "Come on, Fortune!" "Come on, Iron Man!" "Fortune and Iron Man neck and neck!"

In a flash of sizzling speed, ears pricked, the black horse stretched out like a frightened rabbit and passed the gray.

"Fortune wins!" "Fortune wins!" chorused the loud speakers.

Thirty thousand deep-throated voices shouted frantic acclaim — thirty thousand voices crumbled into thirty thousand agonized groans, thirty thousand shrieks rent the air.

"What happened? What happened?" Nicholas demanded of the man next to him.

"Didn't you see? Didn't you see! The winner's jock! Pitched over his head! Iron Man trampled him!"

Chapter XXIV

The band swung into "I love a Parade!" Colors waved madly. The crowd cheered itself hoarse. The sun, like a great brazen plaque hung in the cloudless blue sky, blazed down on winner and loser alike. Jockeys, in bright stains, on their way to the scales, rode their quivering, excited mounts by the judges' stand, saluting as they passed. Tears were running down the face of Piggy Pike on Iron Man.

Nicholas Hoyt, leading Fortune, was unaware of the clamor; his thoughts were on Curtis Newsome. What had happened? His anxious inquiry had been evaded, and he had been swept toward his winning horse. Mrs. Pat's box was empty. Something serious must have called her away. She was too good a sport not to wait to see the horse which had defeated her favorite receive his laurels. It was incredible that

Curt, Curt Newsome, the superb rider, had been thrown. Had that detestable note from Estelle shaken his nerve, or had Fortune played a nasty trick on his rider?

Nicholas looked up at the black stallion whose satin smooth neck arched as if he were proudly conscious that the ovation was no more than his due. His ears were pricked; his sleek coat was barely ruffled after his victorious swing around the oval; he pranced a little on the perfect feet below his tapering ankles. As if he were a mind-reader, he turned his head and looked down into his owner's eyes. Nicholas stroked his neck and whispered:

"Forgive me for doubting your sportsmanship, old boy."

The cheers thinned as the crowd noted the empty saddle, then swelled and roared into acclaim. No matter what had happened to the jockey, he had helped win the race. Fortunes of war. The show must go on.

Nicholas broke away from the radio men who were importuning him to speak into the microphone. The gong was sounding for the next event on the card when he entered the Club House. Jed Langdon met him on the threshold and pulled him into a deserted game room.

"How's Curt?"

Langdon gulped and shook his head in answer to Nicholas' anxious query.

"Is he — has he — is he . . ." Horror blocked the last word.

Langdon nodded and with difficulty cleared his throat. "Keep your voice down. The stewards don't want the news to get out yet. They are saying that Fortune's jockey had a nasty smash."

"Why — why did I let him ride!"

"Don't take it so hard, Nick. Curt wanted to ride. He begged me to make you give him the chance. He said that if he could help your horse win he might get his self-respect back. He said, 'Tell him to give me my chance, remind him that he said that a Thoroughbred isn't judged by his winnings, he's rated by the fight he puts up against strong odds.' Did you tell him that?"

Nicholas nodded. He was seeing the white-faced boy facing him in the softly-lighted music room, was hearing his broken voice:

"Good gosh, life is an in-and-out, all right; guess I'm kind of hopelessly lost in it."

"Pull yourself together, Nick. You gave him his chance." Langdon lowered his already low voice. "Curt had me make a will here in the Club House, giving whatever he won to Mrs. Pat. Do you suppose he had a premonition?"

"A premonition!" The eyes of the two men met as Nicholas repeated the words. Through his memory echoed Curtis Newsome's declaration:

"From now on I ride straight — if I find I can't — well . . ."

Nicholas brushed his hand over suddenly blind eyes. Had life and Estelle been too much for the boy to fight?

"Did Pat get to him — in time?" he asked brokenly.

"No. He — he must have gone quick."

Nicholas started for the door. "Come on, Jed! Let's go to her; she'll need us. Where is she?"

"In the trophy room — with — they took him there. B.D. is with her. I left to find you."

"Did Estelle see — the accident?"

Langdon settled his tie with fingers not quite steady. "Yes. She tried to get into the room, but Mrs. Pat seemed to grow a foot as she shut the door in her face. As Curt would say, 'I guess that is that.' Have you seen Rousseau?"

"No."

"Fortune's victory will be a knock-out for him. He had staked his last penny on that horse."

"He won't have to starve long. He will have the Hoyt estate handed him on a gold platter tomorrow."

"Don't say die yet, Nick. Boy — I know that guy is an imposter!"

"So do I. But how can we prove it? Bridie! What are you doing here?"

The woman, who had been darting uncertainly about the hall, ran to Nicholas. Wisps of rusty hair fringed her hot, red face; she gasped for breath.

"Mister Nicholas! Oh, Mister Nick . . ." Her voice broke.

Nicholas put his arm about her and led her to a chair. "Shut the door, Jed." Langdon's eyes met his. They intimated plainly: "If this woman has heard of Curt's passing, the news must be all over the enclosure."

"Sit down, Bridie. Pull yourself together."

"Mister Nicholas . . ."

He patted her shoulder. "Take it easy. Don't try to talk till your breath stops pumping."

"But Mister Nich-olas! I must — she's gone!"

"Who's gone?"

"Miss Sandra! She . . ."

Langdon caught Nicholas' arm. "Don't shake the poor old girl, Nick. She's about all in."

"I know. I'm sorry, Bridie. I went crazy for a minute. Take your time — but talk as fast as you can! Hurry! Hurry! Hurry!"

"I'm tryin', Mister Nicholas. Ye see, I waited in Miss Sandra's room — till she come from — the ball."

"Who came to the door with her?"

"To the door with her! No one, that I knows of, Mister Nicholas. I didn't hear her say good-night to any one. She was tired, that child was, an' I rubbed her pretty feet an' brushed her hair an' —"

"Cut that and get going, Bridie," Jed Langdon interrupted. "Nick's cracking up with anxiety. What makes you think Miss Duval has gone?"

"Because the lamp was lighted — she must have left the room while it was still dark — an' her bed hadn't been slept in an' her dresses is all in the wardrobe. The pink neg-li-gee she was wearin' whin I left her was in a heap as if she'd dropped it suddin-like, only them pretty blue velvet pyjamas she likes was missin', an' — an' this is what frightens me, the empty case her di'mond bracelet was in was on the dressin' table."

Nicholas clamped his teeth to keep back an exclamation. Huckins had seen Sandra and Rousseau at the girl's door, and she was in blue velvet pyjamas — but the Kentuckian wouldn't abduct her for diamonds; he was too near coming into a fortune.

"Where were the dogs?"

"Shut out on the balconies, Mister Nicholas. They were most crazy whin I opened the French window; they wint whinin' an' sniffin' round the room."

"How long since you found this out, Bridie?"

"It was noon. I didn't go to her room till thin 'cause Miss Sandra had told me as how she had her work for today done, she would sleep late. Mrs. Newsome wint to the track early. Whin I knocked at Miss Sandra's door an' she didn't answer, I thought she might of changed her mind an' gone with the family."

"Why didn't you 'phone me?"

"Didn't ye have a horse in the race? Ye had enough on yer mind. I couldn't find any of the upper servants. Mrs. Newsome had let thim all go to the races. I found Emma —"

"Emma! Why go to Emma?"

Jed Langdon's excited question penetrated the fog of apprehension. Bridie looked up with faded, tear-filled eyes.

"Shouldn't I have gone to her, Mister Nicholas? She was in her room packin'up. She said the housekeeper had fired her, said Mrs. Newsome didn't like her round. She looked terrible. These are hard times for them as lose their jobs."

"Had Emma seen Sandra?"

Bridie's heavy-veined hand patted the fingers biting into her shoulder.

"Ye're kind of hurtin', Mister Nicholas." With a muttered apology he thrust his hands into his pockets. "That's better. Whin I told as how I couldn't find a trace of Miss Sandra, she stared at me wild-eyed, an' thin she laughed an' laughed crazy-like till she choked into a kind of cackle. I was that mad I said:

" 'What's so funny about Miss Sandra's bein' missin', Emma?'

"She laughed again — 'twas like a witch croakin'. 'My mistake,' she says, 'Believe me, it's nothin' funny — it's a break! You go along Bridie, I'll hunt for her too.' "

Could a heart burst from racking, agonizing anxiety and suspense, Nicholas demanded of himself? Emma, who had found the letters in the secret drawer, laughing at Sandra's disappearance! What did it mean?

"Listen to Bridie, Nick." Langdon's steady voice recalled him to the present. "She says that no one at Seven Chimneys had seen or heard of Sandra this morning."

"An' I wint to Stone House to ask Nanny O'Day. The child hadn't been there. But I found this."

Nicholas snatched the flashlight she had drawn from her pocket. He turned it over. S.D. Sandra's!

"Where?"

"In the road opposite where the brood mares and the colts are pastured."

"Notice any tire tracks, Bridie?"

"Jed! Jed! Why stand here asking questions? Let's get busy. Come on!"

"Where to?"

"Anywhere out of here, so long as we are moving. We'll make a break for the roadster. If we don't get out before the crowd starts for the gates, we'll never get there. Jed, go to Pat, will you; tell her — tell her that Sandra is missing, that I have gone to find her. Do what I would do for her. Come, Bridie."

With one arm around the little woman, Nicholas elbowed his way through the crowd. People turned to look and turned quickly away. A few banged him sympathetically on the shoulder. He knew by their faces that in spite of the care of the authorities the news of the tragedy had seeped out. That made it easier for him to get away to find Sandra. Where was she?

He swung Bridie into the roadster. In an instant more he was tensely guiding it through the congestion of home-going and on-coming cars. He drew a sharp sigh of relief as he turned into a back road. He smiled reassuringly at the woman beside him.

"We can go faster here, Bridie."

"Try to take it easy, Mister Nicholas. Sure an' we're all of us actin' as though somethin' terrible happened to Miss Sandra. She may jest have decided to go to the city or — or something like that."

"In blue velvet pyjamas? Sorry I snapped, Bridie, but I've been almost out of my mind over the disappearance of Sharp —"

"Eddie Sharp! 'Where's he?"

"He's gone too."

"Gone, has he? Thin who rode Fortune?"

"Mr. Newsome."

"Sure an' what do ye know about that! I wonder was it because he was goin' to ride that his wife —"

"What did his wife do? Quick, Bridie! We've got to know everything that has been said or done if we are to find Sandra."

"There, there, Mister Nicholas, we're goin' to find her, sure." Bridie patted the white knuckled hand on the wheel. "I was lookin' after the new maid — it's the fourth new one in the last month — who was doin' up Mrs. Newsome's bed, whin I heard the mistress in the next room say:

" 'I saw you last night by the fountain, Curt. Sometimes I wish you were a jockey again. It would be worth a fortune to see that snooty girl friend of yours turn you down flat.'

"An' he said, 'Has it ever occurred to you that I might be trusted, Pat?' Then I saw the new girl's ears were standin' out straight listenin' an' I shut the door between the rooms, quick."

Half of Nicholas' attention was on what the woman was saying, half of his mind was suggesting and rejecting possibilities. Sandra's pocket flash had been found on the back road to Stone House. Didn't that indicate that she had been on her way there when she had dropped it? Had she been coming to him? If so, at what time? It must have been after eleven this morning or she would have seen Nanny O'Day. At that hour the housekeeper and the maids were to leave for the track, taking a picnic lunch — Charity Race Day was the supreme holiday in the county, it ranked every other — but it couldn't have been after eleven; hadn't Bridie said that she had found the lamp lighted in the boudoir? Bond and a couple of swipes were on duty at the stables. Would Sandra appeal to them if she could not get into the house?

"We can't do much for Miss Sandra if we get smashed to jelly or jailed for speedin'," reminded Bridie practically.

Nicholas reduced speed. "I'm sorry. Did I frighten you?"

The faded eyes gazed back at him adoringly. "Jest fer a minute ye did, an' thin I said to meself, 'He ain't takin' any chances till he finds Miss Sandra,' but I thought I'd remind ye of how fast you was going, jest the same."

"You bet I'm not taking chances, Bridie."

The glimpse of the stone and clapboard house at the end of the tree-bordered drive as the roadster swung between the iron gates at Seven Chimneys reminded Nicholas of the day he had brought Sandra from the station. Little he had thought then that the girl would come to mean all the world and a little bit of heaven to him. He should have known from the tingle in his veins when she had held out the bill crumpled in her hand and had said:

"Please take this for smokes or talkies."

From that moment she had been in his heart, and now — he snapped out of his torturing reflections as he stopped at the front door. He swung Bridie to the step.

"Hustle up to Miss Sandra's room, Bridie; she may have come back. I'll go over the lower floor. After that we'll beat it to Stone House."

A hush brooded over the hall as he entered, an ominous hush, as if already the long, dark shadow of death was stealing across the threshold. His footsteps on the tiled floor gave back a ghostly echo. He glanced into the library lighted only by the glow above the M.F.H.; a half completed puzzle was spread on the small table. He swept the pieces into their box and dropped it into a drawer of the desk. No need for Pat to be hurt by that when she came back.

The still living room seemed to be holding its breath, seemed to be listening for a footstep. Sunshine was streaming in through the studio window; it turned each blossom on the mimosa trees to gold; lingered, as if tenderly, on the worn violin case on the piano.

Nicholas' throat contracted. It seemed incredible that Curt never would enter this room again, never would — what was that sound? The tinkle of silver on china? Men's voices? The high tea! Had no one told them?

The dining room was fragrant with white flowers in silver bowls; great candelabra held tall pale yellow tapers ready for lighting; the refectory table with its scarf of rare lace was laden with piles of plates, platoons of cups and saucers, salvers of sandwiches and cakes, ornate dishes of nuts and candies. Silver chafing dishes, two or three of which already were sending forth delectable aromas, were in line on the buffet. Nicholas followed the sound of voices to the pantry.

The caterer listened in shocked silence as he told him that there would be no tea, and why; with a low command to his startled men, silently the boss began to fold his tents.

What next, Nicholas asked himself, as he returned to the hall. Here was Huckins — surely Huckins would know —

"Mister Nicholas!"

Nicholas charged up the stairs to meet Bridie who was half way down. She was wringing her hands; her eyes were popping with excitement. He clutched her shoulder.

"What is it?"

"Come quick! Come quick! Softly! Softly! I don't know how to tell ye!"

Chapter XXV

In the hall at Stone House Sandra clutched Sharp's arm. "Look! Look! The knob moved!" she repeated in a husky whisper.

"Perhaps it isn't a person, Miss, perhaps it's the wind," encouraged the jockey under his breath. "Go back, I'll find out. No one will get past me. I'm all set to give some one the works. I don't care much who."

Sandra barely breathed as she listened behind the hanging. She glanced at the opening between the bookshelves. Could she escape if necessary through the frame? That letter would be snatched only from her dead body! Sharp had turned the knob! He . . . had he let in a whirlwind?

"Bud! Buddy! Were you looking for Sandy?"

She dropped to her knees and flung her arms about the dogs who frantically licked her face and hair.

"Sweet things! They must have been nosing that knob! It wasn't . . . I forgot! We must get away from here. You can drop me at Seven Chimneys on your way to the track, Sharp. Hurry!"

"I'll be at the side door with my own car, Miss."

"Hurry! Hurry!"

Sandra paced the hall with the dogs at her heels. No wonder the commotion she and the jockey had made had been unheard. Everyone was at the races. The side door probably locked when it closed.

The clock again! Fifteen more minutes gone. Would the big race be held up to wait for the missing jockey? Doubtless that question showed her ignorance of the methods of the turf. Wheels on the gravel!

The dogs bounded after her as she ran to the car.

"We've got to take them, Sharp. I may need them terribly. Who won the race?"

"Shove the dogs in back. Scram, fellas! All set? No one saw me take out the car. The boys were in my room listening to the broadcast. I didn't want to hear who won. The big race came off, all right. They wouldn't wait for me. I'll bet Mr. Nicholas is cussing me for a dirty double-crosser."

One great tear rolled down his check.

"Hurry, Sharp! I went to Stone House to help him. Every second lessens my chance. The man who kidnaped you may be on my trail. Don't worry. Mr. Nicholas will understand when you explain."

"What can I explain, Miss, except that some one who said he was Mr. Langdon 'phoned me in a soft voice to meet my boss at the Hunt Club an' I went? I'll be picked for the All-American dumbbell team, sure. I had just sense enough to give one of the two men who seized my arms a fierce kick on the shin — I'll bet he's limping — then I didn't know anything more till I came to in what you said was the underground passage. Will Mr. Nicholas believe that yarn?"

"Of course he will. You never have failed him before, have you?"

"Never, Miss."

Walls, fields, fences flew by. Sandra's hair blew about her face. She breathed deeply. Glorious air! It had the lift and tangy buoyancy of mid-September. She turned to look at the dogs who were sitting upright on the back seat. Their sensitive noses sniffed the wind which ruffed their tawny coats. Their brown eyes met hers and shifted.

The remembrance of her immediate

problem wiped out the smile their dignity had brought to her lips. What would she do first when she reached home? Hide the envelope in her room, of course; then she would drop a pound or two of bath crystals into the tub and . . . The high tea! She had forgotten that. She must be in the living room before the first guest arrived. Could she make it?

At the side door of Seven Chimneys she jumped from the car; the dogs leaped after her.

"Don't worry, Sharp. Even if you didn't ride him, something tells me that Fortune won." She flung the scrap of comfort over her shoulder.

The house seemed deserted except for voices in the kitchen end. She tiptoed in. Stealthily she reached her boudoir door. It was ajar. She withdrew her outstretched hand as if the knob were red-hot. Voices! Whose? She gripped the collars of the dogs. Knelt. Applied her ear to the crack.

"You didn't lose time getting away from the track, did you? Must have burned up the road. I know. I know who won. Bridie's gone crazy because the Duval girl hasn't showed up. I told her I'd wait here so that if she came I could let her know. Perhaps you can tell where she is?"

Emma, the waitress, talking. Talking? Sounded more as if she were setting her teeth in some one. In whom? Sandra strained her ears to the cracking point, but she could hear a murmur only.

"Speak up! Don't mumble!" the woman's bitter voice prodded. "There's no one in the house to hear. You've begun to drink again, haven't you? Just when you need a clear head. Oh, you won't show it, you never do, but you're not a safe person when you drink. Why couldn't you wait till . . ."

The voice thinned to a whisper. Sandra's hands were ice-cold. Emma and Huckins! Hadn't Mrs. Pat suspected that he drank? Time some one stopped their little game. She banged open the door with her foot. Gripping the dog's collars, she demanded:

"What are you do . . ."

Surprise choked her voice. Emma's eyes were steel points of hate; beside her stood Philippe!

"Well, see who's here!"

Rousseau's face was drawn and haggard, but his greeting was a jaunty imitation of hers in the library not so many hours before. Sandra blinked as if to clear her eyes. Philippe and Emma again!

"What are you two doing in my room?"

At her sharp question, the dogs, who had been motionless, took purposeful steps forward. She tightened her hold on them, jerked them back on their haunches.

Rousseau laughed. "What are you doing in those pyjamas at this hour? Don't tell me that you didn't get to the races. I wasn't in Mrs. Pat's box, so I didn't know that you weren't there."

"Never mind where I have been. You'd better sit down, both of you." Could that be her voice, cold and steady, when her legs were folding at the knees like a jack-knife? "You may be here quite a long time."

The maid dropped to the bench. Her cheek bones were splashed with red, her eyes were sparks, her fingers tense. She is loaded with TNT, Sandra thought. It looked as if the rough touch wouldn't be lacking to set her off with a bang right here. Rousseau remained standing. He twisted the end of his small mustache with his long fingers. His dark eyes were tinged with wistful melancholy.

"What a flair you have for dramatization. Perhaps it looks —"

"It looks like a hook-up to me," Sandra interrupted crisply with a fleeting glance at the maid.

"But — dearest . . ." The last word brought Emma's head up as if galvanized.

"Don't dare call me that again, Philippe!"

Not until the color flowed hotly into his face did Sandra realize how white Rousseau had been.

"What has happened since we parted at daybreak?" he reproached. "Oh, I forgot," he cast a meaning glance at the maid, "we have an audience. Emma, you may go."

"Sit down, Emma!"

Sandra's command cracked like the whip of a ringmaster. "Better sit down yourself, Philippe. You'll both stay here until some one comes from the races."

"Will we?"

His hand slid into his coat pocket. Sandra's pulses stilled. Had she the right to hold the two here merely because she felt that they were conniving against Nick? Emma had accused Philippe of drinking! Hadn't she said that he was not a safe person? He had had a gun this morning. Suppose he had? The prospective heir of the Hoyt fortune wasn't shooting himself into the headlines yet, drunk or sober. Perhaps the flesh and blood Philippe wasn't looking at her with a slight sneer, perhaps this was another dream. Perhaps she was still behind the panel, might reason herself out of this nightmare. She shut her eyes tight, opened them.

It was not a dream. The cool green walls touched with silver were real; so were the turquoise taffeta hangings, the crystal and silver laden *poudreuse;* the apricot cushions, the tick of the clock were real. Thank heaven, time was passing! She would keep the man and woman here until she heard a stir in the house; then she would let them go and follow them. Suppose they snatched the precious letter? But they didn't know about it. The dogs knew something was wrong; the collars she was clutching registered every nervous twitch of their lithe bodies.

"Sit down, Sandra, if we are to make an afternoon of it," Philippe Rousseau suggested sarcastically. "Why you have elected yourself a committee of one to hold me here only you know. Why should I care for the reason so long as I can look at your lovely self? If you will play sentry in front of that door, let me get you a chair. First, though, put those dogs wise to the fact that I'm your friend."

"Friend!"

"Why the scorn? What have I done to *you* that you speak like that?"

His hurt amazement was not fabricated. He had reason to reproach her. She had liked him and had shown that she had. But, day by day, in spite of her knowledge of the letters which should prove his claim, her liking for him had trickled away. Philippe and Emma together here! It took a crisis to clarify a situation one had not understood. It was like lightning picking out and showing up streaks of human nature which had been unnoticeable before the tearing, revealing flash.

"Don't bother about a chair for me." Sandra pulled the growling dogs back with her as she perched on the edge of a chair near the door. Pity she didn't smoke — a cigarette might help her to appear nonchalant. She didn't care for the hand in Philippe's pocket. Was she afraid of the man she had liked?

"Why did you come here?" she questioned more in disappointment than in anger.

"I like that tone better." His eyes narrowed. "I came back from the track — because my horse was beaten and —"

"Iron Man lost! I'm sorry, Philippe!"

"Sorry! Oh no, you're not! I came here the minute the race was over because this woman had told me that Nick Hoyt has letters which prove my claim. You know it, she says. Have known it for days!"

How had Emma discovered the contents of those letters? She had read them, of course, before she took them to Stone House. They were both unsealed. What should she say? Oh, if only Nick would come! The maid started for the door.

"Sit down, Emma!"

"I — I — heard some one outside, Miss. Some one's listening. I'll lose my place if Mrs. Newsome thinks I'm helping you get a man into your room."

"Emma!"

Was that livid-faced girl in the mirror herself, Sandra wondered.

"Isn't she right, dearest?"

"If you call me that again, Philippe — I — I — Come in! Come in!" Sandra called frantically in answer to an authoritative tap at the door.

"Stay out!" Rousseau warned. "Unless you —"

"Sstt! At him, boys!"

The dogs sprang at Rousseau's sleeves before he could bring his hand from his pocket. The door was flung open by Nicholas Hoyt.

His eyes burned into Sandra's soul — it seemed to her as if there were two men standing straight and tall on the threshold — before they flickered over the maid and fastened on the man by the window.

"What are you doing here, Rousseau? This house isn't yours yet. There are some rooms you can't enter. Call off the dogs, Sandra."

"Don't call them off, Nick! Don't! Philippe has a gun!"

"Drop him! Come here!"

Bud and Buddy gazed at Nicholas Hoyt with unwinking red eyes as if questioning his meaning.

"Come here!"

They backed away from Rousseau, their fangs gleaming, savage growls rumbling in their throats. Sandra caught their collars. The man they had released took a step forward.

"Stay where you are! What are you doing in Miss Duval's room?" Hoyt persisted.

Rousseau twisted his mustache. "I might ask you that question. If she doesn't object, why should you?"

"Philippe!"

He ignored Sandra's angry protest. His eyes burned. A nerve at one corner of his mouth twitched incessantly.

"I'll tell you why I'm here, Hoyt. You've beaten me on the track, you have been prejudicing my girl against me, but I'll turn you out of Stone House tomorrow. For over two weeks you've held letters which proved my claim."

Nicholas Hoyt's eyes widened. "How do you know what is in those letters?"

"You acknowledge you have them! How do I know? I've seen this woman Emma sneaking round whispering to the butler. She found two letters in my father's, Mark Hoyt's, desk. Took them to you, didn't she? I've put the screws on her, and —"

Emma's face contorted with rage. "Screws! Screws!" she hissed. "Think I'll stand for that? You're crazy! Screws! Who sent me to this house? Think I'm so dumb that I'll let you walk off with fortune and this girl — *Slick Fingers?* You . . ."

The TNT had gone off! Blinding. Stunning — for a second only. Rousseau sprang. The woman choked on a shrill note. Nicholas caught his hands from her throat and twisted them back. He gripped his wrists.

"Call for help, Sandra! Quick!"

Emma flung herself against the door. "You'll call no one! Let him go! If you don't . . ."

She jerked open the door. Screamed. Huckins faced her, Huckins, smiling his furtive, secretive smile.

Sandra set her teeth sharply in her lips to keep back a gasp of terror. One more against Nick! She gripped the collars of the dogs. This time when she let them go they would do their work. Silence. Tense. Vibrant. Rousseau sneered at the maid and the butler.

"'What did I tell you? He didn't expect to find us here. He's come to divide the jack you paid the woman for those letters, Hoyt."

"Yeah!" Huckins pushed aside Emma who was staring at him with big, terrified eyes. He closed the door and leaned against it. "Come to divide the jack for those letters, have I? You've got me wrong, Rousseau. I've come to tell Mr. Hoyt that I saw your girl friend here plant those letters."

Nicholas' face was colorless. "Take Rousseau's gun!" As the butler deftly removed an automatic and slipped it into his own pocket, he released the Kentuckian's wrists. "Now, explain about those letters, Huckins."

"I saw the woman put them in the secret drawer. I've waited for other facts before telling you, but . . ."

Rousseau's laugh was ugly. "Good, but not good enough. You can't put it across,

Cousin Nicholas. That man is in your pay. I've suspected it. Of course he would lie about those letters. Didn't intend to produce them, did you? Perhaps you've disposed of them already. As for this woman being my girl friend! It's a frame-up! Never saw her before she came to Seven Chimneys. Will the Court take her word against mine — I ask you! It's part of your game to have her lie —"

"Lie! Lie!" Emma's repetition shook with fury. "Is that the thanks I get for turning myself into a housemaid? A housemaid! Me! Lie! 'The girl you're going to marry!' *'Dearest!'* You've called Sandra Duval that for the last time! You've been crazy with the idea of this fortune! You've cast off one after another of your friends and now — me! You'll have to pay for that! Things don't come so easy. Go to court tomorrow —"

"Wait! Wait!" Sandra interrupted frantically. For the first time since Nicholas Hoyt entered her room she thought of the letter under her jacket. The pin stabbed viciously at her shaking fingers as she loosened it.

"I found this, Nick . . ."

He caught the mauve envelope from her hand.

"A registered letter from Kentucky! The return address A. P. Rousseau! He looked up at the man intently watching him. Another of your plants, 'Slick Fingers'?"

Sandra caught his arm. No! No! I found it in your uncle's book, THOROUGHBREDS. See, he has written on it, 'Nick must see this at once.' He must have received it the very day he died."

As he read, Nicholas Hoyt's face darkened. His lips twitched. He nodded toward Rousseau.

"Hold on to him, Huckins."

Rousseau tried to shake off the hand on his arm. "What's the big idea, Hoyt? Staging a melodrama? Got a movie camera concealed about your person?"

"No, only a letter to read to you, *Philippe Rousseau.* If he so much as stirs, Huckins, take him out and lock him up. This letter was written by Anne Pardoe Rousseau. From the date on the envelope, Mark Hoyt must have received it shortly before he died."

Was Nicholas waiting to get his unsteady voice in hand? Sandra looked at Philippe. She never had seen a face so white; he was staring at the floor. The eyes of Emma, the waitress, were dilated; Huckins' lips were parted as if in suspense; the dogs kept tense, red-eyed vigil. Would Nick never speak?

The sheet of paper he held quivered. He gripped it with both hands and read:

" 'Dear Mr. Hoyt:

" 'My doctor has told me that I may go at any moment. I don't care. Life lived in a fog of remorse that one has been a coward, has run away, doesn't mean much, but God won't take me until I have written the truth to you.

" 'Little Philip did die! I swear it. I have reason to think that after I am gone my son, Philippe, will try to prove that he is your son. Never mind how I know it. The scars of burn on his shoulders are a coincidence; he looks something as your boy might had he lived — how could he help it when for years your Philip's face was in my mind?

" 'My Philippe has a fatal gift with his fingers — I won't use an uglier word. He has forged my name to get money — only mine, I am sure. It is unnatural for a mother to testify against the son she loves, but I owe you the warning.

" 'Philippe may never try it, perhaps I

am misjudging him — I pray every night that I may be — but —' "

"That's enough!" Rousseau slashed into the sentence. Nicholas held up a paper. "Your *mother* enclosed your birth certificate from the South American city where you were born."

"Didn't I say I'd had enough? I know when I'm licked. It's just my luck! Well, it was a good try — if that woman hadn't squealed . . ."

Emma defiantly met his glare, but her body shook as with a chill.

"What are you going to do about it, *Cousin* Nick? Send me to the hoosgow?" Rousseau demanded cockily. His hunted eyes betrayed his bravado.

Nicholas Hoyt's face whitened. His gray eyes were black. His voice was bleak.

"Not for trying to steal the estate, but the turf authorities will take care of you for stealing my jockey."

"For what?" Huckins jerked Rousseau back as he plunged forward. "What do you mean? That I would pull anything crooked about a race! Why you —"

"Mr. Nicholas! Mr. Nicholas!"

Nicholas pulled open the door in response to the frantic call. Bridie caught his sleeve. Her eyes were red, her voice was choked with sobs.

"Oh, Mister Nicholas! Come down! Quick! Ain't it terrible! Mrs. Newsome wants ye!"

Chapter XXVI

"Excuse me, Miss Duval, for interrupting. When I saw your rose-color dress from the hall, suddenly I felt that I couldn't leave without explaining one or two things to you. I've only stayed on this week to help if I could."

Sandra looked up from the pile of music she was sorting on the piano in the living room. Huckins stood on the threshold, very straight, very spruce, impeccably appareled for the street. His mouth was firm and honest, his skin had lost its tell-tale redness. Had the color been make-up for his part? She smiled.

"You were good, Huckins. By the way, is that your name?"

"Not so good as you were. Never mind my name. When I saw you coming out of the projector room, I didn't know for whom you were working. I knew that

Langdon had planned the phantom scheme; that Mr. Hoyt had told him to lay off because the wrong person had been frightened. When Rousseau almost went to pieces at dinner and threatened to block the underground passage, I started it up that night on my own responsibility. I scared the life out of him."

"You reduced me to pulp with your mysterious warning that afternoon in the library after I had discovered the projector."

"Sorry. Was sure you liked Rousseau —"

"I did like him."

"He has his points, he's a good horseman, but he's pretty dumb. A man faking a long-lost son shouldn't bring his sweetheart along on the job. She's sure to gum the game."

Sandra regarded him with interest. "I've never met a secret service man before. It must be a thrilling profession."

"It is, Miss Duval, if you stick to sleuthing. I wasn't so good as a butler. The way you found that letter! You're not so bad a detective yourself."

"That was pure accident — was it, I wonder. The gods provide the thread when the web starts to unravel. That's my own version of the adage. I recommend the correct one for your coat-of-arms, Mr. — Huckins. 'The gods provide the thread when the web is started.' I suppose you knew that Emma was a — a confederate?"

"Yes. I suspected it the day she arrived. Something in her make-up. I slipped up on Sharp. I had tried to be fratty with him for his own safety, offered him a drink to test him. I 'phoned him about fifteen minutes before he was shanghaied to make sure he was at the stables. Felt sure he was safe. I should have stuck by him. I'll be pleased purple to take you on as assistant any time you're looking for a job, Miss Duval."

"Thank you. Good-bye and good luck, Mr. Huckins; I won't forget your offer."

Sandra listened to the diminishing sound of his footsteps; his tread wasn't so catlike now. A week had passed since Race Day, a tragic week. It seemed as if she could still smell the funeral flowers. They had come by the truckload, mostly in designs of horseshoes, saddles, trophies, jockey caps; they had crowded the lower floor. She shook off the memory.

Philippe Rousseau had left Seven Chimneys a few hours after his deception had been discovered. Had Nick let him off without punishment? He had come to her to say good-bye. She had wanted to tell him that she had liked him, that it had hurt when she had found that he was just a common imposter, but he had been so full of self-pity, of hatred of Nicholas Hoyt, of fury that he had been suspected of "pulling a dirty trick" in the turf world, that she had merely stood looking at him in amazement at his sense of values. To him impersonating a dead boy was an adventure, kidnaping a jockey was a crime.

He had taken punctiliously polite, if slightly theatrical, leave of her. He had not told her that he loved her. Was Emma responsible for that omission? In the moment of parting she had liked him again; it was as if she had a sudden understanding of his weakness, his worse than fatherless boyhood, his wild youth.

How much had happened since she had first entered this room not so many weeks ago! It looked exactly as it had then. The studio window framed by the gold of mimosa trees. Choice furniture. Touches of luscious orange-pink in the rug. Little licking flames reflected in the ebony and silver tea service. She restlessly crossed to the window. Shriveled blossoms in the garden. Great scarlet medicine balls on the breeze-ruffled surface of the azure-lined pool. A cold autumn sky. Wind in the clouds. White frills on the river.

Her eyes rested on the worn violin case on the piano. She had liked Curtis Newsome; he had been a real person. Her lashes were wet as Jed Langdon entered the room.

"Why the tears, Sandra? The rightful heir is in the saddle, yo ho! And the Peerless Pretender is trekking south."

"I had been thinking of the changes here. Have you found out who kidnaped Eddie Sharp?"

"I still think Philippe Rousseau was back of it."

"He was so furiously angry when he was accused that I can't believe he was acting."

"I know, there never has been a breath against him on the turf — but he needed money. Being a rightful heir is expensive. Well, that fight is all washed up now. We didn't rely wholly on Anne Pardoe's last letter; Nick insisted that the experts should pass on the diary. They went at it with their magic microscopes, proved by the handwriting, by the watermark, which was of a much later date than the paper on which the rest of the journal was written, that the pages which contained her alleged confession were forged. The letters that

Emma person planted in the secret drawer were forgeries too. Boy, Rousseau had the nerve to try to put that stuff across these days!"

"I haven't recovered yet from the discovery that Huckins, whom I suspected was a racketeer on location, was really a plain-clothes man."

"And Nick hired him on the job! I didn't know it. B.D. didn't know it. I was red-hot when I found he had held out on his attorney, but he was right when he insisted that every person who shares a secret makes it so much less a secret. Huckins — to use his alias — had been employed by Mark Hoyt years before to follow up Raoul Rousseau. When Philippe set out to claim the estate, Nick sent for him, got him the job here. Luckily I'm a better lawyer — I hope — than a sleuth. The real heir is a great boy. And don't people know it! I've been staying at Stone House this week. I've been on the jump answering the 'phone, congratulations and invitations for Nick, slews of them."

"All from ladies."

He looked at her quickly. "What has Nick done to you, Sandra?"

"Nothing. I — I just am not interested in him."

Peter denying his Master. Why should that irrelevant thought flit through her mind? She had to be flippant to keep from being bitter. A week had passed since she had found the letter for Nicholas Hoyt, and he had not tried to see her once. Had he been so busy answering 'phone calls that he couldn't come, or was he afraid that she had taken his invitation to drive to the ball — immediately withdrawn — his offer of the diamond and emerald clip to mean something which it didn't?"

She had an instant's temptation to unload her heart of its ache. Jed was sympathetic. Would he understand? She shut her teeth into her lip. Selfish! Wouldn't Jimmy Duval say:

"It should be spare ye one another burdens, instead of 'Share ye,' Sandy."

She said hurriedly, as if she feared that her thought might flash across space to him:

"Do you know that Mrs. Pat is leaving here?"

"Leaving! Why? What becomes of you?"

"Out of a job. I'll strike my tents, be once more on the march. That's been said before, but it's still good. I'm off on the next train for town, with an offer from our late butler to be his first assistant, an extra month's salary in my pocket, and a new beret on my head."

"That-a-girl! The sparkle's back in your voice. If only Nick weren't ahead of me . . . Here he is! Nicholas Hoyt in person! I'll be seeing you in town, Sandra." He raised her hand to his lips in Philippe Rousseau's most ardent manner. With a sigh which shook him from head to foot, he vanished into the library. Sandra's eyes shone with laughter. Jed was a dear. She glanced at Nicholas Hoyt in the doorway. Did he see the humor of his imitation? Evidently not. Even his lips were colorless as he asserted:

"So Langdon's in love with you too?"

In spite of the band which seemed tightening about her heart, Sandra retorted lightly:

"Now that Philippe has gone, it would be wonderful to have some one like me."

"Like you! Why shut me out?"

"You!" All the heartache, the strain, the disappointment of this last week, when she had hoped and longed for him to come to her, surged in her voice. "You have not been interested enough to ask where I found that precious letter! When I think of the way I raced to Stone House, sneaked behind the panel — I — I might have died there! A lot you would have cared so long as you had your fortune. You let me tear myself to pieces —"

"You're tearing me to pieces." He caught her and kissed her roughly on the mouth. Sandra . . ."

She twisted free. "How — how . . ." Her laugh tightened his lips, darkened his eyes. "I almost said 'dare.' Good old melodrama. Do you know, if I *had* to have one of you kiss me, I would much prefer Philippe. He may have had his faults, but at least he knew how to make a girl like him."

She caught the back of a chair to steady her trembling body. His kiss had shaken her very soul. How could she have flared at him like that? Why ask? Hadn't the sight of Estelle snuggling against him loosed a primitive self she had not known was in her? Estelle. She seemed a mere shade back in the dark ages.

The man looking down at her was not the friendly Nicholas Hoyt of the last two weeks; he was the trainer with the inflexible mouth, burning eyes, voice which pelted like icy hail.

"And you think I don't know how to make a girl like me? In case you care . . ."

"Oh, here you are, Nick. Sorry to keep you waiting." Mrs. Newsome spoke from the threshold. Her deep mourning accentuated the grayness of her face, the tragedy in her eyes. "Don't go, Sandra. Close the door, Nick — the doors to the library too. This house has a hundred ears and a million eyes. The servants don't like me any better than they ever did."

"If this is a family conference, please excuse me, Mrs, Pat. I don't belong here."

"Nick may have views as to that. I want you to hear what I have to say, Sandra."

Nicholas drew forward the wing chair. "Sit down, Pat. You are shaking. Take your time. Remember, there is nothing you need tell me unless it will make you happier to get it off your mind."

"Happier! What's happiness? You think you have it and it's gone. Life is brutally cruel."

From behind her chair Nicholas Hoyt laid a tender hand on her shoulder. Was he standing there that he might not see the anguish of her face? It twisted Sandra's heart unbearably.

"Life itself isn't cruel, Pat." No ice in his voice now; it was protectingly gentle. "There are cruel hours, perhaps days, sometimes months, but there are radiant spots in between — otherwise we couldn't bear it. Go on, let's get this over."

Mrs. Newsome clenched her large,

capable hands on her knees. She stared at the fire. "I told you, Nick, that I was leaving Seven Chimneys."

"But you are coming back. This is your home."

"Never!" She sprang to her feet as if inaction were unendurable. "I'm never coming back. This house is a nettle scraping my raw heart. I suffered the tortures of the damned here — seeing Curt — getting to — to — hate me. Don't stop me, Nick! I've got to talk! I can't live with this thing on my mind! I had Sharp kidnaped the night before the race."

"Mrs. Pat!" The horrified exclamation escaped Sandra's lips before she knew she had spoken. Mrs. Pat had worked with Philippe? Incredible!

"Swear at me, Nick, it will ease my mind. Do you know why I did it? To force Curt to ride for you. Hadn't Estelle said she had no use for a professional jockey? I thought if he rode she would turn him down. He was always crazy about you and I counted upon his helping you. I fooled myself into thinking that the results of the race would be the same with either Sharp or Curt up, that the public betting on the horses would not be cheated. The rider in this case didn't make any difference — say that you think it didn't, Nick!"

"I am sure it didn't, Pat. Fortune would have won in either case."

"That makes it easier. I'll tell you how it was done."

"Don't! I know."

"You know! How?"

"Mac Donovan has been limping since Race Day. Sharp kicked the man who kidnaped him. The Donovans did a good job with their falsetto voices, fake mustaches, and slouch hats — but — they should have tied the jock's feet first. They are new at the racketeer business. Huckins found out. He was my man."

"I thought he was a rotten butler." Mrs. Newsome's voice was more normal than Sandra had heard it since the tragedy of the race track. "I've been almost out of my mind with regret, thinking how Curt would despise me if he knew."

She brushed her hand across her eyes. "I'm through with horses forever. The stables, everything at Seven Chimneys go back to you, Nick. Mac and Sam Donovan will stay until you get their successors. Don't be too hard on them. They — they tried to help me."

"I'll be glad to keep them, Pat."

"I'm sorry I took Rousseau in. I started

something when I let him come. Everything broke into pieces like one of Curt's puzzles, and now — now the scraps have been put together in a different picture. It was giving you a mean break, Nick, but — well, I wanted to hurt you. That's over too. Old Damon told me that you sent Rousseau off with a cheque big enough to pay his lawyer's bill and to make a fresh start. Why did you help the fake heir?"

"I owed him that for accusing him of having shanghaied Sharp."

"You needn't go so red, Nick. Any one, who knows you, knows you'd do a thing like that. I'm leaving tonight. Decided this morning. What would a lone woman in the fattening forties do with this big house? Think I'll spend my income running it, and the rest of my life fighting with servants? Not a chance! Bridie will pack my things and send them after me. I can't stand this place and its memories another day!"

She gripped Nicholas Hoyt's arm. "Nick — Nick — Curt's fall was an accident, wasn't it?"

"Sure, Pat. Something — something broke and — and he pitched over Fortune's head."

Mrs. Newsome's drooping mouth trembled; tragic skepticism hardened her eyes. She shrugged her heavy shoulders.

"Something broke in equipment belonging to you? That's a joke. Trying to let me down easy. I get you. Curt's heart broke. Good-bye, Sandra. I'm giving you a raw deal to send you off on such short notice, but I can't stay another hour. No, don't come with me; I'd rather be alone. The chauffeur has orders to take you to your train."

Sandra listened to her heavy footsteps along the tiled hall. Instinctively she looked at Nicholas Hoyt. He smiled.

"Blink those tears out of your eyes, beautiful. She'll come through. In a year she will have another stable — she can't keep away from it — and she'll be happy again. Now you will listen to me. Nicholas Hoyt announcing. Do you think I wasn't almost off my head when Bridie told me that you were missing? Ask her. Do you think I haven't been mad to get to you this last week? I've been kept away. Haven't had five consecutive minutes to myself. I had so much to say that couldn't be said in the fog of tragedy which has been hanging over this house. Are you listening? Look at me. Don't stand there as if poised to fly. Come back by the fire."

"But the car will be here —"

"You're not going by train. I'm driving you to town — in case you care."

"Oh, king, permit thy servant to pack her bag?"

Flippancy camouflaging emotional ecstasy. That "beautiful" had set Sandra's pulses racing. If she hadn't laughed, she might have cried. Nicholas caught her shoulders.

"You and I have been playing at cross-purposes long enough. You know I love you, don't you? You know that I've been almost out of my mind with jealousy of Rousseau, don't you? You wouldn't rather have him kiss you, would you? Remember that you told me once that you'd better marry me?"

"I! When?"

"That night at Stone House when you were hurt. You thought it was — was some one else who held you in his arms, but it was I — it was I who kissed you."

Sandra glanced down at the hands gripping hers, looked up.

"So it was you all the time! You know — I love you, don't you . . ."

Somewhere a clock struck. Sandra withdrew one arm from about Nicholas' neck to hold him off the fraction of an inch. Her eyes fell before the eyes looking down at her.

"If we are going to town, we really ought to start, Nick."

He caught her close again. "Believe in me now?"

"Yes, and — and like it." Laughter rippled her voice as she reminded:

"We were about starting for town, weren't we?"

"We were — we are. Come on!" Nicholas kept his arm about her as they crossed the tiled hall. At the foot of the stairs he stopped.

"How soon will you come back to stay? This is a big house for a lone man."

"How soon do you want me?"

"How soon!" He caught her up in his arms, kissed her throat, her eyes, her lips. With his cheek against her hair, he admitted huskily:

"That's how soon I want you! Say, 'I, Cassandra, take thee, Nicholas . . .' "

With her eyes on his, Sandra repeated unsteadily:

" 'I, Cassandra, take thee, Nicholas . . .' "

Abruptly he set her on her feet. He cleared his voice. "That will do for *now!*"

The employees of Thorndike Press hope you have enjoyed this Large Print book. All our Large Print titles are designed for easy reading, and all our books are made to last. Other Thorndike Press Large Print books are available at your library, through selected bookstores, or directly from the publishers.

For more information about titles, please call:

(800) 223-1244
(800) 223-6121

To share your comments, please write:

Publisher
Thorndike Press
P.O. Box 159
Thorndike, Maine 04986